A Candlelight Ecstasy Romance™

HIS HANDS TRAILED WILDFIRE ACROSS HER BACK. . . .

"You're a very beautiful woman," he crooned.

"Last time I was 'plain' and 'scrawny,' to quote your own eloquent description."

"Last time I was wet and tired and angry. Now I can see straight." Strong hands glided down across her middle, drawing her back against the hard length of his body. A magnetic force tilted her face up toward his. Her lips parted in helpless invitation, to be met a breath's stop later by his in descent. His ardor came through, hard and bold, against her, as he crushed her slim form to him. Her fingers wound through the thickness of his hair, forcing his lips more vibrantly onto hers. She was oblivious to all reality but the fiery need within. . . .

LILAC AWAKENING

Bonnie Drake

A CANDLELIGHT ECSTASY ROMANCE™

Published by
Dell Publishing Co., Inc.
1 Dag Hammarskjold Plaza
New York, New York 10017

ISBN: 0-440-14588-0

Printed in the United States of America
First printing—October 1982

To Our Readers:

We have been delighted with your enthusiastic response to Candlelight Ecstasy Romances™, and we thank you for the interest you have shown in this exciting series.

In the upcoming months we will continue to present the distinctive sensuous love stories you have come to expect only from Ecstasy. We look forward to bringing you many more books from your favorite authors and also the very finest work from new authors of contemporary romantic fiction.

As always, we are striving to present the unique, absorbing love stories that you enjoy most—books that are more than ordinary romance.

Your suggestions and comments are always welcome. Please write to us at the address below.

Sincerely,

The Editors
Candlelight Romances
1 Dag Hammarskjold Plaza
New York, New York 10017

To my father,
who gives so much,
yet asks so little

CHAPTER ONE

Nightfall was the last resort in nature's bid to blot out her own splendor. For much of the afternoon across the upper Vermont countryside, an ominous bevy of dark clouds had lurked among the forested peaks, swarming, breaking, then regrouping in a macabre arabesque, succeeding not in stifling beauty but adding to it with a muted gray softness sifted over the deep greens of the hillside. The age-old power of the land was an awesome one, subtly stated through all eternity by the proud posture of the pine on the hill, the free flow of the river winding through the valley, the indomitable gaiety of the orange Indian paintbrush swaying in the breeze amid well-grazed meadow grass. Darkness was but a makeshift shield for this natural beauty to which Anne Boulton had been privy on her escape from the city.

The past summer had been an oppressive one in New York. Heat and humidity had vied to surpass each other, stubbornly clinging to highs that brought beads of sweat to foreheads and furniture alike, lending a stickiness to even the hard concrete of heavy-aired avenues. As the skyscrapered congestion closed in about her, so had the throng of well-intending friends and family, coaxing her out to lunch, when all she wanted was a tall cola and a salad at home, urging her off to the theater, when all she wished for was a quiet evening alone, spiriting her away for a weekend of noise-filled companionship, when all she fancied was a good book and healing solitude. In the end all she craved was Jeff, but he was lost to her.

Now, as darkness provided a cushioning cocoon about the large upholstered chair in which she curled, the wood fire in the hearth offered the only source of light, its orange and gold flames flickering hypnotically before her dark eyes. If this first evening at her hilltop retreat was a harbinger of the peace she sought, then she had truly made the right decision in renting the house for the week. Time was a precious commodity, yet here time abounded. There would be time to read, time to walk, time to work, and, most important, time to think. This last item had high priority in Anne's mind.

Late September in Vermont seemed the perfect opportunity for soul-searching. With promises of misty mornings and golden afternoons, newly ripening apples and sweet corn in abundance, deer and squirrels and crisp mountain air, it was a fitting antidote for her malaise. The small house on its high perch was everything the rental agent had promised. The jostling of her small Chevette over the bumps and ruts of the steadily climbing dirt road had held instant reward at its end, for the house was charming. Brown weathered shingles and a silver slate roof blended easily with the earthen road and the gray of the sky, and it rested peacefully in the arms of the giant maples and towering firs that bounded the road, the yard, and the landscape beyond. Low shrubbery, agedly verdant with the oncoming autumn, bordered the house, save the taller lilac bushes, their fragrant blossoms but a poignant memory, straddling the ebony front door.

Within, the cottage was as compact as its surroundings were generous, an open-hearthed living room at the front, a kitchen, bedroom, and bath at the rear. A narrow stairway on the far side led to the multidormered attic, which Anne promptly relegated to the realm of the superfluous, for her own purposes at least. Decorated functionally and comfortably, the whole was a far cry from her more elegant New York apartment, yet its very difference pleased her. For this was a neutral spot, a place of few luxuries and fewer memories, a place where she could simply face life for the pleasure of the day. And this had been a tiring one, from a morning filled with a rash of last-minute errands—to the bank for money, to the library and the bookstore for the week's entertainment, to the university for a delivery and a pickup, to the market for the food she would need in the wilds—to an afternoon of continual driving. Having stored the groceries and unpacked her bags, the fireplace seemed the sensible retreat for a bone-weary Anne, whose very stamina had been sadly lacking for weeks.

As the wing-backed chair held her slim form the dancing flames lulled her into recollection of the dinner she'd had with her parents the weekend before.

"I don't understand," her mother had tried to reason with her, "why you feel the necessity to take off like this, all by yourself. We've tried so hard to do what's best. Have we failed?"

Anxious to ease the look of hurt that crossed her mother's gentle features, Anne had forced a semblance of a smile. "Of course not! I'd just like to get out of the city for a while. You know," she quipped feebly, "fresh-air-and-color-on-my-cheeks type of thing?"

"You could certainly use that!" The deep voice of concern was that of her father. Tall and distinguished-looking, Anthony Faulke's sturdy frame belied his near-sixty years. It was from him that Anne took the darkness of hair and eyes, though her willowed shapeliness was her mother's. "But we would have liked to have you join us on the shore in several weeks. Won't you reconsider and wait until then?"

Slowly Anne shook her head, disturbing not a hair in the somber knot at the nape of her neck. "Now is the time; I've already made the arrangements and paid for the place."

"But, darling, you've never enjoyed traveling alone like this before. Wouldn't it be better to have someone with you? If I didn't have the charity luncheon on that Wednesday, I would go with you myself. You need company, Anne." Once more her mother's pained expression tore at her. Her parents had suffered nearly as much as she, having to stand by and watch helplessly as their older daughter's life fell apart. Now, as her mother scanned it, the pallor in Anne's oval face appeared accentuated, framed as it was by the pitch black of her hair and the dark navy sheath she had donned for the dinner.

"I really have no choice, have I, Mother? I suppose I've been more fortunate than others, always having someone to be with. When it wasn't you both"—she widened her sad gaze to include her father's compassionate one—"it was Peggy, then my roommates at college, then—then Jeff." Eyes downcast, her voice broke at the last. Tears had been long-since spent, yet that catch in her voice, in her very breath, persisted.

Marjorie Faulke spoke quickly, grasping at straws. "Why don't you call Peggy, dear? She won't be starting classes for another few weeks. I'm sure she'd like to make the trip with you." The glimmer of hope in her pale green eyes died quickly with her daughter's staunch headshake.

"No, Mom. Peggy is terrific. For a sister, I couldn't ask for finer. But she is involved with her own life, her own friends, as well she should be. It's not her job to baby-sit for her older sister. No, I would really prefer to be alone. After all, I'd better get used to it." Anger, regrettable as it was, was inescapable. It had plagued her relentlessly during the last eight months, refusing to relinquish its grasp on her battered emotions. Unfortunately the only cure for the ailment would be through the courts, but that process was to be months more in resolution.

For long, drawn-out moments, a silence had hung over the intimately round table, its elegant place settings and sumptuous gastronomical offerings all but forgotten. It seemed to have become a pattern, this family gathering turned wake. Somewhere the circle had to be broken. Somehow Anne had to start to branch out, to live a new future. Perhaps the trip to Vermont would be a first step.

As the initial full blaze in the fireplace simmered to a more sedate crackling, the patter of raindrops, gentle but distinct, broke through Anne's reverie. Stretching barefoot legs, she stood, smoothed out the bunched denim of her jeans, then padded quietly to the front window. The chill of the evening air had precluded raising the windows earlier. Now, staring out into the darkness through panes dotted with moisture, she was grateful that habit had bidden her to shut the car windows and lock the door when she'd finished bringing her belongings and supplies into the house upon arrival. The idea of going out to do it now did not appeal to her. For, as she stood, hands by her sides, eyes straight ahead, she could see nothing, nothing but the black of night . . . and her own grim reflection.

It hadn't taken friends to tell her that she looked gaunt and spectral despite her innate beauty. Where once her cheeks had warmed with color, now they bore a pale creaminess, hollowed by the weight loss that had robbed her body of the gentle curves in which Jeff had once delighted. Where once her lips had tilted in a perpetual smile, now they were more often drawn thin and straight. Where once her dark eyes had danced with happiness, now they spoke of the loneliness that reached to her very core. Where once her hair had flowed freely, swinging from shoulder to shoulder as she walked, now it was tied back stoically with a thin piece of black velvet, the ends of which lost definition in the ribbed wool of her black turtleneck sweater. This too—this ghostly appearance—would have to change if she intended to make a go, in her heart, of what her good sense dictated.

Following the cataclysm of the January before, she had suffered weeks of stunned inactivity until her strength finally returned in sufficient quantity to allow her to ponder the future. The future without Jeff—the thought was still alien to her. They had been married for seven years, though it had seemed forever. Anne was a sophomore in college, a language major, when she had first met him during a summer of study in France. He had been one of the few Americans she'd seen during her three-month stay with a family in the small village west of Limoges. His means of transportation had been a bicycle, his means of communication a brilliant smile—until he had discovered she spoke English. From that point on they had been inseparable, his touring plans being revised to accommodate her own plans. When they had returned to the States at the end of August, the friendship had blossomed into true courtship. He was also from New York, his family home a mere hour's drive from her own. By January she had transferred from her school in the city to his midwestern university; they were married the following summer. With but two years' difference in their ages, they literally grew up together, passing through the college years of flux and idealism with hours of carefree camaraderie, more of first love. Both had come from hard-working, upwardly mobile families that helped them out financially until they had gotten on their own feet. But money hadn't mattered, even as it came to them through Jeff's burgeoning success as an investment consultant. Rather, it had always been Jeff and Anne, Anne and Jeff. Then, abruptly, it was Anne . . . alone.

When the stupor finally began to wear off, she forced herself to analyze what she did have. She had a home—a fine, totally furnished, stylishly decorated, fully equipped, and spacious apartment. She had sufficient money to live in it comfortably, with a further source of investment capital when all the paperwork would be completed. She had friends. She had family. She had her own car, perhaps not as sporty as Jeff's manual-transmission Audi, but small, reliable, automatic, and gas efficient. And she had her work.

Fluent in both French and Spanish, Anne had worked as

a free-lance interpreter through most of the years of her marriage. At first the money had been an important addition to their joint income; later, it faded in significance. But she had enjoyed her work, and with no other responsibilities—such as the children they hoped to have one day—to keep her at home, she happily filled the hours during which Jeff was at the office, with her own career. It had been ideal. If they planned a trip, she merely accepted less work for the week or two. If Jeff was to be away on a business trip and his hectic schedule precluded her attendance, she took on more, satisfied to keep herself ever busy until he returned.

More than once, during those long months of recovery from the suddenness of losing him, her mind had taken a more morbid spiritual tack. What if, she had wondered, what if she *had* been with him on that last, fateful trip? Perhaps they would be together still.

But they weren't. She was alone. Little by little she took on more work, branching off into the realm of translating textbooks for several of the local universities. As opposed to interpreting, where she had to be personally on the spot at a given time on a given day, there was more flexibility in translation. Once the material to be worked had been picked up—or dropped off, as was the case with more than one overeager professor—she could tackle the job on her own schedule, in the secluded comfort and privacy of her apartment. Mercifully there was a deluge of such work from which to choose; it seemed that her skill, availability, overall competence, and unerring promptness of delivery had put her very much in demand.

On occasion, as she reflected on those overeager professors, Anne had suspected that her newly altered marital status was in part responsible for the attention those particularly young, particularly attractive academicians paid her. And, though she deeply appreciated the work and struggled to be ever courteous to each client, her rebuffing of any and all advances, subtle or less so, was instantaneous. It disturbed her, even angered her, that men thought she could begin to date, want to date, so soon after the ordeal she'd undergone. Perhaps men handled things differently, she had reasoned, in a token bid to explain and to forgive their insensitivity. For her, the desire to date was nonexistent. Memories of Jeff were too near, too vivid, too dear, to allow her to contemplate sharing with a different man that which she'd once shared with him. In time the memories would find their proper place, and she might then seek male companionship once more. For now, however, the thought was unwelcome and inappropriate. To open herself again to love and the pain it entailed—that would take a very, very long time, she feared.

Perhaps this was another reason why she had sought to get away. Here was an excuse-laden trilogy—getting ready to leave with a million errands left to do, being out of state for the week, and just having returned to a huge pile of work—to protect her. And certainly where she was going, to the backwoods of Vermont, the male of the species would cause her no problem. No aggressive men in this serene locale, she guessed. After all, she had every intention, barring an unforeseen emergency, of meeting no one all week. Pretty reclusive for a former socializer, she mused without a hint of remorse.

From the hearth, the sudden crumbling of an ash-split log startled her. Whirling around, eyes widened in alarm, it took her a moment to recall herself, so deeply had she been enmeshed in her melancholy daydreams. Even then her clenched fists did not register until finally the pressure of fingernails against palms approached pain. This too would have to stop, she mused, as, looking down, she slowly uncoiled each digit, lifting them to study the nails, which, after months of gnawed shortness, had finally grown to tapered tips, long and slender as were her hands. Her eyes caught in a poignant trance on the wide gold band, gleaming with deceptive brightness, on the third finger of her left hand. Then the fire spoke again, its command for fuel cackling through the room. Kneeling down before the warm stone, she took a piece of split, dried birch from the large wood basket and carefully laid it over the broken embers, watching with satisfaction as the log heated, caught, then burst into rollicking flame. It was an omen, she vowed, as she picked up her book from its resting place on the floor by her chair, slipped the oversized tortoiseshell frames of her beige-tinted glasses over the bridge of her straight nose, and settled back once more between the chair's wide wings. They were a comfort, these wings, she realized, serving, much as the blinders on a horse, to keep her sights on the fiery illumination before her, rather than on the darkness all around.

She had her friend, her ticket to freedom, in her lap. Ever an avid reader, Anne had taken great comfort in the written page over the past months when all else had failed as a sedative. She had discovered that, as a friend, a book had many advantages over the human variety: it was there whenever she needed it, it vanished as easily, and it never asked questions, expected witty rejoinders, made awkward suggestions, or otherwise overcompensated for its own inability to rectify the wrongs of the world. Yes, she had decided, as she'd packed a friend-a-day supply for this trip, her books would be all the company she'd need this time around.

For starters, it was a biography she had snatched from the bookbag she'd dropped, with her luggage, in the bedroom. Determined to make good her escape, she opened the hardback book with deliberate movements . . . only to be helplessly caught up once again in the world she so desperately tried to flee. For there was an inscription on the inside cover of the volume, one that she hadn't noticed earlier, but which brought back a storm of memories. "To my favorite sister-in-law. Have a marvelous vacation and be sure to spend a week with *us* when you get back. MaryEllen."

From the very first Jeff's family had adored her openly, insisting, with a laugh, that, should anything ever happen to the marriage, they would hold Jeff personally at fault. True to that sentiment, they had stayed by Anne's side to the point where she had had finally to declare her independence. Only then, and with great reluctance, had they eased off.

Her own parents had persisted even longer, urging her to give up the apartment and move back into their home. But she had refused, knowing that the apartment, crammed as it was with reminders of the past, would be better than the Westchester home in which she had spent her childhood. Somehow to return there would have been tantamount to an admission of failure—failure to make a life of happiness as had her parents.

A rueful ghost of a smile lifted the corners of her lips as she thought back on that childhood. How happy it had been, even during those awkward adolescent years when she was, by modest accounts, an ugly duckling. Oh, her parents had argued with her verdict, but the mirror could not lie. Mercifully the ugly duckling had become a swan well before the time of the Senior Prom. A quiet, graceful, and very beautiful swan she had been then, thriving academically, socially, and emotionally. In fact, nothing in her rosy first twenty-seven years had even remotely begun to prepare her for the heartbreak at the start of her twenty-eighth.

Brought back to the present by a sudden pang of hunger, she closed the untouched book with a clap of resignation and padded toward the kitchen, flipping on only what light she needed to assist her in the work of mixing a can of tuna into salad, putting on a pot of coffee to perk, and toasting two slices of rye bread. Then, sandwich plate in one hand and coffee mug in the other, she retraced her steps, flipping lights off behind her with a deft nudge of the elbow.

The extent of her hunger surprised her. She finished the late supper in a rare move, and, noticeably revived, relaxed back into the chair, the mug warming her hands much as the fire warmed her feet, toes wiggling in delight before the dancing flames. It was this sense of awareness that suddenly welled, then burst within her, seemingly eager to compensate for the months of numbness, when she had been oblivious to things such as the rich smell of coffee or the barefoot plushness of the carpet. Now something in her body reawakened. The coffee *did* smell divine, wafting through the heady aroma of burning logs and the rusticity of the house itself, swathed in the evergreen bouquet of the hills. And her feet *did* exult, albeit in the smooth-sanded oak planks rather than in thick carpeting. Her very senses seemed to be freed from the self-imposed restraints of home, that home that carried *his* mark on every sofa, chair, pot, pan, pillow, sheet, and towel. But she had loved him deeply; never would she wish to wipe out that memory. To live with it, yet without him—that was the challenge.

Pushing the glasses higher up on the bridge of her nose, she lowered her eyes to stare at the biography. No, perhaps it wasn't a night for biography, she sighed, as she jumped up and returned to her room for a replacement. Mystery or romance—the choice was simple enough. While a romance might appeal to her later in the week, when she was less sensitive to her own loss, the mystery now beckoned.

The addition of several logs to the fire sparked an exuberant blaze, one by which, as she edged her chair sideways, closer to the hearth, she would have no trouble reading. And so she began, shedding her own identity for that of the heroine of the compact paperback. Only marginally was she aware that the rain had gained in intensity, beating now with increased force against rooftop, windowpane, and clapboard. It was a fitting background symphony for this story of a young woman stranded in the deep woods in a cabin not terribly unlike her own. Anne shuddered momentarily at the comparison, debated switching to the romance after all, but was drawn inexorably back to the tightly written piece. Shifting in her seat to burrow more soundly into the chair's protective cushion, she surrendered herself to the intricately developed plot line.

For an hour, perhaps two, she read, pausing once to refill her coffee cup. Her thin-banded gold watch read nearly eleven o'clock, yet despite the length and exhaustion of her day, her mind was wide awake, exhilarated both by the new surroundings and by the riveting edge of the story. As Chapter Four fell before Five, and then Six, the mystery deepened. Accidents were neither accident nor coincidence. Someone was after the heroine; no, some*thing* was after her, or so it appeared from the bizarre markings left by footprints, paw prints, or what have you in the winter snow. Terror slowly mounted; the woman was trapped, hunted, doomed. Futilely, as Chapter Seven ended and Eight began, she hatched her escape plan against seemingly insurmountable odds. Then, to complicate an already desperate situation, came the blizzard. Gale force winds, blinding snows, chilling temperatures—all conspired to keep her in the clutches of the beast of the wild that stalked her.

With a thud, Anne put the book facedown onto her lap, heart pounding in vicarious fright. *Mystery, my foot,* she mused regretfully, *this book is sheer horror!* Had she picked it up last night or last week, in the urban luxury of her New York apartment, she would not have thought twice about the setting. Here, however, she was all alone, isolated from the familiar, with the nearest shred of civilization a good three miles over dirt roads and through a torrential downpour. She cringed. Spooked, it took her a minute to realize that what she'd assumed to be the thundering of her pulse through chilled veins was, instead, the rain. Lightning followed quickly, brightening the dark side of the room for a shocking instant, its blue-white gleam an icy one in comparison to the warm orange glow of the fire.

Hastily she added another two logs to the fire, desperately needing to put the ghostly book down, desperately needing to read on, knowing that sleep would not come this night until the last page had been turned and the mystery solved. Shaky hands raised the book again as another roar of thunder deafened her, vibrating through the house in the accompaniment of tongued bolts of harsh white light. Suddenly Anne's every nerve end prickled. For in the thunder's wake came another noise, one more human and even more threatening, given her state of heightened awareness. It was the sound of a car, approaching steadily from a distance, growing nearer and louder, louder to express itself above the storm. When it seemed no further than the front door, it stopped, abruptly, returning dominance to the pounding rain.

Huddled in the chair, Anne froze. The rental agent had not alerted her to visitors. Who could be here, at this hour? At a quick glance, fearful eyes noted the time as twelve thirty-five, certainly beyond the normal calling hours of even a thriving metropolis, which this was not. Perhaps the storm had created a problem about which one of the villagers felt called upon to warn her. Perhaps someone was lost. Perhaps . . . perhaps . . .

All such speculation in the world could not have denied the furious pounding at the door that commenced. Had it been a gentle knock, Anne might have mustered the courage to answer it. Anger resounded in each thud, however, intimidating her even further. At least, she reminded herself, the door was locked, though she wished fervently for the dead bolt she had in New York.

"Open up! It's wet out here!" The voice was deep and gruff, echoing the anger of clenched knuckles. "Open the damn door!"

In the face of such imperiousness, sympathy eluded Anne. This was *her* cottage for the week, and she had the papers to prove it. No one was going to appear, an angry vision in the middle of the night, and shatter her peace. But then, she mused, he already had. Coming on the tail of the mystery, which had set her pulse to racing, this stranger's arrival had caused a knotting in her stomach that several long, deep breaths failed to ease.

The banging continued. "Come on, whoever you are. Open

this door! I'm getting wetter and I can't reach my key." *His* key? Surely she had the only key around. Or was this a common visiting place? Had the realtor forgotten to tell her something?

Guilt-ridden at being warm and dry, chiding herself for suspicions that were more appropriate to the concrete jungle of the city, curbing the wild imaginings of her near-climactic reading, and stifling the indignation the unexpected visit raised, she approached the door slowly.

"Who is it?" she yelled, resting her forehead against the smooth oak.

"It's Mitch, dammit. Open up!" An impatient hand assaulted the doorknob from the outside.

"I don't know any Mitch." The loud shout of her voice was necessitated by the racket of the storm, continuing unabated through the drama. It disguised the frantic pitch that tinged her words. "What do you want?"

The returning growl was menacing. "I just want to get dry. For God's sake, open up. I *do* have a key, but if I have to put these bags down to get it, I'll be madder than ever when I do get in there!"

Assuming she could believe him, he had a point. If it was simply a matter of time before he retrieved his key and opened the door himself, she might as well save him the effort—and perhaps blunt his anger. Haltingly she reached for the knob and slowly opened the door a few inches, leaving her weight in readiness against the door, in case she didn't like what she saw.

Without warning, a heavier weight thrust it full open, throwing her back into the room. Startled by the unexpected force and cursing herself for her naïveté, Anne lost her balance and tripped, falling backward onto her bottom with a thump. From that vantage point she watched, wide-eyed, as a huge man entered, dripping water savagely, tossing several large bags to the side before slamming the door shut and leaning against it.

The fire had begun to die, leaving but the faintest glow to illuminate the stranger's features—enough to reveal the tautness of a jaw, the sneer of lips, and the unfathomable depth of eyes that impaled her.

"You bitch! What took you so long? Why didn't you open the door? Can't you see what the weather is like?" The thunder outside was nothing compared to that within. "And who sent you anyway? Was it Joe?" His eyes narrowed maliciously, raking her form with an insolence that shook her. "No, it must have been Lennie. He always did go in for the plain, scrawny type." Even in the darkness the repeated perusal he gave her sprawled form was humiliating, yet astonishment at this sudden turn of events in what was to be an uneventful getaway held her speechless. It was a monologue he seemed intent on finishing. "What? No denials? No coy protestations?" As he spoke his right hand released the buttons of his heavy wool jacket, then he slipped the sodden covering from his shoulders with a shrug and deftly tossed the material onto an empty chair. He was an imposing figure, dressed, ironically, much as she was, with snug-fitting denims and a dark turtleneck. To her horror, he advanced a step, then two, until he towered directly over her, hands on hips, legs wide apart. "Well? Haven't you got anything to say? Or are you just going to lie there, all helpless and inviting?"

His implication fired her; Anne found her tongue at last. "You shouldn't be here. Get out!"

A coarse laugh filtered through the sounds of the storm. "Ah, having second thoughts, are you? Reneging on your little deal so quickly?"

Slowly Anne slid backward on the floor. "I think there's been a misunderstanding—"

"You bet there has!" the intruder declared soundly. "I don't know who you are, but I don't want you or any other woman up here. So"—he quieted his voice with a deceptive calmness that failed to relax his jaw—"I'd suggest that you pick up your little carcass and get out of here."

Anne was incredulous. "I will not!" she snapped on impulse, her eyes not leaving his for a second as she inched further away from his decidedly intimidating presence.

In one fluid and unanticipated movement he crouched before her, steel-muscled shins imprisoning her own, making movement impossible. "What did you say?" He goaded her on, amused at her insolence.

Willing a strength she did not feel, Anne continued to hold his gaze boldly. "I said that I would not leave. I'm here for the week, and if anyone is leaving, it will be you. Now!" The last she practically shrieked as frustration and fear conspired to rob her of what little composure she had.

To her instant chagrin her order had exactly the opposite effect on the man. Purposefully he moved forward, resting his weight on his right hand, which flattened on the hard floor inches from her hip. "So this is a new kind of game," he taunted, puzzling her with reference to the plot of which she was supposed to be a part.

Her lips trembled. "I don't know what you're talking about. This is no game." It was a whisper that broke off when his face moved infinitely closer. Edged by the pale orange cast of the fire, she could only see his lips, firm and well-formed and shaped into a wry grin. All else was blurred by the ravishes of the storm, the darkness of the room, and the sudden terror that erupted from the pit of her stomach. His own eyes narrowed on the quivering of her lips, giving but an instant's warning of his intent.

"No game?" He echoed her words as she struggled to pull herself free of his leg-hold. Then, with the grace of an athlete and the power of a lion, his body stretched over hers, flattening her onto the cold floor. Panic gripped her.

"Let go! Get off me!" Futilely her palms strained against his shoulders to wrest him from her. But his body weight was awesome, stealing from her the very breath she needed to scream. Gasping, she continued to push as his lips came within a feather's breath of her own. "No . . ." she whispered, twisting her head from side to side.

"No game, you say?" he murmured against her mouth. "We'll see about that!" With firm intent his lips seized hers, stilling her thrashing with a steadiness that held her head flush against the oak planks. Startling in intensity, relentless in duration, his kiss jolted her senses with its animalism, raw and primitive.

Engulfed in fear, she fought desperately, writhing beneath him. In a movement she could not believe, his large right hand seized both of her hands and pinned them to the floor above her head. Only then did his lips finally release hers. No longer did the lingering raindrops blur his image; now tears swam in her own eyes.

The seconds ran together as she gasped for the breath she'd been denied. All the while he studied her. Calmness reigned when he spoke, though the cynicism of his tone was unmistakable. "What's this? Tears? Uh-uh, that's not part of the game plan." In an effort to raise himself further, his hand tightened on hers, forcing them to bear the brunt of his weight. She cried out in pain as her wedding band dug into her fingers.

Strangely it was this expression of sheer pain that affected him as her panicked thrashings had not. In the instant of freedom when he sat back on his haunches, she recoiled, crawling backward until she hit a wall, then turning, bounding to her feet, and racing toward the fireplace. Acting instinctively, she grabbed the only weapon in sight, the heavy iron poker, which had lain so innocently against the hearthside.

"Don't come near me," she warned in an unrecognizable high-pitched whine. Her threat reached its mark. Not a muscle flinched in the hard form, which knelt as she'd left it.

Silence hung heavy in air that moments before had been rent with the sounds of battle. Even the rain had eased to a gentle patter on the roof. The storm had abated within *and* without. But what was she to do now? As the gravity of her predicament settled in, a fit of trembling shook her with such force that the poker waved precariously back and forth in her unsteady hands.

Sensing her state of terror, the man got to his feet slowly, palms open by his sides. "Take it easy, woman. I won't hurt you."

"You already have." Her breath caught on her words as she raised the poker higher.

"Put that thing down," he ordered, but gently, all anger gone now from his tone. "You're apt to hurt yourself." Silently she shook her head, her pose promising imminent attack should he approach. "Look." He sighed, running his fingers through the damp swathe of hair that had fallen across his forehead in the fray. "Let me turn a light on here. At least then I can see what manner of woman has gotten the upper hand with me." His attempt at humor eluded her, though she did ease up on her stance, in subtle acquiescence to his suggestion. Light would serve her purpose also.

A calculated stride took him to the nearby lamp, which, when lit, bathed the room in a warm yellow haze. "That's better," he stated calmly, turning to face her once more. Despite her fearful state, Anne's eyes made a thorough appraisal of the man who had attempted to assault her. He was tall and rugged, thinner than she had first suspected, though the breadth of his chest and shoulders spoke of the full-sinewed strength that his earlier behavior had demonstrated. His sweater was black, his jeans faded, though darkened in dampness at the hem, falling over sodden brown leather boots. If she had expected a dark and ominous visage to top the outfit, she was mistaken. For his features were strong yet gentle, his skin but faintly tanned, his hair a thick mass of blonde, turning silver, in rain-coaxed waves. There *was* an underlying gentleness, yet it warred with the sternness of his lips, the taut leanness of his cheeks, the grim set of his jaw. And his eyes—silvered hazel and bespeaking chameleonlike change—bore into her mercilessly. Then, beneath her dogged scrutiny, his lips twitched in mockery.

"If you've finished, would you please put down that poker? Surely you can see that I'm not a thug."

She lifted the weapon even higher in reminder. "How about a rapist?" More steady now, she was not to be deceived by a sweet-talking, good-looking—for that he was—man.

The flex of a muscle in his jaw belied his composure. "I am no rapist. I would not have forced you into anything. Particularly"—he paused, his eyes taking in the shining gold above her head—"once I saw that wedding band. I don't fool around with married women." Any doubts she might have harbored on that matter were driven from mind by the note of disgust in his sneer.

Unbidden, tears welled again in her dark orbs. It was a bittersweet thought that this symbol of marriage, a marriage that was now nothing but a memory, should have saved her from an unspeakable fate. Once again she had Jeff to thank.

"Who are you?" she whispered.

"You really don't know? Come on, you're holding all the cards. You can confess." Again the mockery.

"Who are you?" Slowly her voice gained in strength.

But he persisted. "It *was* Lennie, wasn't it? He's been trying to set me up with a woman for weeks now!" Something in the frustration underlying his words struck a chord of sincerity.

Determinedly she repeated her question. "Who *are* you?"

With a sigh of defeat he thrust his left hand into his pocket. "Mitch."

That much she knew. "Where are you from?"

"New York."

"You just drove up?" Suspicion lingered in the dark eyebrow she raised.

"Yes."

"Why?"

Under the direct grilling, he shot her a surprised look.

"Why what? Why did I *just* drive up, or why am I here?" The earlier mockery was gone, fallen victim to her utter and persistent terror at his appearance. Only a first-class actress could maintain the aura of innocence she had, and, though Lennie's girls were all first-class, none were actresses.

"Both." As Anne's pulse steadied she slowly lowered the poker, keeping a tight grasp on it nonetheless.

"I just got here because I had a late meeting this afternoon and couldn't leave the city until it was over. I'm here because I need a week's rest, free of all human contact. *All human contact.*" His emphasis was a pointed reminder of his previous accusation. She didn't flinch.

"Why are you here?" Her dark eyes challenged him in a way that no woman ever had. Another vote toward her innocence.

"I just told you."

"But, why *here,* in this house?" Finally she felt herself thinking straight. As he suggested, he did *not* look like a thug. And he could have taken advantage of her when he was on top. Could it be that he was as much in mystery at her presence as she was at his?

A large hand reached to massage the muscles at the back of his neck, much as she had done when she'd completed the long drive earlier. "I come here often. And I'm sure I booked the weekend with Miles."

Well, she mused, he did know the realtor. For that he had to be credited. Slowly she put the poker down. "Then there has been a terrible mistake," she began, her eyes falling to the floor in puzzlement. Absently she ran a faintly shaky finger over the tender curve of her lip where his had battered it. If he caught the movement, he chose to ignore it, intent only on relieving her of the potentially debilitating weapon. Taking advantage of her momentary distraction, he made a deft movement forward, wresting the poker from her hands before she knew he was there. The black-eyed gaze that met his lighter one bore renewed terror, the fear that she had been duped. This too he used to his benefit.

"All right, ma'am. Now *you* answer *my* questions," he ordered triumphantly. Intimidation took her back a step until broad hands stopped her, placing a firm clamp on either slim shoulder. Standing erect, facing one another as they now were, Anne was acutely aware of the discrepancy in their heights. Albeit exaggerated by her barefoot state, Mitch overshadowed her by nearly a foot.

"Who are *you?*" The command in his voice was not to be taken lightly, any more than the physical threat he posed.

She began to tremble again, silently cursing her own timidity. "Anne." If first names were all he had offered, she would do no more. He didn't seem to mind.

"From . . . ?"

"New York."

"So"—a smile touched his mouth but went no further—"we are of the same stock."

"Hardly." Her sharp gaze and clipped response erased his smile.

"When did *you* arrive?"

Deep within, she resented his questions. After all, *she* had every right to be here. Protest bubbled forth. "Look, I don't see that this—"

Hard fingers dug into the flesh of her upper arms, stopping short of a shake. "Answer me. When did you get here?"

Stifling further protest, she sneered her response. "Early this evening."

"And why are you here? . . . Both versions." Correctly anticipating her rejoinder, he relaxed his grip on her shoulders.

Desiring only to escape his clutch completely, she cast an imploring glance up the distance to his face. "Can't I . . . can't I sit down? My legs are rather . . . wobbly."

Cocking his silvered head to one side, he freed her, holding his hands off to the side of her arms for a moment before dropping them, the right to his waist, the left to his pocket, as seemed his habit. "Sit, then."

Stiffly she retreated to her old chair, soundlessly watching as the tall intruder skillfully dropped more logs onto the fire with his right hand, his left remaining in its pocket. It occurred to Anne that he avoided its use, yet she was given no time to question.

"All right," he began, approaching her again, adopting an arrogant stance, tall and imposing, his back to the fire, his own hazel beams impaling her. "Why did you come?"

A defiant tilt to her rounded chin was her only show of objection. "I'm here on vacation. And I did arrange and *prepay* with Mr. Cooper for the week."

"You have proof?"

"Of course!"

"Let me see."

Her dark brows drew together in anger. "Why? Why should I show you anything? You're the one who has barged in here uninvited."

In answer, he leaned forward, resting his hand on the arm of her chair, bringing his lips infuriatingly close to her ear. "Get it," he demanded under his breath, the threat obvious though unspoken. Slowly he straightened to let her pass.

Moments later she reappeared to find him, arm on the stone mantelpiece, deep in contemplation of the soaring flames. Quietly he turned and took the paper she offered.

"Looks authentic enough." It was a reluctant admission, tinged with bridled anger. "That fool," he murmured to himself as he turned back to the fire.

"Where's *your* proof?" she challenged, placing both hands on her hips with a boldness that astonished even her.

His jaw clenched visibly. "You'll have to take my word for it."

Stubbornly she shook her head. "No, thanks. I want proof, or you can just take your things and leave! I didn't drive all the way up here to share a cabin with a man I don't even know."

His lips, even in profile, thinned to a grimace. "It looks like you're stuck with me, lady."

What had moments before been defiance, then annoyance, was suddenly pure anger. "No way!" she contradicted him, holding her stance and her gaze unfalteringly. "I came up here to be alone, and that's exactly what I intend to do. If there was a telephone, I'd call the local police to oust you. But since there is none, and I don't relish the thought of driving out in this weather, I'll ask you to leave like a gentleman."

"Whoever said that I was a gentleman?" His eyes looked fiercely, scornfully, on the flames.

"I'll give you the benefit of the doubt. Now, do you leave, or do I . . ." As her voice trailed off she realized how helpless she truly was. He too realized it.

Slowly he straightened and turned toward her. ". . . Or do you . . . what?"

Frustrated at her predicament, infuriated by his very calmness, she yielded to the need to shout. Loudly. "Look . . . Mitch . . . I don't know who is to blame for this—this fiasco, but I'd like you to leave. It's been a very long day and I'm tired. There's obviously been a misunderstanding, but I have every intention of spending the week here—alone—and I'm paying for that time right now. So, do you go?"

His expression was firm. "Tonight? No."

"What do you mean, no? You have no right to be here—"

In the instant his anger matched hers. "I have every right to be here, but that is between Miles Cooper and myself. Let's get one thing straight." His eyes deepened in fury, to a charcoal green. "I don't want *you* here any more than you want *me* here. It seems, for tonight at least, that we're stuck with each other. In the morning we'll have to work something out."

Steadfastly she shook her head. "I'm sorry, but you *can't* stay here tonight."

"Why not?" For an instant amusement toyed with the grim lines about his mouth.

"Because I'm here, that's why!" she yelled, pushed to distraction.

"So?" Charcoal green had leveled to the more neutral hazel.

A flush crept to her cheeks. "I thought I'd made it clear that I wasn't part of a conspiracy. Well, let me take it one step further." Her breathing faltered as she finally voiced arguments that she'd yearned to scream to the world for weeks. "I'm not interested in you, or any other man. Can you possibly understand that?"

His cynicism mocked her. "Oh, I can understand it, but I'm not quite sure I believe it." With maddening audacity his eyes fell from her face to her neck, then down to her breasts, their full curve outlined by her sweater and accentuated by the rapid rise and fall of her chest. Finally he looked to the wide band on her left hand. Then, frowning briefly, he pulled his lengthy form up tautly. "I think I've had it. Good night." As his arm brushed past her she broke from her trance of disbelief, grabbing out without thinking.

"Where are you going?" Her eyes widened in alarm.

"To bed." His words were blunt, his tone chilled.

"Oh, no, you're not."

A fair eyebrow arched. "And are you going to stop me?" Slowly he looked down at the white-knuckled hand on his arm. As though touched by fire, she released it.

"You can't *stay* here!" Despite her repeated protestation he continued his movement toward his bags. Unable to think of a better course, she followed. "I said, you can't stay! There must be some place in the village. . . ."

Luggage piled deftly under his right arm, he headed wordlessly for the stairs on the far side of the room. Then, abruptly, he stopped, turning his head only enough to call over his shoulder, "I assume you're sleeping in the downstairs bedroom?"

Flabbergasted by her lack of power, she could only continue the apparently pointless argument. "Yes . . . but you've *got to leave.*"

With deliberation he swiveled full front to face her, the dazzlement of his white smile iced instantly by his frigid glare. "I will . . . in good time." Then, taking the stairs two at a time, an astounding feat, considering his bulky burden, his dark-clad form disappeared into the attic, leaving her stunned, incredulous, and at a total loss for words.

CHAPTER TWO

Long moments did not budge Anne from where she had taken root, arms limp at her sides, bare feet flat on the floor, eyes glued to the attic door, which closed with a resounding bang behind the presumptuous stranger. Even the faint sounds from within—the scrape of a chair leg, the creak of the mattress beneath one bag, the thud of another on the floor, the lighter jangle of metal hangers on a wooden rod—failed to break through her stupor. It was, in the end, a stiff neck that brought her back to reality.

Hands bracing the muscles of her lower back, she lolled her head in a circular motion, releasing the tension as she attempted to grasp the situation. It was bizarre, this real-life drama that had usurped the force of the fictional one, discarded now on the floor by the fire. As she reflected on it good sense returned, and with it the awareness that, for tonight, there was absolutely nothing she could do to alter the fact that *that man* was irrevocably ensconced in her attic. Retreating to her own room, she closed the door tightly and, in a measure of desperation, propped a chair against its knob, much as her heroine had done in Chapter Six, or thereabouts. Undressing quickly, she slipped into her long flannel nightgown, brushed loose her thick black mane, then buried herself beneath the heavy quilts of her bed.

Strangely, aside from the precautionary measure to bar an unwanted visitor from her room, she was no longer frightened. His story, irritating as it was, was believable. Or, rather, *he* was believable. There was something about him—his intelligent manner of speech, his clean appearance, his refined air—that spoke of a breeding belying his initial crudity of behavior. Even *that,* his physical attack on her, the brutality of his kiss, was excusable in light of the apparent foul-up of both of their plans. He seemed neither personally malicious nor vengeful, but as angry as she at the rental agent's error.

What was to be done? She had no choice but to sleep on the matter. Come morning, as this Mitch had himself dictated, a solution would be found. It would *have* to be found, for, as *she* had told him, she had no desire to sacrifice her week's peace to any man.

Exhausted as she should, by all rights, have been, sleep was not an easy state to claim. In her tossing and turning, she cursed the two cups of coffee that stimulated her body, the unfinished paperback, which pricked her imagination, the man himself, directly above her, his every move creaking through the ceiling to recall her predicament. The longer she lay awake, the more angry she became. This was her first night in the country, the start of a week of supposed rest and relaxation. She had neither. Yet it suddenly occurred to her that neither was she brooding on her tragic loss, as she had done for every night running for the past eight months. On that ironic note she finally fell into a restless sleep, only to be awoken at intervals by every slight noise, only to be infuriated anew at the realization that practically each one came from above. It was nearly dawn when finally, thoroughly worn out, a deep slumber overtook her.

Seemingly moments later a deafening clatter from the direction of the kitchen jolted her to awareness. Livid at this final intrusion on her peace, she bolted out of bed, threw her disheveled tresses back over her shoulder, whipped the chair from the door, and stormed from her room toward the source of the racket, barefoot again and oblivious to the chill of the cold wood floor.

"What, in God's name, was that noise?" she roared, rounding the door of the kitchen in time to see the tall figure stooping to retrieve the first of a scattered mess of pots, pans, and metal utensils that covered the linoleum beside the stove. Dressed in a navy velour robe that barely touched his knees, Mitch too was barefoot. And disheveled. And very, very cranky.

Casting her a sidelong glare, he bellowed, "What kind of housekeeper are you, to pile these things in that cabinet like that? Did you really expect things to stay put once I opened the door? And where in the hell is the orange-juice press? My Lord, woman, get to it and clean up this disaster!"

The many friends who knew Anne to be an easygoing, even-tempered, understanding, and accommodating woman would never have recognized the spitfire who exploded now. It had been too long a day yesterday, too long a night last night, too disturbing an ordeal for months, to permit an ounce of poise. Dark eyes flashing wildly, she confronted him. "*You* clean it up. I didn't make the mess, and I'm not your slave! It happens that I didn't touch that cabinet when I arrived. Put your blame on whomever you please, as long as it is *not on me*! And what right have you to wake me up like this? This is my vacation . . . or didn't you hear that last night?" Only a deaf man could have missed a word now. Goaded by his indignant stare, she ranted on. "This noise was enough to wake the dead. Not that I needed anything as loud as *that* to disturb me; your twisting around up over my head all night was bad enough! Just because *you* have insomnia doesn't mean that I have to catch it!"

His returning stare chilled her. "You certainly wake up in a lovely mood, don't you? Very different from my usual women . . ." His low voice trailed off as his eyes skimmed her, head to toe. "And that's quite an outfit, also very different from my usual women . . ."

A brief cry of frustration marked Anne's realization that in her temper she had left her robe hanging in the closet. Whirling on her heel, hair flying out behind her, she retreated to her room, donned the robe, then, with a wave of weariness, sank down onto the edge of the bed, elbows on knees, face buried in her palms. What had come over her? She had acted like a crotchety wretch. Where had her self-control gone? What good would this snappishness do? Inhaling deeply, she tried to still the throbbing at her temples. The thing to do, she realized, was to face this man reasonably, to find a fast and satisfactory solution to the problem. His women . . . his women, indeed! She was certainly neither his woman nor anyone else's! A sharp pang of sorrow hit her at the thought. If Jeff could only see her now! Ashamed, she gathered together a towel and soap. A long, hot shower might ease her tension and return her to better humor.

For a short while it did. The water pressure was strong, sending steamy trails of moisture to massage the taut muscles of her neck and back. Rich-lathering shampoo left her hair squeaky-clean and shiny, hanging in damp clusters about her shoulders when she finally emerged, toweled herself vigorously, and returned to her room to dress.

Her ablution had blotted out all other sounds, all other thoughts, until, half an hour later, she headed for the kitchen, clothed in a fresh navy sweater, jeans, and sneakers, to make some coffee. It was already hot on the stove. To her surprise the floor was free of its recent debris, the offending cookware having been stacked neatly in the cupboard from which it had earlier tumbled. A satisfied smile spread over her lips. So he *had* cleaned up himself; so much for male chauvinism! And he had made himself scarce. Fair boding for the morning coffee, she mused, helping herself to a mug and filling it with the dark brew, before sitting at the table to ponder the day.

In light of her outburst she was chagrined to discover that she had indeed slept until ten thirty, rather than the earlier hour she had assumed it to be. From the looks of the man whose ruckus had awakened her, he had just arisen also, with no more of a rested look than she. Now, as she wondered where he had gone, the sound of footsteps on the stairs answered her query, followed by the slam of the bathroom door in blatant proclamation of his intention. At least he had waited until she was done, she admitted gratefully. All she had to do now was to wait until he'd finished his own shower and dressed, then they would calmly tackle their dilemma like adults.

As the sound of the water started she relaxed back in her chair, combing her still-damp hair with her slender fingers, spreading it out over her shoulders to dry. Her eyes were drawn through the three-sided window of the breakfast nook to the backyard, which darkness had withheld from her when she had arrived yesterday.

The rustic scene sent a surge of pleasure through her, the well-kept lawn, the scattering of maples and pines, the intermixing of apple trees, their fruit hanging ripe and ready for picking. The morning mist had begun to burn off, penetrated with increasing strength by bright yellow shafts of sunlight. It was exactly what she had hoped to find, so peaceful and quiet, that she was totally unprepared for the roar behind her.

"I don't believe it! You used up all the hot water! Haven't you got a considerate bone in your body?"

Jerking in alarm toward the angry holler, she saw Mitch standing in the doorway of the kitchen, dripping wet, clad only in a towel draped tightly across his hips. Whereas last night she had been frightened by the unknown, now a totally different force frightened her. Here was the embodiment of virility in perfection, a specimen of rugged masculinity, which, against her will, livened her sensitivities. Arms and shoulders of granite flanked a chest tanned, sinewed, and matted with fair hair made darker by the rivulets of moisture that coursed downward. His stomach was flat and firm, his slim hips a solid start for the thighs and lower legs, which echoed the muscled strength of his torso. An imposing figure he was, without a doubt, whether clothed or unclothed. Swallowing convulsively, Anne forced herself to look away.

"I'm sorry," she murmured. "I didn't realize there would be a shortage."

"You didn't realize?" he mocked loudly. "Well, next time, *realize.* Because I like my showers long and hot, too!"

Annoyed at his persistence in spite of her apology, which he barely deserved since this was *her* house for the week, she took a sip of the hot coffee to calm herself. Therein came her revenge. "My God," she exclaimed vociferously, "this coffee is like mud! What did you do to it, anyway? Or should I ask"—her dark eyes narrowed as they returned to his—"how *much* of *my* coffee did you put into that pot? I don't seem to see any groceries of *yours* around here, or had it been your intention to impose on me all along? I'm glad to see you've made yourself right at home." Her sarcasm amused him.

Lips twitching in suddenly forgotten anger, he leaned nonchalantly against the doorjamb. "And why shouldn't I make myself at home? I plan to spend the week here, after all." His cocksureness infuriated her.

"Oh, no, you're not," she cried out, rising quickly, forgetting every good intention to keep calm. This man seemed to have a knack for bringing out the worst in her, she mused, as she moved toward him. "You'll have to find some other place. I'm sure you'll have no trouble, with your delightful personality and winning smile." Her sneer fell on impassive ears.

An arrogant shift of his shoulders brought him away from his post; placidly, he headed back toward the bathroom. "*You* find the substitute," he called over his shoulder. "I'll be staying here."

Unthinkingly Anne trailed him. "But—but you can't!" The conversation of last night repeated itself as she pursued him. At the bathroom door he turned so suddenly to face her that she nearly bumped into him, catching herself at the last minute, gasping aloud, taking a defensive step back. In a nerve-racking gesture he raised his right arm to rest high on the door, his left, an angry red scar glaring from its upper half, fisted against the terry at his hip. His body was a solid wall—maddeningly magnificent—that thwarted her.

"Are you going to stop me?" The drawl in his voice was unmistakable, the glint in his eye, silver and insolent, likewise. "Hmm?" An arched eyebrow punctuated his probe.

Anne stared silently as the seconds passed, struggling to find a sensible rejoinder. When none came to her, she merely turned and retraced her steps, her soft-whispered "If only I could" beyond his hearing.

Perhaps she needed breakfast, she told herself, searching for a diversion—any diversion—from her dilemma. But the scrambled eggs and toast sat uneaten on the plate while she rummaged through her mental storehouse for solutions. Still none came. If she wasn't so far away from home *and* so badly in need of that very distance, she might have simply packed up and left, to return another time when privacy could be assured. Anne Boulton was no match for this Mitch Whoever-he-was. He was bigger, stronger, and evidently equally as, if not more, stubborn than she. What chance did she have?

"Aren't you eating?" Again his voice startled her, though now, she noted with mixed relief, he was every bit as good-looking but fully dressed. His jaw was clean-shaven, the faintest lingering of after-shave accompanying his arrival; his hair was neatly combed, the fullness of it just reaching the collar of his wool plaid shirt. A wide leather belt hugged his hips, dark blue jeans his thighs. On his feet were desert boots, their tan fabric color-coordinating with his hair. The light green hue of his eyes suggested his becalmed state, even before he lightly repeated his question. "You're not hungry?" His focus on the untouched food indicated that if she was *not*, he definitely *was*.

With a sigh of defeat she shoved the dish to the opposite side of the small table. "Help yourself," she offered indifferently.

His glance touched her for a second, preceding his exaggerated "Thank you." Then he lowered his tall form into a chair and took her up on her offer, leaving her to wonder if, after all, he did know some manners. The thought was short-lived. She couldn't believe his next words.

"No wonder you're so thin. You've scrambled these eggs so dry, they are impossible to swallow. If this is a sample of your skill at the stove, it's a miracle you can eat *any* of your own cooking!"

Anne's jaw dropped in astonishment. Jeff had never, never complained about anything, least of all her cooking. Anger quickly surfaced, sparking her dark eyes with a flame of fury. "You are phenomenal! If you don't like my cooking, then *don't eat it!* As a matter of fact, I don't like *you* very much, so why don't we dispense with breakfast completely and get to the point of finding some sort of solution to this—this mess." Only when she stopped shouting did she sense the tears in her eyes. Jamming her knuckles against her mouth, she looked down into her lap, oblivious to the eyes that stared at her.

"How did you get into this mess, as you call it, Anne? Why aren't you with your husband?"

"That's none of your business." Her voice, muffled against her fist, was audible nonetheless.

"I see. . . . Are you divorced?"

"No."

"Then this is some kind of new arrangement—the separate-vacation concept?"

"No."

"He doesn't know you're here?" The surprise in his voice brought a bitter laugh to her lips.

"No."

"You've run away?"

Her fragile composure suddenly cracked. As tears sparkled anew on her long black eyelashes, Anne's head shot up to face him. "Will you leave me alone? Just go! Get out! *Let me be!*" Her voice lowered with a beseeching lilt. "That's all I want—just to be alone."

But his jaw was tight and unyielding. "Why did you leave your husband?"

"That's none of your business."

"But it is!" he returned angrily. "Marriage is a precious thing to hold to. Some people prize it, only to have it taken from them through no fault of their own. Others throw it away. Irresponsibly. If we're going to spend the week together, I want to know which it is. So tell me—why did you leave him?"

The full implication of his words escaped her, so upset was she at his relentless questioning. This was precisely the reason she'd escaped the city and come here—to avoid such pestering. But the man was persistent, goading her on.

"Come on, Anne," he taunted. "If it was just your lousy cooking or your selfishness in the shower, *he* would have left *you.*" He paused as the thought registered. "Is that what happened?"

Brimming with thunder, she looked up at him. "No! No!" she shrieked. "He didn't leave me. I didn't leave him. We loved each other. He . . . he was in an . . . accident, and now . . . he's dead. *Dead!*" Her chair scraped across the floor as she stood abruptly, reached angrily for the plate of food before him, stormed to the sink, and slammed the food face-down in it. Then emotion overwhelmed her. Bracing shaky arms against the counter to give support to suddenly spindly legs, she hung her head as tears began to fall. Helplessly she surrendered to the quiet sobs, unaware of the slow movement behind her.

There was a genuine softness in his voice when he spoke. "I'm sorry. I would never have pushed you, had I known. It was thoughtless of me."

Her hand brushed a tear from her wet cheek as she shook her head. "It doesn't matter." But it did. For some reason his words had released a torrent of emotion she'd thought long since under full control. It had been months since she'd cried, even longer since she'd lashed out at anyone as impulsively as she had at this man, a total stranger. As much as she tried to stem the tears they persisted, then multiplied, reducing her to a sniffling bundle of misery.

Had she been thinking clearly, she would have shied from him the instant his hands touched her shoulders. But clear thought was beyond her grasp. At the moment the only thing that mattered was comfort. And that he offered, turning her into the circle of his arms, pressing her head against his broad chest, holding her tightly as her body shook with the irregular spasms of weeping.

Time and place became irrelevant, as did identity. In Anne's distraught state she only knew that she had craved this very kind of comfort for weeks—strong arms about her, warm breath in her hair, the steady beat of a heart against her ear. Had he turned around and assaulted her anew, she would not have regretted the need filled by these few, silently physical moments.

"Better?" he murmured softly when she finally quieted. A large hand stroked her hair, fingers smoothing loose strands from her damp cheeks as she nodded against his chest. It was only when he raised both hands to frame her face and hold it back for his inspection that she realized where her own arms had taken hold. Somehow, in the midst of her upset, they had wound around the leanness of his waist. Now she dropped them, awkwardly and with a blush, stepping back and out of his reach, leaving his own arms to fall loosely to his sides.

Avoiding his gaze, she turned to leave. "Wait!" he ordered gently, halting her. "Why don't you sit down. I'll make some breakfast for both of us. You can even water down the coffee if you'd like." He hesitated. In the silence, her liquid gaze met his to find a glint of humor there. "Funny. I've taken my coffee strong and black since I was sixteen. Someone told me it would put hair on my chest. I guess you don't want *that,* do you?"

Anne couldn't suppress a sad smile. "Not quite." Her voice still quivered, though her eyes were drying fast and she felt relieved of an immense burden she hadn't realized she carried. The brief smile in *his* eyes, however, didn't reach his lips before it disappeared as quickly, yielding to the hardness that seemed his norm.

"Why don't you sit down while I cook. Then we'll decide what's to be done about this . . . mess," he said, the use of her own word intentional and apt.

Anne helped herself to a fresh cup of coffee, adding hot water from the tap in deliberate movements, then took the seat she had left in such haste moments earlier. Silence reigned as he worked, cracking eggs into the heavy iron skillet, toasting a fresh batch of bread, pouring two glasses of orange juice—if he did have his own fresh oranges to squeeze, he didn't bother with them now—then toting it all to the table.

The tempting warmth of the gay breakfast plate stimulated the appetite she thought she'd lost. Matching his portion, egg for egg, slice of toast for slice of toast, together they downed his handiwork quickly and still in silence. Then he poured her a second cup of coffee, filling the creamer with water and putting that too before her. Expectantly she eyed him, waiting for him to broach the critical subject. Seemingly as eager as she to find a resolution, he began as soon as he sat down, while he waited for his own coffee to cool. His voice had already cooled significantly.

"I spent a lot of time last night thinking about this." The sharp look he shot her warned against a repeat of her complaint about his restlessness. Wisely she held her tongue. "I planned to do some fishing, some hiking, some reading, and a lot of sleeping. What had you wanted to do?"

With a slight tilt of the chin, she answered him directly. "I have books to read, and work to do. I had hoped to get fresh air, wander about some, and enjoy the solitude."

His gaze strayed to the window, where bright sun now poured in. "Look, this may sound absurd, but I think we can both stay here." He held up a hand to still her imminent protest. "We seem to want the same things—quiet and solitude, above all. There's no reason why we can't each go about our own business with a minimum of interference." He paused to look back at her dubious expression. "I know this area, and take my word for it, there will be no other place to stay, on such short notice, within a twenty-five-mile radius."

Idly tucking a wayward strand of black hair behind her ear, Anne pondered his suggestion. This was definitely *not* the manner of vacation she had foreseen, yet he did have a point. Ruling out her own return to New York—and she assumed he would be as vehement against his—there did not seem to be an alternative.

Her thumb absently traced the texture of the ceramic mug. "This isn't quite what I had planned. . . ."

His lips thinned to a grimace. "It's not what I planned either. But it seems the only fair thing. If I have to put up with your hot showers, you can just put up with my black coffee."

"What about the beds—every move you make rattles on the ceiling. I had hoped to sleep!"

Quickly his anger resurfaced. "I wanted that too. But the bed up there is so damned small and uncomfortable. Why don't *you* try sleeping there?"

"Because you're there!" She glared in answer.

"Then why don't I sleep downstairs?"

Her voice raised a pitch. "Because I'm there!"

"Damn it, woman," he seethed, "I don't want to *share* your bed. Why don't we just switch?"

A dark eyebrow lifted. "After you've told me how small and uncomfortable the attic one is? No way!"

His hand clenched on the table. "Then don't complain about the noise." With one swift move he was up, stacking the dishes, dumping them in the sink. Only then did he turn to her, a fallen wave of silver crossing his frown-creased brow. "You clean up. I cooked." He left the room so quickly that Anne's protest met thin air.

"But—it was—my food—" Slowly she faced the dishes, a scornful pout masking the vulnerability in her mien. If this was a preview of the week in companionship, things looked grim. For, she mused, as she began to punish the plates with a soapy sponge, this Mitch was a volatile man, capable of both violence and tenderness. The first frightened her, the second soothed her. But what she really needed just now was something in between—a neutral zone, so to speak.

Perhaps if they went each his own way, as Mitch had suggested, a middle ground might be achieved. The scouring pad moved briskly over the surface of the skillet as she poured her doubts into the task. Given the fact that she could do nothing about his presence, the only sensible course was for her to carry on as though he weren't around, to blot out his existence and immerse herself in her chosen activities.

This she did with marked deliberateness, beginning with a long walk through the woods, following the line of a low stone wall across the hilltop and down a gently graded slope until the road intersected her path. The view was spectacular from several points where the forest door opened to reveal the village far below, its tall white church steeple catching the afternoon sun in a spiritual sparkle. As she followed the dirt road back toward the house, the climb steepened, forcing a rest stop or two along the way. All was peaceful about, the murmur of the breeze in sharp contrast to the grating sounds of the city she'd fled, the lush fern floor of the land edging the road a far cry from the stone sidewalks of New York, the occasional chipmunk skuttling toward his haven a clean and healthy switch from the guard dog on a leash by the curbstone. Accustomed to the gray of the pigeon, she marveled at the black cap and white bib of the chickadee, the vibrant red breast of the robin. The sun, playing through the boughs of still-fully-clothed trees, tickled her. The crispness of the air, sharp yet short of chill, invigorated her. It was a thoroughly pleasant outing.

Her luck held. When she finally ventured back to the house, Mitch was nowhere about, the only car in sight being her own. With an exhaustion brought on by fresh air and lack of sleep, she promptly collapsed atop her quilt and remedied the situation, falling into deep and restful oblivion. The tension of the past weeks took its due; when she finally awakened, it was dusk. After freshening up in the bathroom, she fixed a light supper of soup and crackers, then settled before the fire as she had done the night before, bent on finishing the mystery, which had been so momentously interrupted then. The continuity had been broken, however, leaving her involvement strictly on the surface. When finally the last page had been read, she sat back in comfort to watch the flames. Their play entranced her, calming, lulling her into a peaceful daze.

This was how it was supposed to be. She sighed restfully. Then it came to her that for the first time and at long last, she felt removed from the tragedy of Jeff's death. How horrible it had been—the news of the plane crash, the limbo as rescue teams set to work, the hope as survivors appeared, the total and utter despair as the worst became reality. Then mourning began.

In all truth Anne believed that now, in this isolated house in Vermont, she could think to shake the awesome black mantle that had cloaked her for too long. Her heart felt lighter, her mind freer than it had been at any point since the crash. But whether it was merely the dissociation of this spot with her real life or whether it was the legitimate start of healing, she didn't know. That would remain to be seen when she returned to New York at the end of the week.

For now she vowed simply to face each day as it came. There was still Mitch to cope with. Though it was after nine, he hadn't returned. Perhaps it was just as well. They seemed like fire and water, the two of them. In hindsight, however, she had to be grateful for his reaction on learning of her widowhood. It was not only a matter of the comfort he'd offered when she broke down, but also the fact that he hadn't gone on and on, as too many people tended to do, about what a shame it was, how young a widow she made, how tragic it was for Jeff to be taken from life in his prime. It was understanding Anne needed, not pity. It was the former that Mitch had offered, briefly and subtly. His arms had spoken with their comforting embrace, his heart with its steady beat. *He can't be all bad.* She smiled to herself. *Even though he does make a bitter pot of coffee!*

The evening passed in tailor-made serenity, drawing Anne from her chair only to refuel the fire. Before long her lids grew heavy and she dozed into a dreamless state from which only the sensation of movement disturbed her much later. When awareness crept slowly back, she was in the arms of her nemesis, her head nestled snugly against his shoulder, his arms under her knees and across her back.

"What . . . what do you . . . think you're doing?" she demanded groggily, beginning to squirm. The arms about her merely tightened.

"Putting you to bed." The voice was gruff, the steady gait already at her bedroom door.

"Let me down! I don't need you to do anything—" With an unceremonious thud she was dropped onto the bed. Startled and now fully awake, her eyes met Mitch's iced hazel ones.

"Don't worry. I'm not doing *you* any favors. It's *me* I'm thinking of." His stance was widespread in arrogant indignance.

"What are you talking about?" she asked, raising herself up on her elbows.

"Very simply, *I* want to sit in that chair!" Before she could begin to call him out, he pivoted and left, slamming the door tightly behind him.

Sunday brought more of the same, both positive and negative. On the plus side, the weather was grand, crisp, and clear once the early-morning fog had lifted its cleansing mantle. Having had her fill of sleep, Anne was up early, putting on her *own* pot of coffee and thereby assuring herself of a tasty cup, before showering and dressing. The door to the attic remained closed; if Mitch was still asleep, his too was a sound one, its previous restlessness markedly absent. In light of the silence overhead she half expected to find *him* asleep in the chair in the living room, but it proved to be empty.

Following breakfast, she rewalked the route of yesterday, this time extending its sphere to the brook that babbled down the far hillside. She marveled at the new day's offering of color, heralding the oncoming season that the nip in the air attested to. In a moment of impulse she removed her sneakers, rolled up the cuffs of her jeans, and waded across the flat granite boulders over which the water flowed more shallow. It was just the kind of thing that she and Jeff would have done. Her spreading smile spoke of fond memories of similar romps that they had shared. Now she was alone . . . yet strangely peaceful. Despite the poignancy of the moment, she enjoyed this for what it was, leaping lightly from stone to stone with near carefree abandon.

Whereas yesterday the walk exhausted her, today it exhilarated. When she returned, she tackled the first of the papers she had brought to translate, making good headway with the English-to-Spanish piece until hunger diverted her attention. By this time there were stirrings from the upper quarter. Studiously she avoided the man himself, lingering at her work until he was in the bathroom, dallying in the kitchen until he had returned to his room. When he finally descended the stairs once more, she was back at work, sitting at the small desk, which stood beneath a side window of the living room.

Then began the minuses. Such as suffering a silent observer over one's shoulder for no less than ten exasperating minutes. Such as having to bear the clatter and bang in the kitchen of the man who seemed suddenly to crave attention. Such as fighting the distraction of the whistling, loud and persistent, of the same country-and-western tune, over and over and over again. Such as parrying the periodic interruptions of the "Hey, where is . . ." type—"Hey, where is the salt?" or "Hey, where is the ketchup?" or "Hey, where is the large spatula?" Only the conviction that he baited her purposely kept her from screeching back at him, though she finally put down her pen, tore off her glasses, and made for the kitchen in an attempt at a civil complaint.

"Are there any more ques— What do you think you're doing?" In alarm, she raced across the room, only to drop her outstretched arms in disgust and roll her eyes heavenward in search of patience.

"What's the trouble?" The innocence of his expression was too much.

"I don't believe it!" she began in a rush, peering once more into the half-hollowed jar in his hand. "That's *my* peanut butter! Have you *any* idea how *precious* it is? I've been hoarding that itty-bitty jar for just this vacation!" It was only for lack of breath that she paused, but it was long enough for him to slip in a fast retort.

"I'll buy you another one! Is money *that* tight?" Clearly he mocked her, particularly when he coated his spoon anew with the gooey stuff and proceeded to lick it lazily.

Anne's brows drew together in frustration. "Give me that!" Reaching for the jar, she clamped on its lid before he could get out a final glob. "It's not the money, but the shortage! Didn't you hear about the peanut freeze last season? My

God, peanut butter is practically nonexistent on the supermarket shelves!"

"I'll get you more," he repeated calmly.

But she was not to be appeased. "And who are you? The Planter's peanut?" For an instant, as a sly smile played on his lips, she realized that for all she knew, he owned the company. He hadn't mentioned his line of work, nor had she asked. Strangely this anonymity suited her, though she wasn't quite sure why. With a shake of the head, she replaced the jar in the cabinet, then turned to face him cautiously. "Can I trust you to leave it alone, or do I have to put it in my room?"

His lips curved now into a more mischievous smirk, Mitch continued to enjoy her show, folding his arms leisurely across his chest as his gaze pierced her thin defense. "I haven't had peanut butter in a long time; I'd forgotten how good it is." He raised an eyebrow for its satanic edge. "But you can trust me . . . at least when it comes to the peanut butter."

It was the satanic element in his drawl that startled her, locking her sight to his beam. The thread of seduction seemed clear. For a moment her breath caught in her throat as the message flashed through her sharpened senses. Then, as quickly, she dismissed it as a figment of her imagination. Without further word, she turned and stalked off.

Monday began without a hitch, as a pattern emerged. While Anne arose early and hiked about the countryside, Mitch slept late, awakening shortly before or after her return, always late enough to ensure a replenished supply of hot water for a long shower. Meals were widely scattered and invariably eaten alone from supplies that remained separate and distinct.

By Tuesday Anne felt well rested and relaxed. If Mitch continued to toss in his sleep, she had either grown immune to the sound or her own slumber was deep enough to blot it out. Whatever the reason, she slept well.

His absence throughout that entire day did not go unnoticed. Arising earlier than usual, he packed a lunch and vanished, leaving Anne to the solitude she desired. Strangely, though, between work, books, and other incidental activities around the house, she found her mind wandering to this enigmatic character with whom she was, in a manner of speaking, living. Looking at the situation objectively, she was appalled by her own acceptance of it. Her friends would have been astounded, her family scandalized. Yet she floated on a cloud of comfort here, both physically and emotionally. This world was divorced totally from that of New York, the man likewise. It was for this reason, precisely, that anonymity was appropriate. Still, she couldn't help but wonder, every now and then . . . just a little.

Wednesday morning brought with it the awareness that the week too rapidly approached its end; by Friday afternoon she would be headed back to the city. Pondering this thought over breakfast coffee, she felt a pang of disappointment. Despite its unexpected turn, the vacation had been a good one. She would miss this country, so open and free, when, of necessity, it was left behind.

Determined to make the most of the remaining days, she spent more time in the woods than ever before, reveling in the natural beauty of the flora, the unmatched freedom of the fauna, and the luxury of time itself, which was, for once, her ally. The sun had passed its high-noon mark when she returned to the cabin, shunning the indoors for the shade of an old apple tree in the backyard. Bracing herself against its trunk, she inhaled deeply of the sweet bouquet, tilting her head back to gaze at the golden sparkle through the fruit-laden boughs. It was in this posture that inspiration came.

Her lightweight parka was quickly drawn off and spread wide upon the soft grass by her feet. Standing, she began to pick apples, bypassing the greener fruit, selecting only the fullest and deepest red of the lot to add to a steadily growing pile. When the last of the best within reach lay on her jacket, she briefly calculated her own agility, squinting toward the upper branches, taking stock of her options. Then, casting prudence aside, she braced a rubber-soled foot against the trunk and carefully hoisted herself onto the first branch, opening a whole new batch of fruit to her grasp. Balanced gingerly, she plucked one, then another, filling her free arm slowly until she could hold no more. Her gaze had been up, her concentration narrowed. Only when she lowered her sight to descend did she see the dark form, arms on hips, legs planted firmly by the foot of the tree.

His appearance startled her, preoccupied as she had been. With a short cry of fright, she lost her balance. Apples barreled to the ground in a crimson storm. As she began to fall she twisted sideways, grabbing back at the low branch to catch herself. Strong arms were there, however, to break her descent, saving her from the ground, but not soon enough to prevent a bruising from the ragged bark and jutting offshoots.

Embarrassment brought a flush to her cheeks. "Why did you creep up on me that way?" she shrieked, when her two feet felt the firmness of earth at long last. The arms released her instantly, but not before she'd seen the flinch of pain on the rugged face. Then, with a gasp of pain herself, she sank onto the grass, rubbing furiously at the knee that had taken the brunt of her weight against the branch.

"Are you all right?" The concern in his voice contradicted his fierce expression.

"Of course!" Avoiding his gaze, she probed an aching elbow.

"Are you always this clumsy?"

"I wasn't clumsy. You terrified me—sneaking up like that."

His deep voice derided her. "Now, who did you think it was? There aren't an awful lot of other people around here, or hadn't you noticed?"

"Oh, I noticed," she challenged him curtly, "but that's beside the point. I was doing beautifully until you came along!"

He bent to gather the fruit that had haphazardly scattered

upon the ground. As she peered up through the filter of her luxuriant lashes, she saw that his expression was grim, rather than the mocking one she might have expected. "You should be more careful. You could break a leg that way," he growled.

Eying him speculatively, she baited him. "Is that the voice of experience talking?"

"You might say so." His lips clamped shut.

Her attention caught on the left arm, which hung idly as the right casually tossed the last of the apples onto her jacket. "Is your arm all right?"

He glanced sharply up to follow the line of her sight. "It's fine." The unmistaken hardness in his tone warned her not to pursue the matter. "Can you walk?" He changed the subject.

As she stood, testing the knee, he pulled the parka around into a bundle and lifted it, awaiting her judgment. "No problem," she insisted tautly, but even as she tried to hide it, there was a slight limp in her walk as they returned, silently, to the house. His long strides outdistanced her uneven ones, and when she entered the kitchen, he had already deposited the load on the counter by the sink and disappeared.

Grateful for the privacy, she collapsed into a chair, twisting her arm to see the scrapes on her elbow, unprotected by the sleeve of the charcoal-gray sweater, which, in the heat of her exertion, she had unwittingly pushed too high.

"Here, let me take a look at that."

Her humiliation was not to be minimized as she had hoped! His order was a firm one. Before she could resist, Mitch deposited a bottle of disinfectant and a washcloth on the table, pulled up a chair, and took her arm for his inspection. The warmth of his touch seared her skin unexpectedly, yet its firmness prevented her withdrawal. When the sting of antiseptic hit her scraped skin, she winced.

"Acch! That's enough!"

But he disagreed, persistently dabbing the dirt from the

wound before kneeling down and reaching for the denim-covered knee that had been marred by the rough tree bark.

"It's all right!" Her repeated protest brought the silver head up even with hers. His jaw was carved of granite, his cheeks hollowed of the same unyielding stone. Yet his eyes were softer in their hazel glow than she had seen them. Something deep within her tripped in response. This he couldn't see, yet the pallor beneath her flush was ample refutation of her words.

"I'll do my best not to hurt you, but it should be cleaned." His broad hand closed around her calf, but it was not until her own gaze softened in submission that he eased the blue material, inch by inch, up over her knee. Now too his ministrations made her flinch, yet it was another factor that startled her more. His touch held a gentleness reminiscent of one other occasion in this same room. Carefully he reapplied the fiery liquid, blotting it gradually to ease her discomfort.

As Mitch worked, Anne's eye caught on the flex of muscles at his shoulders, boasting a latent power beneath the snug mold of his dark green turtleneck sweater. His head, bent before her, was rich and full, silver interpersed with blond in a wealthy spread. Her fingers ached to touch it, to plunge into its obedient waves. Instinctively she clenched her fists to deny the urge.

"There, now," he murmured softly. "That wasn't so bad, was it?" With both hands cradling her leg, he surveyed his work a final time. A shiver of emotion raced through her at his gentle tone and even gentler touch. When he raised his head, her breath faltered, for the deep green of his eyes threatened to drown her, and her pulse quickened independently from the shock of the fall.

His own breath caught at the image of simple beauty before him. Her sculpted features had softened with vulnerability; her dark, rounded eyes suggested a loneliness that he knew, too. Driven by an unbidden force, his hand raised to curve lightly around her neck. Mesmerized, she didn't resist when his thumb feather-touched the soft swell of her lips. For an instant he hesitated; Anne's breath held.

Then, with eternal slowness, he raised his mouth to hers, testing her response with the tantalizingly light movement of his firm lips. When she made no protest, his pressure increased, his lips coaxing hers to open to a kiss that was the total antithesis of the one he had so brutally imposed on her that first night. No thought could infiltrate her trance, save that of the wildfire coursing through veins that had, for so long, been clogged with ice. With sensual expertise he caressed her lips, his tongue playing against her teeth until, swept up with delight, she offered her own. Bespeaking months of starvation, she yielded to the every demand of his kiss, her own hunger furthering his until, with a reluctant and unexpectantly rough grasp of her shoulders, he pulled away.

Only then did sanity return. With a gasp she bolted out of the chair and to the far side of the room, oblivious to the remnant of a twinge at her knee. Mitch stood slowly, his back to her as his breathing steadied. When finally he turned to face her, the rich green depth of passion had leveled to its normal, placid hazel.

Trying desperately to understand what had happened, she raised unsteady fingers to her lips, still moist and throbbing. He was a man; perhaps that was his excuse. But what was hers? Under his intent stare, she lashed out irrationally. "You had no business doing that." But her voice held more bewilderment than anger.

His gaze held steady as his lips thinned. "I don't seem to recall your objecting at the time."

"You didn't give me much of a chance." Her words were apt. His sexual prowess was such that, given their closeness, the tenderness of the moment, all rational thought had fled.

Seemingly indifferent to her defensive barbs, he approached, his eyes studying the luminosity of hers, the blush of rose on her cheeks, the telltale quiver of her lips. "It's been a long time, hasn't it?" The reference was to himself as much as to her, though of this she was ignorant. She only saw the rueful smile that he bestowed, and promptly misinterpreted it.

"Don't give me your pity!" The words were out before she realized her mistake. In her heart, she knew her accusation was unjust. Not once in the week had he hinted at pity, and he had known about her status since that first morning.

Now anger hardened his features, jolting her insides as his words finished the job. "I don't deal in pity. I've seen enough of it in the past year to make me sick. No, Anne, if you can't recognize a basic physical need, then you are deluding yourself sadly." His gaze narrowed sharply. "Let's just say I took my reward for playing nursemaid to a bad-tempered tomboy!"

Her gasp of dismay met his broad back as he turned and stormed from the room. He was right. She did delude herself if she refused to acknowledge the sensations his kiss had aroused. His had been a breath of life. Could she deny it? But she had to. It had been only a kiss—*only a kiss*—in this northern land of make-believe. Come next week, this would all be but a pleasant dream, enjoyed for the moment, savored in memory, never to be relived.

With her slowly calming mood came the return of purpose. One by one, she pared the apples, slicing each, piling the skins on a piece of paper towel, turning the slices into a large glass pie plate, before sprinkling them with cinnamon. Rummaging through her dwindling supplies, she produced the proper amounts of flour, butter, and sugar for the topping. It was only when the masterpiece was in the oven that she stopped to ponder the unused apples. Washing each, she dried and polished it to a high gloss, filling a dish in the center of the table with gleaming red orbs. Only then did she notice Mitch's arresting form, eying her intently from the doorway, where his casually lounging length had apparently been for quite some time.

Defensiveness surged anew as she eyed him warily, her voice tinged with huffiness. "Is something wrong?"

"Just looking to see that you're all right." In truth, she had forgotten about her bruises. Informing him so, he nodded. "Glad to hear it." Then, with a suave inclination of the head, he left as silently as he had come, leaving Anne to admire his fine looks in hindsight.

At his departure from the house soon after, she immersed herself in the last of the work she hoped to accomplish before she returned to the city. The scent of the apple pie wafted through the cottage as it baked, then cooled. It was delicious, by her own immodest estimate, a perfect finish for the early dinner she ate in solitude. Dusk found her, again, reading before the fire.

"Anything good?" The deep voice broke into her concentration.

A guilty smile stole over her lips. "Just a romance." So, she *had* picked it up and was thoroughly enjoying it. A surprise, to say the least! And her own motivations were as much an enigma to her as those of the man whose momentary intensity cut sharply through her. When Mitch turned to head for the kitchen, she stopped him. "There's some apple pie on the counter. Help yourself." Then, prompted by his raised brow and slow-spreading grin, she added, "Even bad-tempered tomboys have their merits." The mischievous sparkle in her eye was acknowledged with a knowing nod.

"Thanks." His tone lightened with the unexpected offer.

"You're welcome."

"By the way, I put the peels out for the deer."

Again, there was a touch of guilt to her smile. "I wondered where they'd gone, but I wasn't about to look a gift horse in the mouth. Do deer really like apples?"

"We'll see." His evasiveness was deceptive. Anne thought that Mitch could probably instruct a zoo-keeper on the habits of the animals of the hills.

That was the end of the verbal interchange for the evening.

To her surprise, however, it resumed early the next morning, when a strong hand shook her gently awake.

"Anne? Wake up. Come on, there's something you've got to see!" The conspiratorial whisper drove away all sleepiness, the warm hand on her arm all resistance. Rolling out of bed, she allowed herself to be guided to the window of her bedroom, where his pointing finger directed her attention. There, beneath the pocket of low mist in the yard, by the base of the old apple tree from which Anne had tumbled, was a young doe, munching at the remains that Mitch had tossed out. Breathlessly, the two watched as the lithe animal stood on her hind legs to pick a fresh apple.

"Deer do like apples, wouldn't you say?" His breath fanned her ear, its warmth heightening the delight of the scene and overshadowing the hint of mockery in his tone.

"That's beautiful," she murmured as the doe, having temporarily satisfied herself, trotted away. "Thank you for waking me." She turned to find his eyes on her already. For a heart-stopping moment gray-green locked with black in wordless communion, before he put a gentle hand to her arm, patted it lightly, then left. He had been wearing only his robe then, but by the time she showered, dressed, and entered the kitchen, he too was dressed. As Mitch gazed absently out the window as he sat on the edge of the kitchen table, the freshness of morning gentled his features.

"Coffee?" she offered quietly.

"Ummm." He paused, slowly turning to look at her. "And a piece of that apple pie. My compliments to the baker."

"Apple pie? For breakfast?"

"Sure. Call it danish, if the thought disturbs you. But it *was* good!"

She set her hands to the coffee-making, though whether the addition of an extra scoop to the basket was accidental, she would wonder later. "Swedish apple pie. My mother's recipe. Easy and good. Actually, now that I think about it, my dad used to have it for breakfast too." Fearful that she'd spoken too personally, she quieted.

"Is your father dead?" His loden gaze bathed her in compliancy, bidding her gently to reveal even more.

"Oh, no. It's just that . . . I live in my own place." As hard as habit was to break, she had managed to leave Jeff's name off the description of her living quarters.

As though sensing her train of thought, he prodded gently, "Isn't it lonely for you?"

"Sometimes." An understatement.

"Children?"

"No." Regretfully.

"You're lucky."

Her smooth brow furrowed in puzzlement and surprise as she lowered the gas under the perking coffee. "Why do you say that? I've often wondered whether it would have been easier . . . to have . . . someone left. . . ."

An abrupt tautness gripped him. "It isn't. Take my word for it."

Unless grossly mistaken, Anne could have sworn she heard the voice of personal experience. But, much as she wanted to ask, she feared they'd already said too much. Anonymity was the best course. He seemed in full agreement, offering no elaboration of his own for his near-bitter statement, vanishing shortly after he'd finished his pie and coffee, tossing a mocking "Getting better!" over his shoulder in passing, a superfluous reminder as Anne added more water to her own cup of the brew.

Late that afternoon, busy sounds from the kitchen announced his return. Anne put the finishing touches on the piece she had translated, stacked her papers neatly, then paused, sniffing the air in horror as a vile smell seeped from the direction of the kitchen.

"You went fishing!" she exclaimed with a grimace, pausing at the kitchen door to bemoan the odorous mess on her previously clean counter. "Phew!" Her nose crinkled in disgust.

"Now, now," he chided in good-natured dismissal of her complaint, "it may smell badly at first, but once this bass is fried, the end result will be worth it. You *will* join me for dinner, won't you?" The sizzle of oil in the skillet precluded her own sputtering. The eyes that lifted suddenly to hers vouched for the sincerity of his invitation. In light of the latter, she could not have refused.

"If—if you have enough."

"Oh, I have enough, you can be sure," he noted with a mischievous twinkle. "And if we don't eat it tonight, it will go to waste. This is a champion fisherman you're looking at!"

"And an immodest one!" she added with a crooked smile. Not for a minute did she doubt his ability. It occurred to her, with begrudging admiration, that Mitch would be good at whatever he did. He had that certain air of competence, well beyond the arrogance of his jaw and the deliberateness of his bearing. Indeed, as it turned out, the fish was delicious. As was the fresh-squeezed orange juice that awaited her at breakfast the next morning. He was, it seemed, a handy man to have around the house.

To Anne's surprise, when she headed for the woods on this, her last morning in Vermont, Mitch fell into step beside her. It was as peaceful a hike as any she'd had, the silence broken only by the sounds of nature and Mitch's intermittent comments. Knowledgeable in the ways of the forest, he had a wealth of information—species of trees and flowers, habits of woodland creatures, history of the area itself—to share, which he did in an easygoing, unpresumptuous manner. He sensed when to speak and when to be still, reading Anne's mood well. She was almost sorry when they arrived back at the cabin, knowing that her next chore was to pack.

With the luggage safely stowed in the trunk and the key in the ignition, a naughty voice inside her prayed that the engine would fail, that, having sat in idle luxury atop the pine landing for the week, her car would simply refuse to budge. But it coughed to life at the first turn, then hummed smoothly as it warmed. With but one thing left to do, she was about to climb out of the car when the object of that "one thing" rounded the side of the house and headed toward her.

"You weren't going to leave without saying good-bye, were you?" When his head bent to talk to her through the open window of the car, the sun glanced off its silver strands in sparkles.

"I was just going to come and find you."

"Have you got everything?" His voice flowed warmly over her.

"I think so. I . . . left the rest of the apple pie for you."

The sparkle in his eyes matched that of his hair. "Thanks. You do make a good one, even though your coffee is still too weak."

"Then you'll be glad to be rid of me." She smiled wryly. "When do you leave?"

"Later this afternoon."

"Oh." There seemed little else to say. Her gaze fell to the strong fingers, more browned now than when he'd arrived, which curved over the window ledge of the car.

"Will you be back up here at all?" he asked softly.

She shrugged. That far ahead she hadn't thought. "I'm not sure. It's been a good week. I'm—I'm sorry to be leaving." Self-consciously she looked away, yet he'd read between the lines.

"It *wasn't* all that bad, was it?" He hesitated, debating whether to say more as he studied her sudden shyness. "Look," he began tentatively, "I'll be coming up for the week before Thanksgiving. Kind of to give myself a boost before the holidays. Keep it in mind." He had stopped short of an open invitation, yet the implication was there, impractical yet tempting.

Slowly she looked back at him. His gaze held a sense of understanding that she might feel the need for escape, also.

"I'll remember." Her voice was a near whisper. Awkwardly she cleared her throat. "Well, good-bye, then."

He straightened, but not before his eyes had fallen to her lips for a last electric moment. "Good-bye." His control held.

As he stepped away she put the car in reverse, backed around, and headed for the road, all the time thinking how nice it would have been if he had kissed her again. His lank image shrank steadily in the rearview mirror as she moved forward, a strange sense of loss toying with her heightened spirits. Then the car traced a curve, and her sights narrowed toward New York and reality.

CHAPTER THREE

How different the road looked on this trip. Blankets of parched brown leaves lay in heaps on the ground, awaiting the first snow. Forests of bare branches blended with evergreens into a blur of gray-green on distant hills. Mountainous rises stood stark, more harsh now without benefit of the thickly piled verdure carpeting their slopes. Hordes of foliage seekers had long since retreated to the warmth of their homes and thoughts of the approaching Thanksgiving, barely two weeks away.

It was this very anticipation that had precipitated this trip, so Anne told herself, as she pushed steadily northward in her small yellow Chevette. In kaleidoscopic progression she recalled the two months since she'd last traveled these roads. The return trip to New York had been uneventful, her apprehension at facing life and its memories eased by the vivid colors of autumn to the right and left, and the bolstered emotional keel of the week behind.

"You look marvelous!" her mother had exclaimed that first night of her return, holding her daughter at arm's length to study the freshly colored complexion. "I like that healthy pink on your cheeks. It becomes you." Anne could not argue. Even after the long drive she had been full of energy, prompting the early-evening call on her parents before she drove the final leg into the city. "Now, tell me," Marjorie Faulke had said, "did you have a good time?"

Anne's smile had been purposely understated when she nodded. "Yes, Mother, I did. It was perfect. Just what I needed." *With perhaps a few added elements to give a little spice to my adventure,* she had added silently.

"Well, sit down and tell me all about it," the older woman had ordered, and Anne had. Almost. Carefully she avoided all mention of Mitch. There had been no point in enlightening her mother *that* far. And, besides, he played no role in her life, her *real* life. Why, she didn't even know his last name. But that had been part of the game. He was her personal secret.

At the time, she gave little thought to the idea of returning to Vermont, as he had suggested, in November. The pace of life had quickened with the blossoming semester, the abundance of translation work filling her time more than satisfactorily. Though she still had had to parry the pampering by her friends, it was with much more patience that she recalled their good intent. They, in turn, sensing her calmer state, had eased off somewhat, finally beginning to respect her need to be independent. After all, hadn't she thrived during that solitary migration in September?

Dating was still alien to her thoughts. However, her enthusiasm for the project of one particular professor had been sufficient encouragement for him to sign her on with his grant as a part-time assistant. Assured of this ongoing project to off-balance other short-range assignments, she had faced the fall and winter seasons with confidence.

Yet the void had persisted. Jeff was gone. And the holidays approached. What would they be like alone? Would the tragedy rear up anew to punish her with its devastating aftermath? Would joyous family gatherings only trigger painful thoughts?

When the first whisperings from the back of her mind had

begun, she had ignored them. Then, as Halloween had come and gone, the whisperings had become a murmur she could not escape. Mitch . . . Mitch . . . Mitch . . . Go to Vermont, the voice had said. But how could she?

That first time had been an accident. Their staying together, innocent as it had turned out to be, had been a makeshift solution to an awkward problem. To return there, however, would be a very different matter. This time she would go *knowing* he would be there. But would he? Had he been serious about his intent to return the last week before Thanksgiving? What if she *did* drive up, only to find a strange tenant in the weathered house?

In the end it had been Mitch's own correct assessment of the holiday season-in-anticipation that had thrown the balance in favor of making the trip. She *would* need bolstering, she knew, to help her face the coming festivities alone. With or without Mitch, the week would be good for her.

This time her parents raised no objection to the trip, nor did her clients, who knew from experience that she would bring back a stack of completed translations. As a precaution she made a reservation at the nearest inn, some thirty miles from the house. It could always be canceled, she had reasoned, if Mitch *was* there and the house was open. But it would assure her a place to stay in the event of others in residence, or a tightly locked front door. For, after much deliberation, she had opted against calling the rental agent. What could she have said: "Is Mitch going up this weekend?" or "No, I don't know his last name, but we spent the week together there last time," or simply "That was quite some mistake you made!"? In truth, she was reluctant to acknowledge Mitch's existence in any form or manner aside from his actual presence in the isolation of the Vermont retreat. He was, she repeated, her own little secret.

The force of the present returned with a sharp turn off the gray-toned highway onto the rutted brown road leading the distance up the hill to the house. Anne was besieged by a sudden attack of anxiety. What *was* she doing? What sort of warped thought had convinced her to drive this distance in search of a . . . a long-forsaken breath of life? Could she really hope to capture the elusive moment for a second time?

The ruts were harder, more jolting now beneath the raw November chill than they had been in milder September. Likewise were her thoughts more sharp-edged, more contradictory in their ups and downs, ins and outs. She shouldn't have come—she had to come. What did she hope to accomplish—why did she have to hope to accomplish anything? What if Mitch wasn't there—what if he *was?*

It was this last thought that sent a shudder through her—of fear, of excitement, of reluctance, of aggressiveness, of frustration, of exhilaration. She was playing on a whim; of that she was certain. As for the rest, only time would tell.

She timed her arrival well. Mindful of Mitch's late drive on that other Friday night, she had left the city early on Saturday morning, arriving on schedule with a minimum of effort, in the early afternoon. If her calculations had been correct, her host—for so he would be, if indeed he was there —would have just awakened.

Her heartbeat quickened when she rounded the final curve to see the sporty blue Honda parked in front of the house. Amidst the dusky November day, it stood out clearly, a bright and promising robin's egg resting in its dried twig nest. The barrenness of winter lent a silence to the scene that accentuated even the slightest signs of life. Now, with her pulse pounding loudly, Anne felt a return of that same heightened sensitivity that seemed to affect her only here.

So he had come. Had he expected her also? A last-minute clash of nerves skittered through her insides as she pondered her wisdom a final time. Then, taking a deep breath of conviction, she pulled up behind his car, slid from behind the wheel, and walked toward the door. Unconsciously she smoothed out the panels of her gray wool skirt, adjusted the waistband of her black sweater, and pulled the navy pea coat close about her, aware of no sound save the resounding click of her heeled leather boots on the broken flagstone walk.

The grass was aged, dying; the lilac was forlorn in its nakedness. Yet Anne could not forget how alive she did feel as she lifted a pale hand to knock, shyly, on the black door. When there was no answer, she repeated the act, with more conviction, designed to bring him from the kitchen, where he may have been breakfasting. Still, silence confronted her.

Glancing back to assure herself that his car *was* there, she wondered for a fleeting moment whether he'd broken habit and gone for an earlier hike. The doorknob refused to yield beneath her twisting fingers. Finally and with a full fist, she gave a forceful rap.

The door opened. Instantly she knew why he had been so long in answering. Mitch had been asleep. Now, bleary-eyed, unshaven, mussed of hair, and rumpled-looking in an old shirt, tails hanging low over wrinkled jeans, he stood before her, tall, lean, and not quite as enthusiastic as she might have hoped. Shyness sent an unsure light to her eye, second thoughts a quiver to her stomach. Determinedly she swallowed it all.

"Hello, Mitch." Her voice was tentative, her smile even more so.

"Where in the hell have you been?" He glared angrily, eyes narrowed in accusation. "I was thinking of sending the troops out after you." Had it not been for his gruffness, Anne might have hugged him. Only at this moment, and even despite his manner and appearance, did she realize how much she had looked forward to seeing him. Yet his tautness held her off. Self-consciously she smoothed an imagined stray hair back toward the neat black coil at the nape of her neck. "Well?" he prodded in subtle warning.

"I—I didn't leave the city until this morning."

"Why not? You knew I'd be arriving yesterday."

"But I didn't!" she answered quickly with growing belligerence. It hadn't taken very long; they were at each other again. Is this what she had driven hours for?

His eyes, cleared now of sleep, and deep, deep green, speared her. "I'm beginning to wonder if you're more trouble than you're worth!"

Her small chin lifted indignantly. "I was just wondering the same about you! Perhaps it's better that I leave!" Spinning on her heels, she was able to take but one step before his long fingers snaked out to place a steel clamp on her arm.

"No!" Then his voice softened. "Don't go." That her own defiance had inspired his gentle plea, she could not fathom. Yet, when she looked back at him, his gaze had softened, spreading its relaxation to her own finely sculpted features. "Come in . . . please."

She had no choice—not that she wanted one—as his arm-hold drew her over the threshold and into the house. The door closed firmly behind, leaving her but inches from his towering form. Strangely at a loss for words, she could only return the depth of his gaze with her own, drinking in his compelling masculinity as he stood before her.

For a moment he seemed unsure himself, his eyes scanning her face, searching for something. Then, slowly, he drew her against him into the full hug she craved. The iron band of his arms circled her back, holding her prisoner against the warmth of his chest, as her own hands slid around his waist. It was a precious moment of silent understanding, each savoring the presence of the other, their hearts in perfect syncopation.

His lips moved against the smoothness of her hair. "It's good to see you, Anne."

His verbal welcome brought a sigh from her. "Same here, Mitch." The sinewed contour of his chest absorbed her words, yet she made no move to extricate herself from the rapturous haven she'd discovered. It was Mitch who made the move, drawing back to visually caress her softness, to realign memory with reality. As though to better study her, his hands framed her face, tilting it back as his thumbs lightly dimpled her cheeks. When one moved to her lips, they parted expectantly . . . and were not disappointed, for his mouth, replacing that thumb, was as tender, as beckoning as his embrace moments before had been. And she welcomed it as eagerly, tasting his warmth and returning her own. The play was light and sensual, an intermingling of tongues and lips in the sweetness of the moment. When Mitch drew back this time, it was to catch his breath. Though his kiss had ended, the light in his eyes smoldered on, sending flickers of excitement through her veins.

Physical self-restraint could not eliminate the low huskiness of his voice. "How about making some coffee while I get cleaned up? You look a damned sight better than I do right now."

A coy smile warmed her mouth, the unreality of the situation freeing her inhibitions for the moment. "Oh, you don't look so bad," she teased, reluctant to deprive herself of his nearness any sooner than was necessary.

His jaw tensed as, abruptly, he felt it *was* necessary. "Get the coffee, woman, if you know what's good for you. I'll get your bags later." Thrusting her from him with a return of gruffness, he strode toward the bathroom.

Humored by his turn and warmed miraculously by his underlying welcome, Anne threw her coat over a chair and followed his instructions, taking it upon herself not only to make the coffee very strong, but to scrounge up some eggs from his meager supplies and to scramble them—moist—for his breakfast. If it occurred to her to question her solicitousness, she parried the thought with her excitement at being once more at the cabin.

With the fare sitting hot on the table, her gaze wandered out the window to the backyard. There too all was bare, a dull red ball or two clinging stubbornly to the lonely branches of the apple tree. The firs stood out majestically, towering triumphantly over the stillness, swaying gallantly to indulge the occasional gust of prewinter wind that sent shivers through the tall grass below. But the chill without remained there; within, Anne was delightfully warm and content.

"You're looking well, Anne." Again he caught her unaware from his post of leisure at the door. "Perhaps a little pale, but better than last time." Straightening, he entered the room, groomed meticulously now and looking devastatingly fresh in an open-necked wool shirt and clean denims. Her eye strayed helplessly to the wisps of manly hair, tawny colored, at the vee of his shirt; then, quickly, she sought his eyes.

"You . . . didn't have much to offer in the fridge. I hope the eggs are enough."

Stiffling a comprehending smirk, he lowered himself into a chair and took a hefty helping from the central platter. "I thought we could go marketing today. Unless . . . you brought groceries with you." A speculative eye studied her over the rim of his coffee cup.

"No, I didn't bring any food this time," she explained cautiously. "I wasn't . . . sure I'd be . . . staying here. I actually made reservations at an inn in Woodstock. Just in case."

His silvered gaze narrowed dangerously. "Just in case . . . what? Were you afraid I might attack you again?"

"No! Of course not!" she denied impulsively, then instantly regretted her sureness. Unpredictable as his mood was at times, he could try easily to prove a point. Choosing to ignore that possibility, she went on quickly. "I wasn't sure you'd *be* here. After all, it *was* tentative when you mentioned it, and since I had no way of contacting you in between—"

"You could have called Miles Cooper," he suggested lightly.

"You know very well that I couldn't!" she contradicted him immediately. "There was really no *comfortable* way of finding out your plans."

"Did that bother you?" The deep timbre of his voice sent

a shiver through her. She could easily ask herself that very question. Yet, for outward purposes, her answer was clear-cut.

"No. For now, it has to be this way. I"—she looked down to avoid his probing gaze—"I don't think I can cope with identities . . . just yet."

The straight draw of his lips was in keeping with the firmness of his tone. "Then we are in agreement on the matter. No more said." Even as she wondered at his own need for anonymity, she let the matter ride.

"No more said." The sadness of her whispered echo gave him pause for just a moment before he returned to his breakfast.

When he finished, he wiped a napkin across his mouth. "You can phone from the village later and cancel those reservations. But I think you should know that there are two conditions to your staying here."

"Conditions?" Her eyes flashed in defiance.

Nonchalantly he leaned back, balancing the chair on its rear legs. "Yes, conditions." His expression of authority brooked no argument. "First, we eat together."

If that was the worst of it, there would be no problem. Relieved and inwardly pleased, she smiled, an even white smile. "And?"

"Second," he continued more daringly, "*I* sleep downstairs."

Her smile vanished. "You can't do that!" she burst out in alarm. "I never said I'd go to bed with you!"

Mischief danced in his eyes. "You know, Anne, there's nothing I'd like better. I'm told that I'm a very good lover—"

"But—" she interrupted, only to be interrupted in turn.

"But I'm not ready for *you* any more than you are ready for *me.*" He eyed her full flush with arrogance. "At some point, our bodies *will* warm each other. Make no mistake about it. When that time comes, nothing will keep us apart. Right now, we both have ghosts to contend with."

Startled by the mutuality in his words, Anne grabbed the empty dishes and escaped to the sink. Mitch, however, was close behind her.

"You're a very beautiful woman," he crooned, inches behind her.

"Last time, I was 'plain' and 'scrawny,' to quote your own eloquent description." Had it hurt her that much at the time to prompt such sarcasm, or was this merely her only defense against his devastating nearness?

"Last time, I was wet and tired and angry. Now I can see straight." Strong hands glided down across her middle, drawing her back against the hard length of his body. His forearms brushed the underswells of her breasts and remained, their faint touch wreaking havoc with her senses, driving all thought of protest from mind. Her heartbeat thudded for his sure detection. With a low groan he turned her to face him, his arms securing the embrace.

A magnetic force tilted her face up toward his. Her lips parted in helpless invitation, to be met a breath's stop later by his in descent. Possession was warm and firm, though gentle. Mindlessly she responded with a fervor she had forgotten was possible. As her arms moved, of their own accord, over his chest to his neck, he strengthened his hold in a sensuous declaration that ignited fires of desire within her. His lips made momentary detour over the fevered planes of her cheeks and the butter-soft lids of her eyes before returning to the moistness of her mouth in heady demand.

If emotional readiness was in doubt, not so the physical. His ardor came through, hard and bold, against her as he crushed her slim form to the lines of his manliness, his hands trailing wildfire across her back, her waist, her hips. Her fingers wound through the thickness of his hair, forcing his lips more vibrantly onto hers. Her small cry of pleasure mingled with his breath when he slid his hands up to tease the sides of her breasts with maddeningly evasive thumbs. Oblivious to all reality but the fiery need within, Anne arched closer, her silent plea having instant effect. His fingers moved in, cupping the fullness of her breasts to his palms, then singling out the pebbled tips, which already strained through the knit of her sweater. A soft purr of delight came from the back of her throat as he stroked her with an expertise she had never doubted. Her own intuitive skill set her hands in motion, mapping out his virility from shoulder to hip. All the while their lips cavorted hungrily, nipping, tucking, devouring in turn. Anne's momentary need was overwhelming. Her fingers fell to curve about the lean muscle of his thigh, then slid sensually upward, upward and inward in their instinctive search.

Mitch stiffened abruptly, then pulled back. In the agony of loss, Anne realized what she'd done, dropping her arms suddenly, hanging her head onto her chest. The ragged breathing above her was little consolation for her own racing heart.

"That shouldn't have happened." Her faltering whisper took the blame for her wanton behavior in allowing both his liberties and her own.

His sneer carried a cruelty that stunned her. It didn't occur to her that his anger was directed against himself. "But it did! Damn it, this was a crazy idea all along!"

Daring not to look at him, she tried to edge away from the sink against which he continued to pin her. The rigidity of his body spoke his feelings all too well, yet he felt compelled to elaborate. Strong fingers seized her chin to raise her eyes to his. "Annie, you try my patience terribly. One part of me aches to pick you up in my arms, carry you into that bedroom"—he cocked his head toward the other side of the house—"and make furious love to you. But the last thing I need right now is to hear another man's name on your lips in the throes of passion." When she opened her mouth to condemn his crudity, his hold constricted with such force that it tore the breath from her. "You are still mourning your husband. Your clothes, your hair, your eyes, tell me that. And"—his voice grew more hoarse—"I too have a past. The last thing *you* need is to hear *me* call out another woman's name."

The venom at the last brought unbidden tears to Anne's eyes. With an unknown strength she shoved him from her, seeking refuge with her back to him at the window. "You are a bastard," she seethed. "Why do you lead me on?"

Silence hung heavily before he answered in begruding admission. "I can't seem to help myself." Then he paused, recalling her own willingness, her own passion. "What's your excuse?" Disgust tinged his tone, though whether aimed purely at her, or partly at himself, she did wonder. Her head bent, a solitary tear trickled down her hot cheek. "Well?" he goaded, his approaching step silent. "Are you *that* frustrated?"

Torn apart by the quandary he posed, she could think of nothing but lashing out at the source of the dilemma. In a flash she spun around and with lightning speed sent the flat of her hand against his cheek. The resounding clap was instantly dulled by his reflexive move, which hiked the offending hand up behind her back, twisting it painfully as it drew her hard against him.

"Don't you ever, *ever* do that again!" he muttered through clenched teeth, his grim jaw but inches from her face. Then, as suddenly as he had seized her, he thrust her away, taking several long steps toward the door before stopping short, as though remembering some last important shot. During the moment's hesitation Anne held her breath, glued to the spot where she stood, fearful of what was to come.

One lithe stride brought him back before her. To her astonishment he framed her face with his hands and placed a hard, impersonal kiss on her lips, then released her to step back again.

"What was *that* for?" Her anger surged with the feeling that she was a pawn in some mysterious game.

A wicked tilt to his lips gave credence to a smile, then stopped just short. "That was for moist eggs and strong black coffee." Flabbergasted by his gall, she could only watch, dumbly, as he retraced his steps to the door. There he half turned. "I have some things to do. I assume you can find something to keep you busy until we leave for the village in about"—he checked his watch—"an hour." It was not a question, nor did he wait for an answer, freeing her of his presence.

What Anne *did* find to keep her busy, as she hesitantly unpacked the bags he dutifully carried to the attic bedroom, was not exactly her idea of vacation fun. For it was her own motive in coming here—to Mitch—that monopolized her thoughts. What had come over her? She was a widow, still officially, if not emotionally, in mourning. What reason had she had to welcome this clandestine meeting?

Worse, what wickedness possessed her to have invited, then reveled in, the physical prowess of this man who she barely knew? His tart question to her—"What's your excuse?"—rang over and over again in her ears. She had avoided a direct answer to him then. Could she escape her own curiosity now? What *was* her excuse for indulging, as she had, in the pursuit of purely physical pleasure? Isn't that what had happened?

Changing her clothes from the more dressy garb of the city to her country uniform of sweater and jeans, she slumped down onto the bed as she pondered the dilemma. Mitch was a compellingly masculine man, oozing sex appeal from every pore. Did she have the strength to hold him off when her own feminine instinct craved satisfaction? But why? Why was this drive suddenly foremost in her mind? Never before, in her twenty-eight years, had sexual motivation determined her course. Indeed, she had been a virgin when she'd married Jeff, proudly wearing her long, lace-edged white gown down the aisle as proof of her victory over temptation. And temptation there had been aplenty; the attraction between Jeff and her had been a strong one. Yet they had sworn their wedding night to be sacred, and it had been. Physically, as in every other way, they were of like minds, with similar tastes, similar tempers, similar thoughts. Sexually too they had fused, each adoring the innocence of the other as they learned together.

Mitch was an entirely different story. He was stubborn and self-centered, yet he sparked a fuse of life within her. It was much as an art appreciation teacher had once told her: A painting, when successful, must evoke a reaction, any reaction, positive or negative. For Anne the months since Jeff's death had been, by and large, numbed, devoid of reaction—until Mitch had come along. He had driven her out of complacency; for that, she must be grateful. But what had he driven her to? And where was she to go from here?

She should shun his company, yet she sought it out. She should keep a distance, yet it vanished at his very appearance. She should be frightened by his threat—or was it a promise—of future lovemaking, yet fear was nonexistent. She was no longer the innocent she had been eight years ago. She was a woman, with the full awareness of the joys her body could give and receive. And Mitch was a man, every inch a man, strong, virile, and very, very attractive. It would be natural. . . .

Appalled at the turn of her thoughts, she scrambled off the bed and headed downstairs, grabbing her heavy ski parka to protect her from the blustery day. A long walk was what she needed to clear her head of such inappropriate meanderings. Unfortunately she didn't get further than the back door, for her attention was drawn to the very subject of her quandary, deftly splitting dried logs for the fire.

Bundled in a sheepskin jacket with its collar up, he did not see her. Turning the tables for a change, she watched, unobserved, as he raised the axe and struck, time and again splitting each new log with one magnificent sweep of the blade, all with his right arm. Once again she wondered how the left had been injured; once again she chided herself for the interest. What she and Mitch had—whatever it was—was restricted to this very time and place. Neither past nor present had a role here. Yet, as before, she couldn't help but wonder . . . What was the nature of the past he had mentioned? Were there women? Was there still a woman? Was he married? *My God,* she accused herself harshly, *I know nothing, absolutely nothing about him!* As the magnitude of the realization settled in on her, she felt an unease that she neither expected nor understood. Of only one thing was she sure—that before she could sleep another night in the same house with him, she needed several pointed answers.

Reluctantly discarding her cloak of invisibility, she joined him in the backyard, perching quietly on a pile of logs while he finished his work, then as quietly helping to carry the wood into the house to be stacked by the fireplace. Shortly after, they left for the village. The intimate confines of the small car exaggerated the fine line of tension Anne felt, as did the latent strength of agile fingers on the wheel and the denimed mold of muscled thighs adjacent to her own. In profile, as she cast a sidelong glance across to Mitch, he looked powerful: full waves of silver-blond hair falling on a weather-creased brow; eyes alert on the road; nose, lips, and chin chiseled of the same classic mold, suggestive of nobility, of command. Here was a man with a mind of his own—but then, she knew that well!

The confrontation came at dinner as the last of the peach melba disappeared. The conversation had been enlightening, though impersonal, a general discussion of politics, the economy, and the oncoming winter season in the mountains. That they disagreed on many, many points did not surprise Anne for a moment; that they could carry on intelligent discussion about their very differences did. Mitch was as interested in why she felt a certain way about an issue as he was in trying to understand her viewpoint. Likewise, she was more open, herself, listening to his arguments as often as she voiced her own. Then for some reason the conversation took the turn both of them had tried to avoid. It began quite innocently with Mitch's question.

"Why did you decide to come up here this time, Anne?" The intensity of his tone avowed that it was not idle chitchat he sought, but an answer that mattered very much to him.

She remained quiet for several moments, sorting out her reasons as she played idly with the spoon by her empty plate. "I . . . guess you were right. The holidays are closing in pretty quickly and they may be very trying this year. I need to fortify myself, I suppose."

"Is it still very bad without him?" he asked softly.

Anne shrugged. "Not as bad as it had been. I can accept the fact that Jeff is gone. It's the others—the people who try to be so helpful—who make matters worse. I can just see it now—Thanksgiving will be one long let's-cheer-up-Anne ordeal," she finished sarcastically, her lips thinning to a grimace of resignation.

"I know what you mean." Surprised by his own admission, Mitch looked up warily.

Anne was not about to let the opening pass. "How so?" she asked quietly, coaxingly. Regretting his lapse, he occupied himself with pouring seconds of coffee. But she prodded. "Are you married?"

His eyes shot to hers, the silver streaks iced at her intrusion. When she boldly held his gaze, it softened, however, as he yielded to her demand. "No." Anne breathed a sigh of relief, only to gasp anew at his cutting barb. "Why the relief? Are you that interested?"

Her answer was quick and defensive. "Interested in marriage? No! But, yes, I am relieved to find that you aren't married. I have enough of a problem with guilt, without worrying about disturbing a marriage."

"That's a laugh!" His remark was bitter. "Nothing much has happened to qualify you as a marriage-breaker! We're no different than any other pair of platonic roommates."

His offhand remark stung for some inexplicable reason,

though he was perfectly right. Riding on that declaration, she pursued the matter stubbornly. "You have to be in your mid-thirties now. Have you *never* married?" The thought was a hard one to believe, given the qualities of the man. For the right woman, he could make a fiercely devoted husband.

Now that very fierceness bore into her in punishment for her curiosity. "Thirty-eight, to be exact. And, yes, I was married."

His anger channeled her thoughts. "Are you divorced?"

"No."

"Separated?"

"No."

It seemed a repeat of one earlier interchange, with the roles reversed. And there was only one other possibility, an uncannily coincidental one. "Then . . . ?" she prompted softly, reluctant to put her suspicion into words.

He eyed her closely, expectantly. "My wife died."

A slow pallor spread over Anne's cheeks with this jolting reminder of a suffering so close to her own. "I'm sorry." She lowered her eyes. Now, finally, earlier statements made more sense. "Did you love her?"

"Yes." Through clenched teeth, his anger was so like her own.

"How did she die?"

His deep voice softened in timbre. "I'd rather not go into that. Besides, isn't that getting a little more personal than we'd planned?" It was the unspoken understanding to which he referred; perhaps he was right.

Choosing her words carefully, she tried to explain her lapse. "I suppose so. It's just . . . that sometimes it helps to talk about it. You seem still very bitter and angry. . . ."

He stared at her now in a totally new light, challenge written all over his sharp features. "Ah, the voice of understanding. What about *your* anger, *your* bitterness? I've heard it, you know. Do *you* talk about it? You have no idea what I may be feeling! None whatsoever! You know nothing at all about me . . . my work, my responsibilities. How can you be so sanctimonious about the whole thing?"

The recognition that she was merely a scapegoat for his own grief was small consolation for his words. Anger welled at his uncalled-for accusation, her dark eyes flashing her mood. "I wouldn't call it sanctimonious, Mitch. I do think that what I went through less than a year ago, what I *continue* to go through, entitles me to try to help. Has it occurred to you that I may need that help myself?"

The thought stunned him even as it stunned Anne. She had repelled the attempts of others to console her, bottling things up within. To a point, the pain had lessened. What, then, was she saying now? Was she admitting her need to discuss the past, or, more specifically, to discuss it with Mitch?

With eyes averted, she missed the passage of anger from him as she missed the entrance of a deeper, more thoughtful cast to his features. "How did Jeff die?"

Swallowing convulsively, she looked frantically around the room for an excuse to avoid the issue. But her mind was as incapable of escape as it was unable to deny the need to talk. The gold wedding band caught and held her gaze. Nervously she began to fidget with it. "He . . . ah, he . . . was in an . . . accident."

Mitch reproved her gently. "You told me that once before. What sort of accident? Were you with him?"

Her shining black hair, pinned as it was, did not flicker when she shook her head. "No," she whispered with a resurgence of guilt. "He was on a business trip. The . . . plane . . . went down. . . ."

All color drained from Mitch's face as he studied Anne's downcast head. When the silence continued unbroken, she glanced up to catch the shock turning to sadness before her eyes. It was as though he felt her very own pain.

"When did it happen?" he prodded hoarsely, seemingly unable to help himself.

"Last January."

Again he flinched, an unfathomable depth to his eyes, which strayed with his own thoughts. It was only when Anne shifted position uncomfortably that he recalled her presence, darting his gaze back to the one that studied him curiously. Quickly he recovered his composure, defensively shifting the center of the discussion.

"It's been almost a year. Do you date at all?"

"No."

"You should."

Spirit erupted. "*Now* look who's being sanctimonious! When did your wife die?"

"Last winter, also." He held her gaze in a challenge she accepted.

"And do *you* date?" It was a foolish question, one she regretted immediately as his lips skewed into a wry twist.

"I'm not sure you'd call it dating." The smoothness of his voice should have warned her, yet she felt too stripped from her own revelations to spare him.

"Then what . . . ?"

Suddenly he glowered at her, resentful of the admission he was forced to make. A strong hand gripped the empty coffee mug with such force, she thought it would shatter. "I'm a man," he growled, "with very distinct needs. Needs, I might add"—he arched an eyebrow angrily—"you share but refuse to acknowledge. When I want a woman, I get one." He took a breath, then paused on the verge of something he dismissed promptly. Slowly he relaxed, his anger dissipating with the exhalation. "At any rate, I have . . . other obligations."

Like a bolt, it hit her. There *was* a woman. Not merely a date. Jealousy flared within Anne for a fast and impulsive moment before she admonished her weakness. She had no right to be jealous . . . no right at all! Yet curiosity wouldn't quite die.

"Female-related obligations?"

He hesitated, eying her closely. "Yes."

"I see."

"No, I doubt you do," he countered crossly. "But maybe that's better, for now."

Puzzled by his comment, she could only shrug. "Maybe." There were so very many other questions she wanted to ask, but again, she had no right to do so. That was not part of the scheme. There was already more personal involvement than she'd bargained for. The whole idea was to divorce oneself from the past, the present, from reality, when up in this mountain sanctuary.

Mitch stirred from his brooding to underscore this very thought. "Do me a favor, will you?" he barked, though the light in his eyes had softened to a more compassionate green. "Take those damn pins out of your hair and put a red ribbon in it."

Startled eyes flew to his. "I don't have a red ribbon!"

"Anything bright will do, then."

"Am I *that* depressing to be with?" she asked, hurt as she misread his direction.

His lips hung between apology and reproach. In the end he said nothing until he had left his seat and walked around the table to stand behind her. "No, Annie." The gentleness of his words matched that of his fingers, which removed each hairpin, one by one. As he combed her loose mane over her shoulders, he knelt down to meet her at eye level. "I have never found you depressing, but I do think you overdo that starkness. You have no need to punish yourself for your husband's death."

"But I'm—" A forefinger on her lips stilled her denial.

"His loss was ample punishment, don't you think."

Her black eyes were wide in astonishment at his perceptivity. He was right, she knew. And he spoke from experience. What was his punishment? His arm? Those other obligations he mentioned? Frustration surged at the realization that he seemed to know much more about her than she did about him. So much was speculation.

His rhetorical question called for no answer. He continued

softly. "You look so pretty with your hair down, Anne." His low croon caused a somersaulting in her stomach, a symbolic turnaround from past to present. And the present was Mitch, and only Mitch, his face so very close, his aura positively hypnotic. Mouth suddenly dry, she moistened her lips, and the movement caught his eye, seeming to fascinate him. When he closed the bare distance between them, she caught her breath, for his tongue repeated the move, circling her lips with devastating leisure. At her gasp, her lips opened even more, offering their inner warmth for his sampling. His tongue touched and explored as his lips merely shadowed, sending quakes of arousal, echoes of frustration, to her extremities. Molten yearnings surged within, shuddering through her body. Feeling weak and boneless, Anne clutched at his broad shoulders for support. And . . . he hadn't even kissed her in that fullest sense . . . !

She had no choice but to respond, for that was part of her need. Her own tongue sidled sensually along the length of his, the textured meeting setting off even greater sparks, both within . . . and without. For, as before, when she had threatened his self-control, he moved firmly back. This time his tack was a throwback to the conversation their tongue-play had interrupted. "About your hair." His huskiness was indulged mutually. "You'll need to wear something bright—preferably red or orange—if you're going for a hike with me tomorrow morning. It's the middle of the deer-hunting season!" He slapped her knee with remarkable playfulness, considering the headiness of passion moments before, as he straightened. "Come on. Let's go see what we can find."

The woods were their playground for most of the following morning. With constant movement necessary to ward off the arctic air, Mitch led her over trails she'd never explored, through gulleys she'd never seen. The red wool cap, which he had produced, kept her head warm as the action—and the company—warmed the rest of her. Bare of leaves, the trees were no barrier to far-ranging vistas. Hand in hand, the two visitors gazed from stone wall to stone wall, appreciating expanses that, with the thickness of summer vegetation, had only been imagined. The land was theirs, and theirs alone. No other creatures stirred in the gray cold. The doe that had once stood on her hind legs to chomp on a crisp apple, now lived in hiding from the hunter's gun. Chipmunks and squirrels that once scampered merrily over the forest floor, now refused to budge from the warmth of tree and earth. The brook that once gurgled gaily, now charged icily toward its frigid destination.

Anne's cheeks were as red as her cap when they returned, tired but exhilarated. It was a harbinger of the days ahead, the comfort of an easy companionship. Not only did they share their meals, but most every other time of the day. Mitch read when Anne did, his eye glancing occasionally to hers, hidden behind the large frames of her glasses, surreptitiously returning his greeting. They discovered a mutual interest in backgammon, passing several lazy evenings before the fire in this endeavor. The weather held, for their benefit, offering pleasant days, clear skies, and an invigorating chill to the night. They walked together and worked together, Anne on her translating, Mitch on a pile of papers that he diligently hauled from an overstuffed briefcase. Each respected the other's privacy on these matters. Though they came to know each other's daily habits well, the "other" life was avoided with plaguelike fear, each too pleased with the camaraderie to risk confrontation.

All too soon Anne's Chevette was loaded and warmed for the return trip to New York. An arm slung across her snugly bundled shoulder, Mitch walked her, a final time, from the house. The silence had been heavier that morning than at any point since that first afternoon and evening. There was no mystery in Anne's mind as to its cause.

"Will you be spending Thanksgiving with your family?" he asked quietly.

"Uh-huh." She paused to look up at his handsome features. "How about you?"

"The same."

Though the makeup of his family was unknown, the answer was sufficient. She seemed to imagine a tightening of his grip on her shoulder when he continued. "Do you have plans for New Year's Eve?"

They had reached the car, and he turned her around to face him. Her sad smile was reflected in his eyes' understanding. "That's funny. I used to be so worried about New Year's Eve. Would I have a date? Would I not? Would he be tall, dark, and handsome? Or would he be the dregs of my high school class?" Her words were exaggerated in self-mockery. "Now it doesn't seem to matter." She looked away, then remembered his original question. "No, I don't have a date, if that's what you mean. I may just plant myself on the living-room sofa with a large bottle of Chablis and a good book," she added, tongue-in-cheek.

"Why not do it here?" The deep green of his eyes reached out to her.

"What?"

"Spend New Year's Eve *here.*"

"Will you be here?" Unpremeditated, the question bubbled forth, softly yet in earnest. It mattered very much to her.

His arms slid from her shoulders to her waist, drawing her closer against the warmth of his body through the open lapels of his sheepskin jacket. "Yes."

"What about your other obligations?" Again the words were unbidden; again the answer mattered very much to her.

Mitch took a moment to compose his response. "She—ah—she goes to bed too early for my tastes . . . and certainly too early to make it to midnight. No, she wouldn't be much fun as a date." An undercurrent of humor laced his words, puzzling Anne. Then he added softly, "Besides, she doesn't drink wine," and a smirk openly gentled his lips.

Despite the mystery involved, Anne responded to his good

humor and relaxed within his hold, only then realizing how quickly that turn of the conversation stiffened her. If he felt her tension at its onset, he made no mention of it. Nor did he make mention of her hands, which came to rest against his chest.

"I don't know, Mitch." She shook her head, loose strands of black silk gliding over the collar of her jacket. "This is crazy. I know so little about you."

"No less than I know about you," he interjected firmly. "Are you afraid?" His hands moved upward in a light, circular motion on her back.

"A little." The truth chose peculiar times to burst forth.

"Of me?" An arched brow accompanied his huskiness.

She was acutely aware of the swell of his broad chest beneath her palms. "No." She paused, eying the ribbed pattern of his sweater self-consciously. "Of me, I guess." It was an unsteady whisper.

"You have nothing to fear, Annie," he assured her gently, taking her chin between his thumb and forefinger and tilting her head back to study it. This was the closest they'd been, physically, since that first day. Now it made parting harder, clear thought even more of a feat. "I know what my own needs are right now, and they are *not* to make things harder for you. Don't you see, by helping you overcome your own grief, I may just help myself to do the same? There *is* a selfish motive involved."

For a split second she nearly drowned in the shimmering depth of his eyes. Then the hand of reason drew her from the whirlpool.

"I don't know . . . I shouldn't really be meeting you like this. It's beginning to resemble a Neil Simon script."

Subconsciously she cried out for reassurance that what she had done by making this trip, what she contemplated doing by joining him for New Year's, was right. Mitch, however, had made up his mind. Now a shrug heaved up the strong shoulders as he dropped his hands and moved back. "It's your choice. I'll be here anyway."

His sudden indifference was a far cry from the embrace her body craved. The way was cleared now, though, for parting, made easier by his abrupt withdrawal.

Nervously she shot a glance at her car. "I guess . . . I'd . . . better be on my way." Without another word he reached to open the door and see her safely behind the wheel.

"Drive carefully," he commanded softly.

"I will." Backing the car around, she put it in drive, giving Mitch a last, longing glance before sliding her foot to the gas pedal. As she moved forward his "Hey, wait!" echoed loudly through the skeletal forest. His long gait brought him alongside the halted car in an instant, and his breath misted the air when he leaned down to the window to speak.

"Don't forget to pack a dress. We'll be going out!" The knowing smile that curved his lips was lost to the shape of a featherlight kiss that he placed on the tip of her nose. "Get going, woman, before that snow gets here!" Stepping back, he watched the yellow car until it rounded the curve and was lost from sight. Only then did he turn to heed his own advice and pack for the return trip.

CHAPTER FOUR

Anne packed her favorite navy knit for the occasion. Its softness offset her darkness, its gentle wrap reinforced curves that had finally begun to reappear. The image was to be one of poise, confidence, and sophistication, none of which she had felt during the days of wavering prior to her departure. Hers had not been an easy decision to make, for something had begun to change—in her life, in her outlook, in her attitude toward Mitch—and it frightened her.

The awareness of this change had actually emerged during that trip back from Vermont in November. She had felt stronger and been able to face the return to the city with greater enthusiasm—knowing that there was the distinct possibility she would see Mitch six weeks hence. He was, in a sense, a reward, promised to her for weathering successfully the potential trauma of the holiday season, a finite period to culminate on New Year's Eve.

Whereas originally the vacation itself had been the escape, now, during this festive period, it was the anticipation of the next vacation—or, more specifically, thought of Mitch—that was the constant incentive. Work continued to fill her hours, one project ending as another began, the ongoing grant work demanding an ongoing professional relationship with Alexander Robie, the psychologist directing the grant. As interesting a companion as he might have made, in light of the many nonprofessional proposals he issued during the period, Anne shunned diplomatically each and every one of them. She had no desire to relate to men in anything but a purely business-oriented domain—with one gross exception. And *that* had little to do with the treasured memories of her husband.

Increasingly she found herself regarding Mitch in a different light. Whereas at first, in September, he had been the man with whom she had been thrown quite accidentally into an intimate setting she was forced to endure, by November there was nothing to "endure" that was not, in one form or another, pleasurable. Even the bickering between them added punch to the stay. And, of course, there was that inescapable physical attraction. As the days passed leading up to the December trip, it was this very romantic aspect of their relationship, if that was what it was to be called, that both excited and frightened her. Against her wishes, she wanted desperately to know everything—*everything*—about Mitch. In her heart she knew she played a dangerous game, for, as the saying went, ignorance was bliss. Mitch stood as a giant, physically, intellectually, and emotionally, in their cabin in the woods. But what was the other side of his life like? And was she ready for the involvement it might entail?

Thanksgiving passed harmlessly enough, with a traditional turkey dinner at Anne's parents' house. It was a pleasant time, even for Anne, whose refreshed outlook enabled her to relax and regard the friends and relatives—even her in-laws—as individuals, rather than as offshoots of Jeff. The major discomfort, in fact, proved to be a mammoth stomachache from eating more heavily than she had in a year. It seemed that she had been mistaken in her prediction to Mitch. Rather than it being a case of let's-cheer-up-Anne, since she was outwardly fairly cheery already, it turned into a let's-fatten-Anne-up situation. Alka-Seltzer was a fast and effective remedy for that particular problem. If only, she had mused at the time, there was a similar solution to the dilemma involving Mitch Whatever-his-name-was and her feelings toward him.

Perhaps the problem would have been simplified if she could have met Mitch two, even three, years after Jeff's death. As it was, there was still unfinished business relating to the plane crash, which kept her legally occupied. At the time of the accident and in the weeks immediately following, Anne's anger at the injustice of it all had been at a high point. She had not been alone. Jeff's family too had shared the frustration of wondering what had caused the crash, whether it could have been avoided, whether Jeff's life had been lost through negligence. A lawyer had been retained to pursue the matter, finally filing a lawsuit against the airline, a small and privately owned one, for the inadequate upkeep and safety-check procedure for its craft. Over the months, as Anne's anger had leveled off, so had her enthusiasm for the court case, which seemed to be, for her, merely a continuation of the agony. It was primarily Jeff's family who kept things going, supposedly on her behalf, even after she asked them to drop the suit. Particularly after the last trip to Vermont her taste for the matter had soured further. Now she only wanted to look ahead, rather than behind. But the wheels of justice had begun to turn; halfheartedly she received regular updates on the progress of the case. At latest report, there would be a hearing in early April. Anne cringed in anticipation of it, praying only that the entire matter be over and done as quickly as possible.

Long hours spent in silent contemplation of the matter had convinced her that only when things were settled on that score, would her life be freed enough of the past to enable her a clearer glimpse of the future. Did Mitch have a role in that future? The prospect of seeing him for the New Year's holiday became so much a part of her daily routine that the thought of his vanishing suddenly from her life was anathema. Whereas she and Jeff had been mirror images of one another, Mitch was the mirror itself, larger, more solid, all-encompassing. It was a new and different image of herself that she saw through him—the woman as a distinct individual, inspiring and infuriating as she was inspired and infuriated, in turn. His bold framework offered safety and protection, stimulation and challenge; she craved all of these things. He seemed, in many respects, larger than life, too large for an airplane crash to daunt. No—she smiled wistfully, as she pondered it—he would look at the burning debris and walk away unscathed, such was his command of life.

Considering the direction of her thoughts, it was some consolation that while in New York, Mitch was merely a bright star, a promising light in her vivid imagination. She moved through each day with the confidence that though he filled her thoughts more and more, there would be no development in the relationship, either good or bad, until she saw him again at the end of December. She had no way of knowing, as Christmas approached, that she had underestimated the force of fate.

Professor Robie, or Alex, as he insisted Anne call him, organized a dinner for the seven people whose efforts comprised the progress on the grant. There were two secretaries, three research assistants, Alex and a colleague of his, and Anne. A long table was reserved at one of New York's finest restaurants, the whole theory being to defy the more modest style of academia, if for one extravagant evening only. After much persuasion, Anne had finally agreed to let Alex pick her up and drive her to the dinner, conceding primarily in view of the larger group of which they would quickly become a part.

In effect this was the first such gathering that Anne had attended without benefit of family present. Her initial self-consciousness, when she and Alex arrived together shortly after the others, was quickly dispelled by the friendly and familiar circle of faces that surrounded her. It was precisely the type of dinner with friends that she and Jeff had enjoyed many times. Did Mitch go in for this type of thing also? Subconsciously her mind veered off on its own tangent as the conversation of the others swirled harmlessly about her.

What *was* Mitch doing now? How was *he* faring through the festivities? As her thoughts meandered so did her eyes, drawn across the room through the crowd of faces, to a gleam of silver in a far corner. The sudden pounding of her pulse drowned out any other sound that may have threatened to divert her attention, which, for all practical purposes, had riveted toward the figure. Profiled in the dim light, he was every bit as ruggedly handsome as her Mitch. (*Her* Mitch?) Dressed in dark jacket and tie, and a crisp white shirt, this stranger had a tailored fineness about his appearance, a gentle intensity about his mien, his attention bestowed unequivocably on his female companion. What if it *had* been Mitch, dressed so handsomely, and *she* had been the recipient of his care?

Chastising herself silently, she averted her eyes. Strangely the possibility of their meeting had never entered her mind. New York was such a huge city, such a busy place. And she rarely went out—at least to places they might accidentally meet. What a cruel trick this was for her own mind to play! Certainly that had not been Mitch; the coincidence would have been too great.

If the rest of the group noted Anne's sudden enthusiasm for their company, they could not have realized that it was her way of chasing off the daydreams that seemed to want to trap her. But several of her comrades did begin to wonder when, shortly before they finished dessert, the maître d' appeared at her side, bending low to utter some discreet word in her ear as he slipped a folded piece of paper into her hand.

"What's this, Anne?" Alex teased. "A secret admirer?"

Puzzled herself, Anne unfolded the paper. No longer was she puzzled. There, in a bold black script, was the short message "Until December 31st." Reeling from its meaning, she shot a glance in the direction in which the silver-haired man and his date had been seated. The table was empty now, clean and reset with linen and silver, awaiting a new pair of diners.

So it was him! Chewing on her lower lip, she looked back down at the message.

"What is it, Anne? Any problem?" Alex's concern made her aware instantly of the others' attention as well.

Self-consciously she refolded the paper. "Oh, nothing. An old friend must have been in and seen us." She smiled feebly, tucking the note nonchalantly into her purse. "Just wanted to say hello." That was, in fact, all he'd wanted, she assured herself, though she was taken off guard by Alex's perceptive quip, delivered mercifully in a low voice for her ears alone.

"That must have been quite some old friend," he whispered. "I wish it had been my note that had brought that delightful color to your cheeks and that very soft look to your eyes."

Anne's flush deepened. "You must be an incurable romantic, to imagine things like that," she chided in a return whisper. Inside, she knew that he had imagined nothing.

Yet Mitch had not even been around to see the effect he had had on her. Perhaps it was fortunate; perhaps it was better that he not know of the awesome power he could wield, even with a few innocent strokes of the pen!

Anne was to dwell on this incident at length in the succeeding days. Annoyance surfaced that he had put her in such an embarrassing situation with her friends. Frustration loomed at having been deprived of actually speaking with him. Anger surged at his failure to make the note more personal. But jealousy was the hardest emotion to face. There had been a woman with Mitch, though the details of her looks, her age, her dress, her attentiveness, eluded her. At the time Anne had not believed the man to be Mitch. How mistaken she had been! And now she ached to know the nature of his dinner companion.

As though these emotions were not enough to keep her mind boggled when it came to Mitch, they were joined, in time, by confusion and indignation—confusion at the nature of her feelings for her little secret and indignation that she should be put in the position of having to cope with this very maelstrom.

Ironically, in the wake of this pre-Christmas run-in, she had many second thoughts about venturing, once more, into his realm. Things seemed to have gotten out of control. She thought of Mitch far too often and with far greater intensity than she had any business or right to. Yet, much as she wanted to stay away, she could not. Much as one part of her insisted she'd be safer spending New Year's Eve at home, alone, as she had originally intended, there was no surprise when she found herself driving the last of the miles to the cabin.

The landscape was bleak now, snow-covered and frigid. Ice hung in stalactite-style formation from the boughs of trees and the roofs of snug-closed farmhouses and cottages along the old, familiar route. Everything about seemed frozen—gray, ash-green, and white—and stiff. With the superhighway left behind, the small Chevette slid occasionally on a patch of ice, where snow had melted, then dripped from the hillside onto the narrower country road.

Bidden by anxiety, Anne pushed the little car as fast as it could travel safely over the crunchy terrain. With bare trees on either side of the road, the midafternoon sun cast its feeble shadow, a grid of bare sticks of lines with railroad-tie regularity for her to traverse. So mesmerizing was the pattern that she lost track of her own gaining momentum until the loud blast of a car horn from the village road to her right caught her attention. The light blue Honda was recognizable instantly. With a smile of unabashed and instinctive delight, she pulled over to the gravel shoulder by the side of the road. The small car stopped just behind. As the large figure stepped from the driver's side, Anne's pulse began to race. For all of her doubts seeing him again was well worth it! Rolling down her window, a smile spreading in excitement over her lips, she called out a breathy "Hi!" even before he reached the door. Past experience should have prepared her, but it didn't. The fierceness of his glower took her by surprise.

"What are you trying to do . . . get yourself killed, Anne?" he bellowed. "That was no safe speed on this road."

Stunned and temporarily speechless, she merely stared back. Finally she managed a pout. "I was only going about forty!"

Despite his anger he was a sight to warm her from head to toe, magnificent to look at, a heated torch amid the bristling cold. From behind the protective shade of her mildly tinted glasses, she drank in his good looks, which, with one dubious exception, she had not seen in six weeks. She couldn't help but smile. His hair looked more blond than silver in the dull sun, lending a younger, more boyish cast to the eyes that studied her with their hazel glow. In a second's insight Anne knew that regardless of his critical veneer, he was as glad to see her as she was to see him.

He took a deep breath in an effort to maintain his harsh expression. Slowly he sent a faint white-misted exhalation into the air. "Look, Annie, you stay behind me for the rest of the trip. Got that?"

In an impish mood, bolstered by her own sense of subtle power to disturb, Anne humored him. "Did you get everything at the market? All the perishables? Plenty of wine?"

"Behind me!" he repeated in chorus with the roll of his strong fingers, drumming against the window impatiently.

"What about hot chocolate? And whipped cream?" Enjoying herself fully, she had finally discovered how to most quickly deflect Mitch's abrupt flares of temper.

He realized it too, resorting to the fastest means of sidetracking Anne that *he* knew. In a swift move he swooped low and wiped her smile away with a hard and fast kiss, capturing her lips for just an instant before releasing them, standing straight, and delivering a you'd-better-watch-yourself glare her way. Within seconds he was back in his own car, pulling around and to the front of her, then leading her at a more sedate thirty-five miles per hour to the cabin.

When both cars stood side by side on the snow-packed drive before the house, Mitch was the model of propriety, thoroughly businesslike as they transferred their luggage inside. Not about to pick a fight, Anne settled for the attic bedroom. In truth, it had not been at all uncomfortable, warmer if anything than its larger counterpart downstairs. Here she was freed of the diverting sounds of this compelling man above her head; it was sufficiently devastating to have to imagine his once having slept in this bed, his sleeping directly below her now. But the bed itself was plenty big for her; *she* did not stretch out the six-plus-foot length that Mitch did!

It was when she was in the process of unloading and storing the groceries that she felt the silent presence at the door, its eyes now assessing her appearance in detail. The gray wool pantsuit had been warm and comfortable in which to drive, and its white cowl-neck sweater was, indeed, a switch from the somber navies and blacks he'd usually seen her in, though as yet far removed from the bright colors she would at some point seek out again. Her hair was down, falling in silken cascades over her shoulders and onto her back.

"Well?" she prodded, with a touch of mischief, when she could bear the silent appraisal no longer. Only then did she turn to face him.

"Come here." His low growled murmur was music to her ears. There was no hesitancy in her step as it took her across the room and into the arms that reached out in welcome. It was a warm and intimate embrace, yet totally devoid of passion. For each, the other's mere presence was enough to satisfy the need for closeness.

"You looked beautiful that night in the restaurant," he

crooned against her hair, as he smoothed a loose strand from her cheek. "Did you enjoy yourself?"

She pulled back to regard him skeptically, her hands locked behind his back. "I hope you know that I didn't realize it was you," she chided, ignoring his question to express her more immediate thoughts. "You looked more like some mirage I thought I had conjured up . . . until I got the note." In the instant the extremes of emotion stemming from that memorable moment washed over her anew. "Why didn't you come by to say hello?"

His gaze hardened almost imperceptibly. "That's off limits, isn't it? Socializing in the—'real' world . . . ?" Cynicism played with his words even as it raced through her own veins. The situation was bound to change, she knew at that moment; it *had* to change, though she could not quite fathom the direction it would take. For now, the only thing that had real meaning was Mitch, standing tall and in person, before her, his arms curved to the lines of her back, his body molding hers aggressively.

Rather than fumble with words, she let her head fall forward once more against the firmness of his chest, absorbing his strength for a long and silent moment. Communication was intense, though nonverbal. Anne's arms spoke of how she had missed him and how much she savored his nearness now. The rapid pounding of Mitch's heartbeat reflected similar sentiment. Their integrated stance seemed to compensate for everything that was, for the time being, off limits.

Finally Mitch swung her around by his side and led her, an arm over her shoulder in lingering possession, into the living room, where he drew her down beside him on the sofa. Tucking her head into the crook of his arm, he stretched his long legs, still cramped from the day's drive, out before him. "How did you make out during the holidays, Annie?"

Intuitively she knew that this was merely an opening, that this time around they would be getting to know each other more fully than they had in the past. If her suspicions were correct, Mitch had been as disturbed by the unknown as she. Yet there was little solace in that fact. For, as much as she wanted to know about him, there was the fear that knowledge would, in some way, alter the precious something that existed now between them.

Inwardly reluctant, she answered him tentatively. "Not as bad as I'd expected."

"No downs?"

"A few." A frown creased her brow in remembrance. "Jeff and I always went from house to house on Christmas Day. It was more simple this year . . . dinner at his parents' home."

"Who were your friends that night?" he asked casually.

"At the restaurant?"

"Uh-huh."

"People I work with." A pause reflected her unsureness, her grasp of his fingers on her shoulder a subtle assurance.

"Tell me about your work." His hazel eyes regarded her with soft intent, prompting her to speak. For the next half hour of relaxed discussion she did, outlining her interest in languages, their birth and development, elaborating freely on the way her career had been shaped through the years of her marriage to the present day. His questions were thoughtful and implied a legitimate interest in her life. One, in particular, took her off guard.

"The professor—what did you say his name was, Alex?—looked very . . . interested. Have you gone out with him?"

"I told you that I don't date," she scolded softly.

His agreement was exaggerated. "Ah, that's right. I forgot. He *has* asked you out, though, hasn't he?" The touch of his gaze was a tangible one, probing pointedly.

Anne saw no point in denying his claim. "Yes. Several times. I'm not interested in dating him, though. That dinner was a group get-together."

Beside her back-tilted head, his jaw seemed to relinquish the fine thread of tension that had subtly held it taut. Anne made her move. "What about *your* date—excuse me, your companion?" Her soft voice emphasized the last term with a bit too much of a drawl. Jealousy was a tough thing to hide.

"What about her?" Mitch played on her weakness with a knowing grin.

"Who is she?"

"Her name is Liz."

"Do you see her often?" Maybe she shouldn't have asked.

"Yes."

"Oh." Her gaze fell to the floor.

"Aren't you glad you asked?"

"Not particularly." In defiance of his smugness, which had remained undiminished during the cryptic dialogue, she pried herself away from him and slid to the far end of the sofa. As though determined to thwart her escape in some form, Mitch lifted her feet smoothly to cross them over his thighs, a lazy hand sliding beneath the wool of her slacks to caress her leg. The feeling was too pleasant for Anne to object.

"Jealous?" he asked, with a devilish twinkle in his eye.

Her answer was a no-less-direct "Yes," though she knew she had no right to be so.

"That's good." He grinned, more broadly than before.

Anne glowered in frustration. "My God, you are an arrogant brute," she began, then, in a stroke of genius, turned the discussion deftly to more pertinent matters. "If you're so cocksure of yourself, tell me a little bit about what *you* do. You must have some line of work. Is it in the city?"

Where she had expected some mild resistance, there was none. He answered her calmly and clearly. "Yes. My corporation has headquarters in the city, but we operate all over the country."

"Your . . . corporation?"

Strangely, where it might have been more appropriate, the arrogance vanished. "Yes. I head a corporation. Does that bother you?" The test was for something beyond his words, yet she could only respond with the truth of her feelings, which, at the moment, verged on anger at his implication.

"Of course not! Why should it bother me? It really has nothing at all to do with me!" Black eyes flashed in accord with her claim; her anger was as much at that fact itself.

Slowly Mitch leaned forward to grab her arm and pull her once more to his side. Again she couldn't resist. "Take it easy, Annie. I meant no offense. It's just that—well, to be perfectly honest, I've been told that I'd make a very good catch for some woman. Being the president of a large corporation doesn't help to discourage overeager women."

It was only when she leaned forward to look back at his face that Anne saw the teasing gleam that might as easily have been haughtiness. "You're putting me on," she chided in return. "Any woman who would want your strong black coffee and your long hot showers has to be a little crazy. As for me"—she tilted her nose into the air—"no amount of money in the world could compensate for your disrespect for peanut butter!"

A low chuckle slid from the back of his throat. "We'll see," he drawled, applying a playful hug to her middle. His arm was too snug beneath her breasts for comfort, depriving her of breath, wholly aside from the hug. Driven by the need to steady herself, she returned to the earlier discussion.

"What does your corporation do?" she asked, nestling deeper into the crook of his arm.

"We develop real estate—office parks, shopping centers, and so on."

"Anything else?" After all, corporations were often multifaceted, weren't they? Instinctively she knew that where a man like Mitch was concerned, there would be more.

"Some . . . other interests." His evasiveness was obvious.

". . . Which you would rather not mention."

When he didn't answer, she glanced up to catch the sudden alertness in his eyes. "Not right now."

"Hmmmm," she teased coyly, "the mystery of the year—"

As always, he knew how to shut her up when he wanted her quiet. Which he did now. In a fluid movement he shifted her sideways and onto her back on the sofa. Before she could begin to rebound, he followed her down, balancing himself on his elbows, much as he had done that first night, when he'd accosted her. Then, his eyes had been hidden by the dimness of the dying fire. Now there was no fire, but rather broad daylight, yet his eyes held the smoldering glow that was nearly as hot as that long-ago flame had been.

"You talk too much, woman." He punished her with his instant dominance over her. As he held her breathless beneath his weight his eyes caressed her features. "You not only look good, Annie, you *feel* good," he drawled huskily. With sensuous daring he inched over her, the boldness of his form driving her to distraction. It didn't occur to her to fight the force of his appeal. And in the instant's realization she knew that her need was not simply physical. It had gone well beyond that.

Impulsively she coiled her arms around his neck, exerting the slightest pressure to bring his lips down onto hers, which awaited eagerly, parting at the first suggestion of his touch. His kiss embodied all the passion that had been absent in their earlier embrace, and her own returned it in kind. A quiver of excitement surged through her nerve endings as his tongue explored the recesses of her mouth and their breath mingled, one into the other.

The muscles of his shoulders rippled beneath her palms as a heady stimulant to her whirling senses. His nearness and the very male scent of him intoxicated her. She protested with a short cry when his body angled off to her side, fearful that he would deprive her of the glorious sensations that raced rampant through her. Then her cry was of a different sort when his skilled fingers circled one of her breasts, caressing its curve with exasperating leisure until his fingertips finally found and fed the pebbled firmness of her nipple.

His lips left a trail of kisses from her eyes, down her cheeks, to her neck, as her hands sought blindly the buttons of his wool shirt, releasing them, one by one, to slide across the warm wall of his chest. His roughly textured skin was heaven beneath her fingers, his sinewed strength a natural aphrodisiac. At the very moment she thought she would burst, his large hand left her breast to curve around her neck in fierce possession, supporting her head against the onslaught of the lips that returned to devour her own. It was a ravishment that she welcomed, arching her body to be closer to him.

"Annie, Annie, Annie," he groaned, his breathing ragged against her lips, "what am I going to do with you?"

Her slender fingers framed his head, then fell to the column of his throat, then his collarbone, before winding their way once more through the mat of tawny hair on his chest. "Look who started it," she accused, her fascination held by the bulge of muscles beneath her fingers. Her voice, quite unintentionally, was soft and sensuous. The flush on her cheeks added buoyancy to her argument.

As quickly as he had tumbled her, he sat back up, hauling her to a seated position, then leaning forward to prop his elbows on his knees and rest his forehead in his palms. In an unconscious gesture of response to his sudden distress, Anne reached out to massage the taut muscles at the back of his neck.

"What is it, Mitch?" Something had upset him; this thought bothered her more than his actual release of her.

His silver-streaked head tilted to allow him a sidelong glance of her furrowed brow. "You really don't know?" Cynicism tied his words with the skeptical slant of his mouth. When she didn't answer, he shrugged off her hand and cornered himself in the sofa, leaning back to eye her. "I want you, Anne," he confessed, an angry gleam entering his gaze and puzzling her all the more. "I thought I'd be able to chalk this whole thing up to a vacation fling, but each time I go home, I can't put you out of my mind."

The excitement generated by his words was nearly as great a stimulant to Anne's pulse as was his physical arousal moments before. At least she had not been alone in her daydreams. Yet where this fact would lead was an even greater source of puzzlement than Mitch's strange anger. It was to the latter that she turned her focus.

"Why does the situation upset you so?" she asked timidly.

Deep hazel eyes stared at her for long moments before he shook his head in exasperation. "You are amazing," he began in taut rejoinder. "If I didn't know better, I'd say you were a simpleminded virgin who just doesn't know any better." Suddenly he leaned toward her, the force of his gaze impaling her. "Do you have any idea what I'm talking about?"

Anne rankled under his implication of her naïveté, which she felt to be both unjustified and inappropriate. Pulling herself straighter in a move to preserve her own dignity, she confronted him. "Yes, I think I do. You're referring to all the things I've spent hours debating myself!" Self-reproach edged her examples. "'What am I doing here? Why did I come? Whatever on earth do I want to happen? Where is my sense of propriety? The list goes on and on." She paused to catch her breath, clutching her shaky hands in her lap. "What do you want me to say? I know what *you're* saying, but *I* don't know what to do *either*!" Her voice had risen steadily in pitch until it was a desperate plea at the end, one that hit its mark. As though unable to help himself, Mitch sighed and reached out to return Anne's slender form to his chest, much as the whole thing had first begun.

"Oh, Annie." A sadness filtered through his low whisper. "It's gone beyond those questions. Now I ask myself whether I'm ready to see you in public, in New York, whether you're ready for that. I ask myself whether I'm ready for a greater commitment than just that physical one I've made to other women, whether you're ready for *that.* You see"—his voice intensified with feeling, as steel fingers cupped her chin to tilt her face up to his—"I want to make love to you, Anne, but

I can't do that and then just walk away from you when it's over. For the first time in so long it's not only a physical need. . . ." In the fade-out of his voice she heard the repeat of her own thoughts mere moments before.

But now she understood the quandary as poignantly outlined by his questions. Much as her feelings for Mitch grew each time she saw him, she was not quite ready to enter into a full-time, open relationship either. There was still that loose end to tie up in court. There was still an emotional barrier to overcome. Could she love again, as she had once? An involuntary shudder shook her at the course her thoughts had traveled. The sadness etched into the hollows of her eyes spoke wordlessly to him.

His strong hand crushed her cheek once more against his chest, where his heart could speak directly with the power of its beat, as his lips moved against her forehead. "I wouldn't want to hurt you for the world, Annie. You deserve the best. You need some guy's full attention and devotion. I'm—just not that—free, yet."

An invisible vise clamped on Anne's insides at the despair in his voice, the discouragement of his words. A lump of sheer misery swelled in her throat, choking off all words. For infinite seconds she clung to him, her arms encircling his waist as his crisscrossed her back. When she finally drew back to look up at him and his thumb gently brushed a tear from her cheek, she realized the depth of her need.

"I won't ask much of you, Mitch," she whispered falteringly. "I'm not sure of what I want any more than you are. I won't make any demands, but one—*be here* for me to come to every once in a while?" The plea was a simple one to state, a complex one to understand. Yet it was from the heart; Mitch knew that as did she. His arms tightened around her in prelude to his own low moan.

"I will, honey, I will."

Satisfied by his promise, Anne's hold eased, though she could not quite forsake the haven offered by his arms. It was all she needed to know, for now, that they could continue to see each other here, in their world away from the world. Only time would resolve the other matters. In the meantime she had his strength to bolster her, his nearness to entrance her, the knowledge that there *would,* indeed, be a next time to keep her daydreams alive.

The New Year arrived with a surge of high spirit that neither of them, weeks before, would have imagined possible. They dined at a small inn where the restaurant was elegant, though intimate and quaint. For Anne it was a first date. The care she took dressing and applying the light makeup that country life usually precluded, was instantly rewarded by the warm measure of approval in Mitch's silver-sparkled hazel eyes as they roamed her length. He too looked polished and spiffed in his fine wool slacks and well-cut blazer. Together they made a stunning duo, drawing the attention of more than one pair of curious eyes. As on a first date, Mitch refrained from all form of intimacy, though he had to guess how even the lightest hand on her waist, when he escorted her to their table, would affect her. Later, back at the cabin, they toasted in the midnight hour with plenty of champagne, the only surefire way, Mitch had insisted with a mischievous grin, of ensuring either of them a good night's sleep that night.

Indeed, the week that followed bore a continuation of their light-headedness, the crisp and frigid air in which they walked daily buoying them both. The forest was an enchanted place during this season, offering a safe harbor from winds that whipped across the meadow but failed to penetrate the thick cloak of evergreen.

Bundled warmly in woolens and down, Anne and Mitch hiked over ponds that formed solid blocks of ice, following the similarly frozen line of the brook from mountaintop to deep valley. Beneath their heavy winter boots, the snow squeaked with every step, the only noise in the whole of the forest aside from their own voices.

Shielded by the spruce, the pine, and the cedar, they walked for hours through winter's blue-shadowed land, returning to the cabin only when their clasped hands could no longer feel. Then they would seek refuge in the kitchen, propped before the window, to watch as the downy woodpecker poked at the pork fat that Mitch had hung on the nearest fir overhang.

It was a time of silence and serenity. Strangely Anne did little reading, even less working. Rather, she spent hours in calm reverie before the fire. Even this was a triumph for her. She was happy. There was no desire for escape of any sort. She wished to be no other place in the world. There were no sad thoughts of what she'd lost, only lovely memories of what she'd been privileged to enjoy, albeit for so short a time. There was the pure pleasure of the moment, of Mitch's presence, silent as was hers though ever warm. And there was, above all, hope that the future might hold a wealth of new and even more beautiful things for her one day.

It was during one of these moments of relaxation, on the last evening of their stay in the cabin, that Mitch suddenly disappeared into his bedroom, to return moments later with a small box, simply wrapped in white with a pale blue ribbon around it.

"What's this?" she asked in surprise.

"Open it," he commanded gently.

Unsteady fingers pulled at the bow. "When did you get this?" Her tone chided him for having given her anything. His presence was all she required.

"I was in Brazil right after Thanksgiving. It was made by one of the local artisans in a small village in the interior."

The top of the box fell back to reveal a ring, a rectangular piece of enamelware framed in gold and mounted on a fine gold band. Anne gasped at the beauty of the intricately painted design, a semiabstract portrayal of sand, sea, and sun, all woven together by a fine meld of blues, greens, yellows, and creams.

"It's—magnificent, Mitch!" she exclaimed. "You never should have—"

"Keep still, woman, and put it on," he growled. Anne had come to know that when he used the term *woman,* it was a good-humored threat that could lose its good humor in a split second if she resisted his demand. This time she had no desire to resist. The ring slid, in a perfect fit, onto the third finger of her right hand, and gave her pale, slim fingers an even greater delicacy.

"There," he declared, surveying the masterpiece with undisguised pleasure, "that's a little color for you. Maybe next time"—his eyes caught hers pointedly—"you'll bring a pretty, bright sweater to wear for me." Without elaborating, his meaning was clear. Held hypnotically by his gaze, Anne could not have refused if she'd wanted to.

"I will. And . . . thank you, Mitch. The ring is beautiful. I will . . . cherish it." She put both hands up to frame his face, to trace the powerful line of his cheeks, his jaw, then his chin, with her fingers. Then she leaned forward to kiss him, a soft and heartfelt means of expression, as words were not enough.

"Only I wish I had something to give you," she whispered finally, resting her forehead against his chin.

His answer, so quiet, was barely audible, yet she caught every word. "You already have, Anne. And I thank you." They were words that she thought of often, during the long four weeks, which stretched interminably, until she was due to return to Vermont once again.

CHAPTER FIVE

As the first huge flakes of snow began to fall, Anne sniffled and reached for another Kleenex from the glove compartment. For the better part of the week this cold had plagued her relentlessly. Had she known Mitch's phone number, she might have called to cancel their rendezvous for this second week in February, she had felt that poorly. But she did *not* have his number, and she wanted desperately to see him. Therefore Friday afternoon had seen her packed and off, praying that her health would improve with the crisp dry air of the country. What she hadn't counted on was the snow.

Now, as she crossed the border from New York into Vermont, the flakes grew larger and more feathery, sticking to anything and everything in sight. Traffic had slowed commensurate with the decreased visibility, a particularly frustrating happening, for the longer it took to travel, the worse the roads became.

Anne's impatience was understandable. Aside from her hacking cough and the steady accumulation of snow on the windshield in defiance of the double-timed wipers, she was anxious to see Mitch. In a strange and unexpected shift, things had reversed themselves emotionally for Anne. To her, now, these Vermont sojourns had become her "real world," while the rest of existence was more a way of passing the time between visits. She was happier, more relaxed, and more alive with Mitch than she felt back amid the hustle of the city.

As the traffic slowed another notch she glanced anxiously at her watch. Two hours behind, already! It was late afternoon; darkness, though not as early as it had come in December, would drop its impenetrable curtain before long. Driving in the storm was tricky enough in daylight; by night, it would be outright hazardous!

The thought of stopping at an inn for the night crossed her mind, only to be displaced by the fear that tomorrow would see no better weather, no clearer path to the hillside retreat. And still there was no way to contact Mitch.

The treads of her snow tires clung tentatively to the road as she angled off the highway at last. There were yet miles to go, but at least the road was a more intimate one. Unfortunately it was deserted. Her small car pushed on through the blinding rage of solid whiteness, vistas on either side blotted out by the blizzard conditions. Only the low fencing at the side of the road kept her on course, though how long that would remain above the mounting drifts of snow, she did not know.

The tension of the drive was reflected in the whites of her knuckles as Anne gripped the wheel tenaciously. There was no turning back, for the snow seemed to have constructed a solid ice background there, too. As she peered nervously through the windshield, she prayed for a plow to hide behind. As each mile passed beneath her tires, grinding more and more slowly through steadily accumulating depths, there was none.

When her pace slowed to a hesitant fifteen miles per hour, and she could see no further than a single car's length ahead of her, she felt a wave of panic sweep through her. The sense of isolation was utter and intense. Fighting a sudden dizziness, she kept her foot to the gas pedal, knowing that her only way was forward.

The world had shaded to dusk's gray-blue sheen when finally the cutoff to the cabin road came into view mere feet ahead of her. Swerving to make the turn on such short notice, the car skidded, fishtailed, then came to an abrupt halt several yards into the private way, lodged firmly in a deep snowbank at the side of the road.

With a muttered oath Anne alternated from forward to reverse, then back again, in a vain attempt to free the car from the drift. Her nerves were already stretched taut by the length and tediousness of the drive. Now she cursed her luck as she fumbled with the door handle and tripped out of the car, promptly sinking in snow midway up her knee-high boots. Even with her rosiest glasses on, the hopes for the car were negligible. There was but one solution. Turning, she gazed up the hill in the direction of the house. It would be nearly a mile's walk, by her calculations. In ideal weather the walk would have been a mild challenge, uphill as it was. But in this blizzard? Could she make it? Was Mitch already there? What if he had become stranded somewhere, himself, and the house, after her long trek, was locked? Sneezing, she raised a down-parkaed arm to her face. She'd break in—it was as simple as that. There was no other choice!

Closing the car up tightly, she packed her pockets with Kleenex, zipped the parka up to her neck, securing the hood over her heavy wool hat, pulled on her gloves, and set off, moving as quickly as she could in the ever-deepening snow. Hiking in these conditions, however, was very different from walking down even, snow-lined avenues at home. Here, as she lifted one leg high after the other through the depths, muscles began to cry out in protest. Tucking her head deeper into the hood of her parka, she plodded on.

Thirty minutes passed, then another fifteen. Exhausted, she looked around for something to rest against. But all was white, lonely, indistinguishable from everything else. Looking back revealed nothing but a trail of weakening footsteps; looking ahead revealed nothing at all. Refusing to believe that she may have taken the wrong road—the thick blanket of gathering snow obliterated any signposts she may have recognized, any landmarks that might have held a familiar ring—she trudged on.

Bone-weary now and weak from coughing, she felt suddenly terrified. Signs of life were nonexistent. Where was the cabin? For another half hour that seemed like forever, she pushed herself forward, pausing occasionally to blow her nose, huffing hoarsely at the exertion, steadfastly ignoring the heat on her cheeks.

Snow continued to fall, creating a fairyland that, through Anne's bleary gaze, took on a nightmare grotesqueness. The thought that she might be lost shuddered through her now-quivering limbs, but she continued to discount that possibility as boldly as she could, moving more slowly forward and up toward where the house should have been. Where was it? Surely the road had never seemed as long when she'd driven its distance, or walked it, for that matter, in better weather.

The oncoming night brought a swirling blackness to her senses. Dizzy, she fell to her knees on winter's padded mattress. But this was no place to sleep, a far voice begged, steadying her, forcing her to her feet once more to struggle on. Tears of fear mixed with melting snow on her fevered cheeks. Despite the cold her clothing chafed against her sweat-dampened body. Yet she moved on . . . on.

When she could go no further, she collapsed upon her knees, sinking gently into the billowing drifts. Head hung forward and panting unsteadily, she fought hysteria as she fought the cold, which seemed to have suddenly sapped the last of her strength. Hugging her own body in a protective embrace, she swayed helplessly in the gusting wind.

"Mitch . . . Mitch . . . please help me! . . ."

"Annie!"

Mirage or reality, she could not have cared. When the

large form knelt down on the snow before her, she fell against it, grateful only of the support it offered her spent body, the warmth it held for her frigid limbs.

"Hold onto me, Annie! It's not too far to the house." Strong arms lifted her free of the wet snow as snowshoed feet began the final trek.

"Is that you, Mitch?" she whispered against the heavy jacket that protected her face from the blowing torrent.

"It's me, honey. Be quiet now. Save your strength for warmth!" Willingly she relinquished all responsibility for her survival to him. In truth, she was too tired to think.

The light from the house filtered through the snow-studded darkness like a beacon, leading them home. When his boot kicked the front door shut behind them, he lowered her feet gently to the floor, only to catch her up again when her knees buckled. Without a word, he strode into the downstairs bedroom, depositing her on the edge of the bed as he began to remove her wet clothing quickly. He paused but once to throw off his own jacket and pull back the bed's quilt, then returned to undress her.

If Anne was aware of what he was doing, she could not have lifted a finger in protest. Chilled to the bone, she trembled uncontrollably. In a voice willed to calmness, Mitch issued orders that he knew Anne could hardly obey, but which were aimed at assuring her that she was safe.

"Lift your arms, like a good girl," he commanded softly, then, one at a time, drew the sleeves of her heavy sweater off and pulled it over her head.

"I thought I was lost, Mitch. I walked for so long and I couldn't find the house . . ." she whimpered.

"Shhh . . . everything's all right now."

She clutched at his shoulders for support when he knelt before her to pull off her boots, then her high wool socks. "Now, I want you to lie down, honey. Your jeans are drenched." With infinite tenderness he eased her back down onto the bed, unzipped her dungarees, and pulled them off, tugging impatiently only when the sodden denim resisted his hands.

"God, I feel so sick," she moaned in a hoarse whisper, throwing an arm up over her fevered forehead as she squirmed in discomfort. In an instant he was bending over her.

"I know, Annie. But you'll be all right now. I just have to warm you up. Okay?" She didn't answer; neither did she protest when he drew off her cold, drenched panties and tucked the lower half of her body under the weight of the quilt before turning to remove her turtleneck and, finally, her bra. With the covers bunched around Anne's shoulders, Mitch crossed the room to his suitcase, pulled out a clean cotton shirt, and returned to the bed, pausing for an instant to note how small and helpless the pale face looked, buried in the oversize bed, her dark hair strewn haphazardly against the pillow.

Unable to resist, he sat down beside her and pressed his cool lips against the fevered skin of her forehead. "You'll be all right now." His promise was breathed against her brow with a conviction she had to believe. Savoring the refreshing movement of his mouth over her eyelids to her cheeks, she lay still. When his fingertips followed the trail of his lips in offer of small comfort, she sighed unsteadily. The faint sound brought him back to the urgency of the moment. For one dumb moment he stared at the makeshift gown in his hand. Then, quickly, he pulled the covers back to draw on and button the shirt, rolling its cuffs to clear her slim wrists before replacing the quilt.

Anne had been aware of every step of his ministration, fading in and out with waves of dizziness and swings from fever to chill. Now a sneeze preceded her hoarse chiding, bringing Mitch quickly to sit by her side.

"You shouldn't have taken off my sweater," she protested weakly.

Misinterpreting her, he scolded in a deep, though gentle,

voice, "Don't be silly. You were soaked to the skin and freezing. This is no time for modesty—"

"I didn't mean that." Her wan smile was broken by harsh coughing. "That sweater . . ."—she managed to somehow catch her breath—"I wore it for you . . . did you notice?"

His lips twitched into a hint of a grin as understanding dawned. "I did notice, Annie. It was pink." He paused to brush a strand of hair from her forehead. "Thank you," he murmured, his palm remaining to assess the heat of her skin. Then he leaned closer. "I'm going to heat up some soup for you."

Her dark head bobbed from side to side. "No. I can't eat. Just . . . stay here with me for a few minutes. . . ."

Unable to resist the pleading in her fever-glazed eyes, he drew her forward, quilts and all, encompassing her in the haven of his arms as his hands massaged warmth back into her body.

"You can't imagine how frightened I was, Mitch," she whispered against his throat. "It was so cold and wet out there. . . ."

"I would always have come looking for you. You know that!" he chided softly.

"I wasn't even sure you were here. There were no tire tracks—" A cough interrupted her argument.

"Shhhh . . ." He urged her to stop talking. "I arrived before the storm began. In this season the snows can be dramatic. It should be very beautiful come morning!"

His attempt to divert her mind from the ordeal she'd been through was successful. The thought of seeing and wandering through a winter wonderland with Mitch was a lovely one, bringing a brief smile to her pale lips before she sneezed once more.

He took his cue. "Let me get that soup now."

"No! Really, I'm not hungry—"

Strong hands imprisoned her head. "You need something warm inside—"

"But I don't think I can keep it down—"

"You will! Just rest now. I'll be right back."

With a throbbing in her stomach she rolled onto her side and tucked her knees up tightly. The warmth of the bed burned all around, yet a chill persisted in quivering from within. Exhaustion claimed her for a few short moments' rest until Mitch returned with a bowl of steaming broth.

His gentle hand raised her head, then he fed her himself when her stiff fingers refused to function properly. When, finally, she shook her head, unable to take in another drop, he let her sleep.

Awakening an hour later, she felt even worse. Mitch was beside her, a damp cloth in his hand to bathe her face and neck. "That's quite some cold you have." He eyed her sharply.

"It lingered all week. I thought it would be better by now." Speaking was becoming more and more of an effort.

"Why ever did you start out from New York in the first place? You should be in bed, not driving in this storm." Peering weakly up through her lashes, she saw the clenching of his jaw. He was angry, and that upset her in turn.

"It wasn't snowing at home," she rasped. "I had no idea I'd run into this mess, or that it would get as bad as quickly!"

Hazel eyes flashed a dark olive green. "Forget the weather. You should have been in bed anyway, with this bad a cold!"

Anne frowned. "My life can't come to a standstill every time I get a simple cold. . . ."

Full anger flared at her continued argument. "Woman, if you don't learn to take better care of yourself, your life may one day soon come to a *permanent* standstill! 'Simple colds,' as you so carelessly dub them, can turn into pneumonia, or worse—or hadn't that thought occurred to you?"

The force of his retort brought tears to her eyes. "I just wanted to be here . . . with you. . . ." It was her last and most powerful point. Having made it, she turned onto her side, away from his glower, and pulled the covers more snugly around her ears.

Her point was well taken, however, and Mitch had no intention of letting her withdraw into herself after having made it. As he had done before, he scooped her into his arms and let her rest in their strong haven. As the seconds blended together he held her with fierce determination, pressing her head against his chest, dipping his head periodically to hers, touching firm lips to her hair, her brow, her eyes in turn. He could not have agreed more with her sentiment, yet the danger she had put herself in terrified him. His voice softened when he spoke finally. "Annie, don't think I didn't want to see you as much. I did. But we could have come next week."

"Someone else may be here next week." Her argument was muffled and weak.

"No one will be here." The declaration was curt. At its finality, Anne glanced up.

"How can you be so sure?"

In a gesture of resignation, though he held her still, he shifted her in his arms and ran one hand back through the disheveled mass of silver-blond waves that had fallen low on his forehead. "This is *my* house, Anne. Miles Cooper takes charge of renting it out for me when I'm not planning to be here."

Sharp eyes took in the surprise on her face, a surprise that gradually faded to understanding with the poor imitation of a grin. "That figures," she whispered. "It also helps to explain that original mix-up . . . and why you prefer this bed. After all, it *is* your own."

"There won't be any more mix-ups, Annie. I've taken the house off Miles's rental list. From now on we'll be the only ones who use it." Determination lent a force to his words, diverting Anne from their full implication. At that instant, however, a new shudder shook her, and she cowered against him, seeking a warmth that continued to elude the extremities of fingers and toes, skirting her core, which burned with fever.

Feeling her shiver, Mitch lay her down gently. "Don't go anywhere," he murmured, cupping her face before he disappeared. At his return moments later he put a firm hand back to lift her head. "Aspirin, Anne," he explained before she could ask. "Open your mouth."

A more docile patient he could not have wished for. She was too weak to protest his pampering, too pleased by it to want to protest—particularly when the reward for her good behavior was the occasional kiss or caress, which, despite her illness, was innately satisfying. He kept her pumped with broth and aspirin for most of the night, dozing himself, stretched out beside her beneath the quilts. One part of his body always touched her—a hair-coarsened leg thrown over her smoother one, a long arm running the length of her side, a warm hand curving protectively around her hip—to know at precisely what moment she awoke. Given other circumstances, the sleeping arrangement would have been heady—skin against skin with a minimum of covering between. But Anne's senses were strangely blunted by fever.

The next day passed as a hazy conglomeration of hours that blurred together in her muddled consciousness. Her fever continued to rage, despite the medicine, and, increasingly, her whole body suffered an agony of pain when she coughed.

"What *is* the matter with me?" she cried out in frustration, when she awoke from a doze feeling as poorly late that afternoon. Mitch had been ever by her side, aside from the time he spent in the kitchen or standing worriedly by the front window. Now, at her arousal, he took her hot hand in his.

"I'm not sure. As soon as the road is plowed, I'm taking you to the doctor."

"Has it stopped snowing?"

"Finally."

"How much is on the ground?"

"A little over a foot. It makes the plowing slower, even though the folks up here are well-equipped."

"Mitch . . ." She rolled onto her back to face him more fully as he perched on the bed beside her. Her voice was weak, yet bolstered by the need for an answer to this one particular question that had nagged at her since their discussion the day before.

"Yes?"

"If you own this house, then you have access to the names and addresses of the renters. Is that so?"

The light in his eye was a placid hazel as amusement played therein. "Yes."

Her own dark orbs widened. "Then you know who I am."

"No."

"But you do have that information—"

His voice was velvet-edged and deep. "*Miles* has that information. I suppose I could see it if I wanted to, and I have been tempted at times, but, so far, I haven't peeked."

It had begun, after all, like a game, in some respects. Yet Anne was not sure whether to be relieved or hurt by Mitch's self-control. Her blanched features reflected the indecision. To her further confusion Mitch laughed aloud, a deep, throaty sound so much stronger than her own nasal rasp.

"What's so funny?"

His eyes twinkled. "You are. Your face . . . it hides nothing!"

"So I'm *that* transparent?"

"In some respects." His expression sobered gradually in vague reference to things that passed, for the time being, over her head.

"It's really not fair, you know," she mumbled defensively.

"What isn't fair?" A tawny eyebrow arched imperiously.

"Me . . . here . . . at your mercy. With my transparent face and all . . . I feel so . . . naked."

For a short instant his eye bore the smoldering light that

she had come to recognize. "Except for the good graces of my shirt, darlin', you are," he drawled.

The flush of embarrassment was lost within her fever blush. "That's not what I meant, and you know it." The force of her disgruntled denial set off a new spasm of coughing, wiping the devilish grin from Mitch's handsome features. When she finally quieted, he ran the backs of his fingers along her cheek. Their coolness felt like shade in the desert; she savored the relief.

"You talk too much, Annie. Rest your voice now."

At that moment, and in an instant of simultaneous recognition, a sound filtered in from outside the house. "The plow!" Mitch was on his feet and walking, stopping only at the bedroom door to call back to her in firm command, "Don't move until I get back!" Then he was gone.

She lay, still and weak, for what seemed hours. Finally, disobeying his order, she struggled out of bed to use the bathroom. The reflection in the mirror appalled her, the pallor on her cheeks broken only by two small dots of fever, her dark and sunken eyes belying the hours of sleep she'd had, her hand visibly trembling as she sorted through Mitch's toiletries for a comb. Barely halfway through the long tangle of her hair, her knees began to knock. Dropping the comb, she clutched at the edges of the sink for support. At that moment the bathroom door burst open.

"What in the devil are you doing out of bed?" he stormed, as, in one lightning-quick move, he picked her up and trundled her back to the bedroom. The chill from his jacket seeped through the thin shirt fabric to her skin, causing a shudder to add to that of her condition.

If her good sense hadn't kept her quiet, the trembling weakness that enveloped her would have. The bed felt like heaven, the quilt like a soft cocoon when he tucked it snugly around her curled form. "Next time," he taunted by her ear, "you're apt to pass out in the middle of the floor. Now, will you stay in bed?"

"I just went to the bathroom . . ." Her whispered protest was feeble.

"Well, then, you should be set for a while. Am I going to have to tie you to this bed?" Silently she shook her head. "Good. Now, where are the keys to your car?"

Even thinking was difficult, particularly when it involved retracing her moves back in time through the blizzard. Closing her eyes, she tried to remember. "I think . . . I put them in the pocket of my jeans."

He disappeared, returning several minutes later with the keys dangling triumphantly from his finger. "Now, listen, Annie. I'm hitching a ride with the plow down to your car. It may take me a little while to dig it out. Do you have snow tires on?" She nodded, suddenly concerned. "Good. I'll be back as soon as possible. Then you're going to see a doctor."

"Mitch—" Her hoarse outburst caught him at the door. "Your arm—is it all right to shovel?"

Had her eyesight been clearer, she would have caught the tension that gripped him. From her prone position, and given her daze, however, she could hear only his hissing intake of breath, followed by a taut grunt. "It'll do." As intimate as was the situation, this had been an unexpected reminder of all that she did not know. But it was something to occupy her thoughts another time. Now she could concentrate only on passing the time in restless discomfort until he returned. Her head hurt, her sinuses hurt, her throat hurt, her chest hurt, the muscles of her legs ached in delayed reaction to their punishment the day before. Curled up in misery, she could only hope for sleep to relieve her of this slew of aches and pains.

Her hope answered, she must have dozed off, for it seemed mere minutes before Mitch announced his return with a gruff foot-stamping at the front door. Lacking the strength to call out to him, she waited, silently, until he appeared by her bedside, ruddy cheeked from the cold, yet eager to pack her up and leave.

"Okay," he began, glancing from bed to dresser, running a finger along the side of his nose in thoughtful debate of the situation. Bewildered, Anne stared up at him, but not for long. Before she could sniffle in protest, she was swept up, quilt and all, and carried from the bedroom into the living room. Her abductor stopped short at the front door, peering down at her in dissatisfaction.

"Damn," he muttered under his breath, "you need a hat." As though she were a sack of flour, he deposited her on the sofa, stormed into the kitchen, then returned to unceremoniously stretch her wool hat, now dry and warm, over her flowing tresses. "Better," he pronounced smugly, scooping her up again and continuing this time until she had been deposited on the passenger's side of his own already warming Honda.

Feeling foolish and very ill, she wheezed heavily for most of the trip into the village. The darkness swallowed up everything but the beam of the headlights, which ricocheted brightly off the clean snow walls, newly built by the sides of the road.

"Here we are." The shift clicked into park, the emergency brake groaned into position, and he bounded out to retrieve his bundle.

"Really, Mitch," she croaked in mindless reaction, "I feel ridiculous. You can put me down."

The eyes that bore into her were incredulous. "You're wearing nothing but my shirt . . . or had you forgotten?"

A soft moan filtered through her lips. She had, and was not about to further the point. The acquiescence in her expression spurred him on, into the emergency room of the local clinic, where the doctor, alerted by the owner of the snowplow, awaited them. An hour later the steps were reversed.

"Bronchial pneumonia! Good show, Annie," he teased gently, as he tucked her back firmly into the car.

Weary eyes caught his. "Have you got the pills?"

His hand patted the spot where the upper-left breast pocket of his shirt would be. "Right here. Are you comfortable?"

"That's a laugh!" she barked hoarsely. "I've been poked, X-rayed, stuck with needles, and carted around as though I had no feelings at all." The grimace on her face seconded her words. "I feel hot and cold and achy. And you ask if I am comfortable?" With a scowl she looked away. "Don't ask!"

For the first time since the ordeal had begun, Mitch's smile was a relaxed one. Slamming the door, he circled the car to the driver's side, slid, with remarkable ease, considering the overall length of him, behind the wheel, then turned to eye his victim. "At least your good humor is intact," he mocked heartily. "Come on, let's go home. The doctor ordered warmth, rest, and lots of hot liquid, so we'd better get to it!"

For the next three days the doctor's orders were followed faithfully, with Mitch in command, dictating when each penicillin dose was to be taken, when she was to eat and sleep. Her physical misery continued for a full day before, finally, the medication began to take effect. Only then did she dare to balk at the strict regimen to which he held her.

"I think that I'll turn into a chicken if I drink one more drop of this soup. It's awful," she complained when, on Tuesday morning, he appeared with but another mug of broth. "I feel much better today. Honestly I do."

A critical eye scrutinized her pale form, propped now against the headboard of the bed, dressed in her own flannel nightgown. "You still sound horrid," he accused, his eyes sparkling in obvious enjoyment of his role as overseer. The length of his lean frame filled her view, intimidating, to say the least, with arms folded across his chest and feet planted firmly in an open stance.

With a burst of returning strength Anne jammed her own arms across one another defiantly. "If you don't want to hear my noise," she croaked, "then don't goad me into conversation. And isn't it about time I went back upstairs to the other bedroom?"

The manly grin widened in its display of even white teeth. "You don't like sleeping with me?"

On impulse Anne blurted out the first thing that entered her mind. "I'm not exactly 'sleeping' with you, as the expression goes. It's more like sleeping in spite of you. You may think that I'm out of it, but *I feel* you beside me. I *know* you're there . . . all night! You touch me just enough to make sure I'm all right . . . but that's all. What fun is that?" The gasp she made at the implication of her own words sent her into a fit of coughing, from which only Mitch's firm slap on the back could rescue her. To her further embarrassment he stayed to rub gently the back of her neck and shoulders, his touch growing more seductive by the minute. She hadn't been aware of his other hand supporting her midriff until it moved upward. Her breast tingled at its sweet touch; though she gasped, she was unable to pull away. His palm passed around and over her nipple, teasing it through the soft flannel, sending that tingling far deeper into her. Her hand gripped his arm, as much to hold it there as for support.

"It *isn't* much fun, is it?" he agreed more tautly, lapsing into a silence of frustration before sighing in resignation. "But you will stay down here for now, where I can keep an eye on you. In a few days you can go back upstairs."

"In a few days I'll be going home." The sadness of her words spread to the ensuing stillness.

At the urging of Mitch's arm she lay back upon the pillow, her eyes, in the turmoil of unspoken emotions, locking into his. Again it was he whose deep voice shattered the silence.

"Something's got to give. You know that, don't you, Annie?" Wordlessly she nodded. Just as they approached the point where the passionate kiss was not enough, likewise were they fast discovering, each in his own way, that the occasional week spent together was inadequate.

"Are *you* ready for more?" he asked pointedly.

Her answering quest was no less pointed. "Are *you?*"

Both asked, yet neither answered. Anne knew that she still

needed more time . . . just a little. There was the legal matter to settle before she could be heart-free. And she had to know more about this man whose "other" life was very much an enigma still.

"Tell me about your family, Mitch." The sound of her voice was clearer and more musical in its softness than it had been since the onset of her illness.

Silver-sheathed waves fell forward onto his forehead as Mitch's eyes flew to her face. His surprise was not so much at her voice, as at what she'd asked. This was, in truth, one very source of his own grappling. Yet he knew he could not avoid the issue entirely.

"There isn't all that much to tell," he purposely minimized, with a shrug of deceiving nonchalance. "My parents are both alive and well and living in Manhattan. My father is retired and has been so for several years now. It's very nice . . . gives him time to spend . . . doing . . . other things."

"What did he do?" she prodded, ignoring the strange pauses between his words. Bringing himself back from a moment of far-off reverie, Mitch looked at her, startled, then grinned.

"He was a concert pianist. I'm sure you would recognize the name if I told you." He did not offer it, nor did she ask it. That part of the bargain, at least, held.

Incredulous, Anne laughed lightly. "That's quite a switch—from concert pianist to business tycoon in one swift generation! Was the musical ability passed on at all?"

One corner of his well-formed mouth curved up in mockery. "If you are asking whether I can carry a tune, the answer is fairly. If you're asking whether I play the piano, the answer is no. I leave that lovely art to my sister."

Her eyes widened. "You have a sister too? Is she older or younger than you are?"

The ceiling absorbed his one-eyed squint of feigned deliberation. "Older . . . by . . . let's see . . . three, no four, minutes."

"Years," she corrected quietly.

"No, minutes," he reasserted, laughing.

"*Twins?*"

He nodded.

"Oh, Mitch! That's marvelous! What fun it must have been growing up!" Her delight, as she lay in bed, was that of a child being told an enchanting bedtime story. With the diminishing of her fever the flush on her cheeks was a natural, more healthy one.

Mitch frowned playfully. "Not really. She was always taller, smarter, and faster than I was."

"And now?"

"Touché! It's safe to say that I've finally caught up."

"There must have been some advantage of being the runt of the litter." She teased him openly.

His reply was no less in that spirit. "Oh, there was. My mother used to pamper me more. She felt sorry for me." A mischievous gleam danced in his hazel spheres. "I suppose that's why I still have the need to touch and be touched . . ." As though given permission by his own words, he reached out to take her hand, running his fingers with rough-textured electricity from shoulder to wrist and back.

But Anne refused to be daunted by his clever diversion. The subject of the discussion interested her far too much. "Are there any other twins in the family?"

He shook his head. "Just Liz and me."

"Liz?" Warning bells sounded in the back of her mind, snapping her back to another discussion during an earlier visit. Slowly a smile spread across her lips as Mitch realized his slip. "Hmmmm . . . Liz," she repeated with an accusing lilt.

He grinned sheepishly. "Now you know my secrets, I'm afraid."

"That was Liz with you at the restaurant before Christmas."

"Uh-huh."

Her dark brows knit. "Is she married?"

"It . . . didn't work out. But lately she's been seeing a very nice fellow."

"What does she do with her music?"

"Actually, though she is an excellent pianist, she would prefer to think of herself playing the harp."

"How beautiful!" she exclaimed excitedly.

"Not while she was first learning," he quipped in a low and conspiratorial murmur, an eyebrow arched knowingly into his brow.

"Oh, you are impossible . . . and jealous of her talent," Anne concluded with a gentle nudge to his middle.

"Perhaps . . . perhaps . . ." was his only response, as he raised her slim fingers to his lips, kissed them in true continental style, then excused himself to see to some work.

That night, perhaps sparked by the discussion of family they had had, Anne had a nightmare, more frightening than any she'd had since she'd been a child. Bolting upright in bed, drenched in a cold sweat, she struggled to catch her breath until Mitch's arms seized her supportively.

"What is it, honey?" his voice rang out in alarm. The room was dim, bathed eerily in the blue light of the moon as it mushroomed over the unblemished carpet of snow in the yard.

"A nightmare—it was horrible," she gasped, trembling in spite of his steadying hold.

"Do you want to tell me about it?"

Several deep inhalations later, she felt stronger. "It's that court case, hanging over my head . . ."

"Court case?" The band of his arms constricted reflexively, then loosened to allow him to look down at her.

The moonlight gave her hair a blue-black sheen when she nodded. "The accident. My husband's family has been pushing me to sue for negligence. At first, when I was as angry as they were and we were all so helpless, I agreed. Now I'd rather put the whole thing behind me."

Mitch sat statuelike for long moments, his face, hidden by

shadow, raised to a focus over her head. "And the nightmare?" If there had been reason to suspect it, Anne might have recognized the sound of defeat in his low voice. But, given no reason, she assumed his tone to be one of gentleness, particularly when his arms drew her back tenderly against his chest.

"The nightmare was terrifying! I dreamed that I was on that plane with Jeff when it crashed, that I wasn't injured, but had to stand by and watch, helplessly, as he suffered. There were no doctors, no medics. Nothing but burning debris, people's screams, and then silence." She shuddered, and the arms tightened around her. "It was awful . . ." Her whisper of horror was smothered against his T-shirt, which, bottomed by briefs, comprised his sleepwear for her stay in his bed. When, after the first night or two, he had failed to produce pajamas, Anne had concluded that he customarily wore none. Wisely she did not ask.

Now he crooned softly against the long silk of her hair. "I know, honey, I know. But it was only a dream." His tone lacked conviction, though her disturbed state could not hear that. Rather, she let his nearness comfort her, falling back quickly to sleep while he stared, for long hours, wide-eyed, into the darkness.

For the remainder of the week Mitch's preoccupation was offset by his diligent effort to pamper his patient. It was only on her last night, before she was to leave, that she looked up from her book to find him glaring in dark and ominous brooding toward the flames in the hearth. He was sitting on the floor, by the base of her chair, legs outstretched toward the warmth; instinctively her slim fingers found the line of his shoulder.

"Is something wrong?"

Snatched from some distant place, his head jerked back toward her. "Hmm?"

"You look bothered by something. I'm very much back to

normal, and you haven't even begun to fight with me." Her teasing smile was only able to spark a sad one in return.

"I seem to have lost temporarily my taste for the fight." The double meaning of his words was lost on Anne, though the undercurrent of despair was not.

"I'm sorry, Mitch. This must have been a really boring week for you. Playing nursemaid to me . . . again." With a soft laugh she recalled her bruised knee and the old apple tree.

His hand moved up to cover hers. "I haven't minded. It's been very restful."

"Too restful. Tomorrow is my last morning here; will you join me for a walk, or do I sneak out alone?"

After a quick shot over his shoulder at her, his gaze returned to the fire. "I'll join you."

She had expected an argument. Its absence left not relief, but puzzlement. Yet the silence of this, their last evening together, was too precious to risk by probing deeper. Something was troubling him; she could only hope that he would, one day, have enough faith in her to share his worries freely.

With the snowfall still fresh and clean atop the deserted mountain, the sight that met them the following morning was one of blinding splendor. The sky was a deep blue, the air cold and still. Days of warm sun and freezing temperatures had put a crisp crust of ice atop the virgin whiteness. The crunch underfoot echoed around them as they made their way across the hillside. Their breath misted much as did the unfrozen brook, running through crystalline palaces of weeds and branches, made gemlike by the vapor-filled air. The only signs of life were those frozen into the snow, the tracks of the snowshoe rabbit or the packed highway of the deer. It was a scene of rare beauty, built to perfection by the long week's wait to see it. Its memory helped to soften the inevitable moment of parting early that afternoon.

"Are you sure you won't stay the weekend? You should

really not be driving such a distance yet." They stood, side by side, putting off that final move for her to enter the car.

The wistful gaze that encompassed Mitch's features reinforced Anne's regret. "I wish I only could. But I promised my folks that I would attend a hospital benefit with them tomorrow night. I really can't let them down."

He turned her toward him, ensuring her nearness with the circle of his arms. "Even if you're letting *me* down?" An arched eyebrow baited her, then lowered before the look of hurt in her eyes. Helplessly his gaze fell to her lips, pausing for a minute to trace their curved form before losing them to his own lips.

It was a gentle caress, sweet, sweet torture to Anne's fast-healing body. Her arms wound around his neck as his tightened about her, exerting a force he had shunned all week. Now, with her imminent departure by necessity containing the situation, each indulged in the other with the intensity of feelings too long pent-up. Slowly and inevitably the fire grew hotter. Their lips consumed in turn, his firm and seeking, hers softer and giving. She returned his kiss with the power of her femininity, her lips expressing the thank-you's and I'll-miss-you's and when-will-I-see-you-again's that her heart cried out.

In an explosion of wildness prompted by sheer desperation, his tongue plunged deeper into her mouth, sending riotous sensations through her, all of which spoke of a need to return to the house, to that same bedroom, that large bed. She opened up to him, unable to get enough, craving even more, when, with a deliberate but reluctant wrench, he stilled her.

"I want you to take this, Annie," his lips rasped in a last fevered caress of hers, moments before he drew back to take her hand, drop something into it, and close her fist, sealing it with his own. "It's the key to this place." He spoke quickly, his breath coming in short gasps. "I've got a few hectic weeks ahead, but I'll be up again at the end of March. If you want to come—at *any* time—I want you to."

Breathless and touched by his sentiment, Anne felt her eyes fill with tears. Then, lest she make a fool of herself, she whispered a soft "Thank you" against his cheek in a last hug, pulled away, and got into her car, heading down the sanded road without a look behind. Parting was getting harder . . . and harder.

CHAPTER SIX

March in Vermont was the time of unlocking, that period during which the frozen ground gradually yielded each frigid layer, in turn, to the power of an ever-strengthening sun, when the brooks and ponds, rivers and lakes, one by one, surrendered their ice-clogged solidity to the rush of the downstream current. It was a time of the loud thrashing of formidably cold waters against their natural earthen and stone bounds. It was a time of mud.

Anne had not quite expected the latter when she left New York, with its wind, its rain, and its prespring dullness, to head north. Taking Mitch up on his suggestion and making good use of the key he had so meaningfully given her, she arrived several days in advance of his impending appearance. The excitement was in being there, in these hills, in Mitch's house. Nothing could have kept her away longer.

"You're driving up there *again?*" her mother had asked in surprise. Anne was prepared for the question, having done her homework well. Her response was nonchalant and lighthearted.

"Sure! It's maple-sugaring time. I wouldn't miss it for the world!"

"Humph!" her father had interjected with a teasing note.

"I wouldn't be surprised if you turned around and bought that place, since pretty soon you'll be spending more time there than you do here."

A rush of blood colored Anne's cheeks a very healthy red. The cabin already had an owner, a hale and hearty one, who appeared to be in no way interested in selling. Fortunately her parents had never learned of the stranded car or the pneumonia fiasco . . . and they still knew absolutely nothing about Mitch. On this last score Anne had grown increasingly uneasy and guilt-ridden. She had always been close to her parents. They had been understanding and solicitous during her past ordeal. Didn't she owe it to them to share her happiness now?

For she was happy; she knew that. With the knowledge that Mitch would be there, with her, at the charming haven in Vermont, she could face just about anything else that would arise. His giving her the key had been a significant gesture. Now she had a steady tie to the hideaway. It was merely a small piece of metal, yet it was that tangible reminder of the contentment she had found, the excitement she had felt, the promise she could now hold for the future.

These past few weeks since she had returned, penicillin tablets in her pocketbook, from the northern snows had seen changes, some subtle, some less so. For one thing, she had found finally the courage to sort through and pack up Jeff's things, as his family had long urged but as she had, likewise, long refused. For another, her physical appearance had undergone a metamorphosis that was attributable outwardly to the recovery from her illness, but which, in fact, had a deeper emotional cause. Though she still dressed in muted colors and styles, her face was more animated, her figure more gentle. At last her self-imposed physical stoicism had ended. And finally she had begun to go out more, to see friends and tolerate new acquaintances. Her social life stopped short of what could rightly be called *dating*, yet it did enable her to escape the confines of her apartment.

How strange it was. For so much of the last year her apartment had been her sanctuary, her private retreat, her personal niche of escape from the demands of the world. Before, the act of living had been painful; now it was no longer so. In truth, of late, her apartment had been nearly as lonely as it had been in those dreadful days following the crash. But the loneliness was for a different cause entirely now.

She missed Mitch. Regardless of how she looked at it, that was the crux of the matter. The longing dug into her, deeper and deeper as each day passed, until her only refuge was in her work and in the company of others. He was never far from her mind, in either case, particularly as the day of their reunion neared.

Now, as the mud spattered its ugly streaks over the once-bright yellow glow of her car, she turned onto the private road that led to the cabin. Twice her tires began to spin in the muck; twice she was able to back down, then charge forward successfully, bypassing the offending mud hole in her bid to reach the house, car and all.

It was early Wednesday afternoon when, turning the key in the lock, she entered the house. Mitch was not due up until late Friday. Everything seemed larger, emptier, and more silent without his commanding presence, yet the thought of his arrival two days hence staved off the loneliness she might otherwise have felt. His mark was in every room of the house, enveloping her in a cloak of warmth as she wandered about.

In his absence she applied herself happily to all sorts of menial tasks that, had he been there, she would have demanded he share—dusting, mopping, scrubbing sinks and the top of the stove. The pile of her own work, which had dwindled further each trip she made, sat untouched. Her mind was too prone to its meanderings for concentration on anything deep.

During the two days she waited she did more baking than she had in the past two years, trying her hand at fresh-baked bread and muffins, with a moderate degree of success. There was something about the rural life that inspired this type of activity, she mused, as she set the dough in the unlit oven to rise. In the hurried life of the city she had never spared the time for such delightfully mundane tasks. Here, she reveled both in the profusity of time and in the innate satisfaction of the activities themselves.

Despite the mud a daily hike was part of her routine. Though spring was yet a way off, the sounds of the world awakening from winter's rest echoed through the forest. It began in the air with the first of the geese winging their way in intricate formation through the pale blue skies above. It stirred in the tallest of the tree branches, still bare, yet blowing with willowy flex in the gusting wind. It reverberated in the scurry of the occasional squirrel testing the air for a hint of the season. And it resounded in the soft squish of the ground underfoot. The snow was gone, for the time being, leaving the naked woodland growth in its predressed posture, waving before the evergreens as though to say "We'll beat you soon." Even the leggy lilacs by the cabin's front door stood proudly, boasting their promise of fragrant blossoms.

Friday night came and went without sign of Mitch. For Anne the wait was devastating. Anticipation had built steadily during the two days since her own arrival. A fine chicken dinner warmed in the oven; a bottle of wine had been opened to come to room temperature. The house was spotless, clean linen on the beds. Anne had showered, then dressed in a pair of soft wool slacks and a paisley print blouse for the occasion, her hair brushed to a high luster and draped about her shoulders. The soft pink glow on her cheeks had needed no reinforcement, though her eyelids bore a sheen of lavender, her long lashes a fine coat of mascara. On the slender third finger of her right hand was the exquisite enameled ring he had given her, gay and graceful.

She waited. The hands on her watch seemed not to move, the minutes dragging out interminably. She paced to the kitchen to check on dinner. She returned to the living room via the front window to search for signs of headlights. She slumped back into her wing-backed chair, listening and waiting, as one log after the other crumbled to glowing embers in the hearth. The round—from chair to kitchen to window to chair—repeated itself again and again as nervousness mixed with impatience, culminating in a disappointment that prompted her, well after midnight, to foil-wrap the food, clean up the kitchen, and retreat with vigilance to her chair.

It was two in the morning when finally she gave up her watch, undressing and going to bed for what would prove to be a predominantly sleepless night. While black eyes probed the darkness, one ear listened, always listened for the sound of the motor that would announce Mitch's arrival. It never came.

Saturday morning found her heavy-eyed and disturbed as the gamut of possible explanations for his failure to appear raced around and around her consciousness. Perhaps he had been merely delayed over some business matter. Unable to contact her, as there wasn't a phone in the cabin, he may just have decided to set off early that morning, in which case he would be there by afternoon. Perhaps he had forgotten that she would be waiting. Now that he had given her a key he no longer had to feel the responsibility to arrive first and open the cabin for her. Perhaps he had decided not to come *at all;* after all, she did have that key and could make herself at home very easily.

These and other possibilities flitted about her brain as the hours passed, one longer than the previous one. By late afternoon, when there was still no sign of the light-blue Honda, Anne's thoughts turned on herself, citing her own romantic imaginings as the cause of her disillusionment. What had she expected? She and Mitch were friends, intimate in some respects, not so in others. Had she blown the relationship into something it was not, nor had any chance of ever being?

What, in fact, was the true nature of her own feelings for

Mitch? She found him attractive, attentive, intelligent, and exciting. No day passed that her thoughts did not touch on him, in one form or another. With no effort at all she could imagine spending the rest of her days with that man in this isolated house. Was it love she felt . . . or merely an answer to the loneliness left by the loss of another love, one that had bloomed from innocence and come to fruition?

The harsh grate of a horn penetrated her quandary, drawing her from her window seat in the kitchen to the front door. But it wasn't *his* horn—she had known that instantly. Whereas everything about Mitch oozed of charm, this sound carried the rough edge—charming in its own down-home kind of way—of a local pickup truck.

"Mrs. Boulton?" the gruff voice barked out as the stocky form of a farmer, clad in heavy wool jacket, baggy overalls, and aged work boots, stepped from the cab of the truck and strode toward her.

"Y-yes?" Her interaction with the locals had been limited to those few she had met in the grocery store and the drugstore. The bearded face before her, topped with a flop-eared hunter's cap, bore no familiarity at all.

"Message for ya. From a Cooper fella. Phoned the police station. Sorry for the delay." He handed the crumpled piece of paper into Anne's outstretched hand, touched a callused hand to his short visor, and returned to his truck quickly, shyly.

"Thank you!" The truck had already backed around before she had a chance to call out to him. Her words were acknowledged with a curt wave out the window as the truck disappeared around the curve. With trepidation she looked down at the folded paper in her hand. Was it good news or bad? Was he coming, or would he be passing up the trip this time around?

Nervously she unfolded the paper. The scrawl was nearly illegible. "Unavoidable delay. Mitch arriving Sunday night. Miles Cooper."

With a tired sigh she cast a glance down the empty road. Sunday night . . . another whole day to wait. Unavoidable delay . . . what had that meant? The mystery continued to nag at her, though exhaustion offered the escape of deep sleep Saturday night.

Sunday arrived to the accompaniment of the pounding of rain on the rooftop. It was a dark and gloomy day and, for the first time since she had arrived, Anne sought the solace of her translating to ease her mind from its preoccupation. It seemed like yesterday that she'd sought this same solace from thoughts of Jeff. Now the obsession was with Mitch. Was she in love with him? Again she asked herself that all-important question. The disappointment at his continued absence was devastating. More than anything in the world, just then, she wanted to see him. But was it love? Life did not consist, alone, of the existence in this hideaway. What would happen if their lives together expanded in realm to New York? Would their relationship blaze there as it had here?

At the sound of the car approaching from the distance, Anne's heart began to race. The light of day had long since fallen beneath the horizon line to give credence to the pitch black of night. A heavy rain had continued to fall all day, and at times she had feared that his small car might become bogged down in the mud. But the steady purr was unmistakable; without doubt it was the Honda.

Excitement welled within as she opened the front door to catch the close headlights before they were switched off. It seemed an eternity before Mitch finally climbed from the car, wrested his bags from the trunk's cramped confines, and bolted through the rain toward the house. The instant he brushed past her without a direct glance, she knew that something was definitely wrong. In that fast moment the answer to one of her many questions had emerged; the delay had had a private cause. Whether Mitch would choose to share it with her remained to be seen.

Numbly she closed the door on the rawness of the night,

turning then to see the tall figure deposit the bags, throw off his overcoat, and head for the fire, all without a word. Strangely unsure of herself, and equally as strangely divested of boldness, she slowly willed herself toward the fire, sinking down onto the sofa to study the broad back before her, to await the turn of its counterpart toward her.

The magnificence of the man reached out to grab her, both physically and emotionally, as she silently marveled at him. The mold of muscles through the beige knit of his sweater was not to be minimized, any more than the suggestion of latent power beneath the narrow sheath of brown corduroy slacks. But it was the attitude of fatigue, spoken through his bent head and the limp hand in his pocket, that made the greatest impression on her, tearing at her insides. She ached to help, yet she feared rebuff. For the present her only course could be the passive one she had taken.

Eyes glued to the fire, Mitch seemed oblivious to her presence. His mood was a dark one, the hand on the mantelpiece clenching and unclenching in turn. What secrets, she wondered, did he harbor within? What sadness could master his spirit so? An uncanny note of familiarity in the scene before her rang out; the similarities to that very first night she had met him, back in September, when the rain had been falling and he had been as ominous, disquieted her.

Motivated to make some small gesture of comfort, she escaped quietly to the kitchen, returning with a tall mug of strong black coffee in her hand. The timidity of her step was repeated in her voice.

"Have something hot, Mitch. It was a long drive."

His silvery head jerked toward her with such suddenness that had it not been for the hot coffee in her hand she would have jumped. That she had recalled him from some intense mental struggle was obvious by the fierceness of his expression. Without a word of either greeting or explanation he accepted the cup and returned to his brooding. Again Anne waited, her heart going out to the man before her. For despite his preoccupation and seeming indifference to her presence, his had made her feel whole once more.

"I'm sorry, Annie," he murmured finally, setting the empty mug on the mantel and brushing his arm across his forehead, as though to erase the worry creases, before turning to face her. His eyes were tired, his face more drawn than she remembered it, yet its ultimate attention and the wan smile that crooked his lips warmed her. "You're looking well," he offered calmly.

She tilted her head slightly, resting her chin on her knees, which were drawn up and secured by her arms around them. "I have been . . . thanks to you. That penicillin did the trick."

"No more trouble?" She shook her head. "That's good." His towering form turned back to the fire, troubled. Conversation was too formal for what they had shared. An invisible barrier had come from somewhere, from nowhere. Anne didn't know how to pierce it, yet she had to try.

"Is everything all right, Mitch?"

"Is everything ever all right?" He answered her question with one of his own, throwing her into a renewed silence. His anger bewildered her.

"Was it a bad drive up?" She took a new tack, even though instinct told her it had nothing to do with his mood. The point was to break through, somehow, and get him to open up.

"The usual." The curtness of his response set her back. A long silence followed.

"I received the message. Thank you for sending it," she offered at last.

"I didn't want you waiting."

Or worrying, she added silently, bitterly. The civility of the dialogue was inane, driving her to thoughts that terrified her. Perhaps the worst was true. Perhaps Mitch had not wanted to come at all. Perhaps he regretted having given her the key and such free access to the house. After all, during that first run-in in September, he'd made it clear that he didn't want any woman here. Over the months he appeared to have reversed his position, having invited her back time and again. What if he no longer wished her to be here? What if he had simply shifted once more? What if those "obligations" he had spoken of had finally taken priority to the relationship, isolated as it was, that they shared?

The words tumbled out beyond her control. "Would you like me to leave, Mitch?"

Abruptly he turned to stare at her. "Of course not! Why do you suggest such a foolish thing as that?"

"Is it all that foolish?" she snapped back, becoming irritated at his distance. "You are two days late, then you walk in here like a zombie, staring at the fire. It occurs to me that you might just want your house to yourself!"

Ironically her own disturbance seemed to have drawn him out of his shell. "If I had wanted that, I would never have given you a key to the place."

Cornered on the sofa, Anne merely stared up at him. "I've asked myself over the last two days exactly why you *did* give me that key. And I can't seem to come up with a satisfactory answer."

His gaze leveled as he shrugged. "Suffice it to say that I wanted you to have access to the place whenever you wanted."

"Why?"

"That's one hell of a crazy question." His jaw clenched.

"And this is one hell of a crazy situation!" she lashed back uncontrollably.

He walked toward the front window to peer out at the darkness. "I never promised you any other."

As always, he was right. A heavy weight settled in Anne's stomach at the realization that she had come to expect much more than he was prepared to give. Hadn't she, herself, claimed at one point that she would make no demands on him . . . other than that he *be* here, every once in a while, for her to see? He had kept his word; he was here. What more could she ask?

Yet there *was* more, much more, she knew in the instant. Though she wasn't quite ready to give it a name, it had become a vital part of her.

Head bowed in defeat, she arose from the sofa, reached for the empty mug, and headed for the kitchen. At its door she stopped without turning to call to him. "Have you had any supper?"

"No."

"I'll make something."

"That's not necessary."

"I'll *do* it." To deprive her of everything was unfair; the least he could do was to let her put together a makeshift meal. Her face was a mask of indignance as she entered the kitchen.

The late-night snack was perhaps the most awkward of any they had shared yet. Actually Anne merely sat and watched as Mitch downed a club sandwich, made with the chicken that had gone uneaten on Friday night. Conversation was sparse and cryptic, compounding her frustration.

"Thank you," he offered, when only crumbs remained on the plate. "That hit the spot." His eyes were cold and aloof, shiny as steel and every bit as hard. The lines fanning out from his eyes reflected a deep, inner tension.

"I'm glad I've finally done *something* right," she murmured sarcastically, standing to clean up the dishes. At his place, her hand was seized with iron-cuff strength.

"Now, what is that supposed to mean?" His eyes narrowed in challenge as his head cocked skeptically, his voice lowering with displeasure.

Anne's dark gaze fell to the touch point of their hands. "I think you know." With one sharp jerk her hand was free and she continued to the sink.

"Anne." Suddenly his warning voice was directly behind her. "You've been vague about something for the last hour. What is it?"

"Nothing." Fierce hands scrubbed at the dish.

"You're angry, aren't you? Because I showed up two days late?"

"No."

"Come on. What else could it be? I sent word. I even did it through Miles so that you wouldn't worry that I'd discovered your last name," he added with a properly bitter note.

"That's not bothering me."

Steel fingers seized her shoulders and turned her around forcibly. "Damn it, look at me, Anne," he growled, oblivious to her soap-dripping hands, which she held out by her sides. "I want you to tell me what is irritating you."

Instantly the flames in her own eyes flared. "Why should I? I don't owe you any explanation for my behavior, any more than you owe me one for yours!"

His smoky eyes held hers for an eternity before finally releasing them. "So, that's it. You want an explanation for my . . . er . . . tardiness, as though this is some kind of a business meeting."

"I want nothing!" she cried out vehemently, whipping out of his grasp to dry her hands on the towel, then thrust the damp rag into his hand. "Here, *you* finish cleaning. I'm going to bed."

Mercifully the tears held off until she was safely upstairs in her attic room . . . and sure of not being followed. Then they came, with the force of a love that seemed destined to bring a whole new scourge of pain. Why had she let it happen? She had loved Jeff and lost him, through powers beyond her own. Why had she opened herself up to the agony all over again?

Yes, from amid the soulful maelstrom of tears and torment came the realization that she was in love with Mitch . . . Mitch, whose last name she didn't even know! Why it should have come to her, this earth-shaking realization, on this night, she couldn't tell. Perhaps it stemmed from missing him, for loving implied wanting desperately to be with him.

Perhaps it stemmed from the depth of his brooding earlier, and her inability to console him, for loving brought with it the need to give of one's self when the other was distressed. Perhaps it stemmed from that lack of an explanation for his delay, for loving demanded an openness in all regards. Perhaps it was merely their failure to communicate, for loving prized communication in any, and every, form.

For long hours she fought the rising despair that threatened to engulf her. While one part of her suggested that the best course might be for her to leave tomorrow and put this entire emotional upheaval behind her, the other, more powerful part told her to wait. Mitch's presence was still of high priority in her life; the extent and precise nature of his feelings was an enigma. The temptation to be with him was far too great to deny. And there was always hope.

On that optimistic note she finally fell into a deep sleep, long after all sound of life from the downstairs quarter had ceased. The rain continued its steady spray upon the windowpanes, yet it was the familiar aroma of coffee, black and strong, that finally woke her up.

Even without raising her lids she felt the difference. The weight by her right hip, and the distinct depression of the mattress, could not be mistaken on her narrow bed, nor could the faint but recognizable scent of after-shave, which blended with the dark brew to tantalize her. And then there was that very subtle awareness to clinch the fact. She was not alone.

Slowly her heavy-lidded eyes opened to focus on the relaxed figure sitting on the edge of the bed. Through her delightful haze of grogginess, he looked soft, gentle, and caring. Freshly shaven, showered, and dressed, he was a powerful symbol of masculinity. His face was one tender smile, broken only when he took an occasional sip of the coffee from the mug he held. He was a lovely vision, this man before her, one that she was reluctant to pollute with words. As it happened, he spoke first.

"Good morning, sleepyhead. I had begun to wonder

whether you would ever wake up. A real sleeping beauty." His voice held the velvet that Prince Charming would have worn, yet he made no other move to emulate that fabled icon of chivalry.

Anne was unable to resist a smile in return for the lovely awakening presence he'd given her. "I'm afraid I had trouble falling asleep. I nearly saw the dawn."

"I know." A tawny brow arched pointedly, his inference drawing a soft laugh from the bed.

"Hah! Got a taste of your own medicine, eh?" Pushing herself higher up on the pillow, she lifted a hand to move her hair back off her cheek.

"What's this?" Mitch's eyes lit up with the movement. "Bare arms? A negligee? Whatever happened to that adorable long flannel nightgown you always used to wear? It's not *that* warm yet!"

A deep flush colored Anne's features, bringing with it a heat of its own, though not so much in embarrassment at what had been revealed to Mitch's eye, but rather what must have been revealed to his mind. "It's not a negligee," she protested with soft scorn. "That implies something . . . daring. This is merely a . . . nightgown." Reflexively she pulled the quilt up to cover adequately the sensuous meeting place of lace and skin, just above the ripe swell of her breasts.

Glittering hazel orbs teased her mercilessly. "We're arguing about semantics, Anne. The fact remains that you look like a woman *should* look first thing in the morning."

"I look terrible!" she burst out, thinking of her sleep-knotted tresses, her tired eyes, her bare features.

"You know," he jibed, "you'd be a millionairess in a week if you could give women the key to that 'terrible' look!"

"And I'm sure you've seen your share of women first thing in the morning—" It was an unfair shot, one which she regretted as soon as she'd taken it. Thankfully Mitch remained undaunted.

"Here, Annie." His arm slid beneath her shoulders to lever

her into a half-seated position. "You need some coffee to get you off to a better start. Jealousy has never been your style." The smile continued to play at the corners of his lips, yet his eyes were serious.

"I'm not jealous," she lied, then sipped at the proferred drink. The very intimacy of drinking from Mitch's cup, of putting her lips on the spot where his had been moments before, made the lie even more poignant. She *was* jealous—of a nameless, faceless something that occupied Mitch's time and thoughts when he was away from her. And even after he had arrived last night, that something had intruded on her time with him. Yes, she was jealous. Annoyingly so.

"Better?" he asked, retrieving the coffee mug to take a drink himself. At her nod he let her lie back down, then placed the empty mug on the nightstand. "Is it symbolic—that nightgown—much as the pink sweater was last time?"

"I suppose so." She shrugged, oblivious to the fact that in the process of having sat up to sip the coffee, the quilt had fallen to waist level, where it remained now. It was so natural to be with Mitch. "I'm getting out a lot more now. I think that I've finally recovered . . ." Her voice trailed off as she remembered the upcoming trial, which she dreaded. As though paralleling her thoughts, a frown split the manly features before her. Disturbed to look back and see it, she sought quickly to recover the warmth they'd shared when she had first awoken. "How about you? Any 'symbolic' gestures of recovery?"

His lips curved into a distinctly sly smile. Anne knew, even before she heard it, that his answer would be evasive. "Some."

"Well . . . ?" she prodded with demand in her eyes, when he failed to elaborate on his own.

"That's better told at another time."

"Why?"

"Because I have something much more important in mind right now."

"Oh?" Her innocence was genuine, until she followed the line of his sight to the curve of her breasts, outlined clearly through the sheer fabric of her gown. Instinctively she crossed her arms over its pale yellow bodice, renewed color suffusing her features, working slowly up from her neck to her cheeks.

In response his hands grasped her wrists and firmly withdrew their protective covering, pinning them on the sheet on either side of her head. "I haven't properly said hello," he murmured, low and husky, as his lips descended to greet her in a nonverbal caress that plunged deep into her, drawing forth the response she could never have denied this man she loved. His mouth tasted and coaxed, his tongue teased and enticed, until Anne burst, at last, into a breathless moan of desire. What had begun as a gentle hello abruptly exploded into multiple flames of hunger, her lips parting and returning his kiss with every ounce of her inner love. At some unknown point he released her hands to lift her free of the pillow, cradling her in his arms, letting the length of her black hair cascade behind her. Her own hands, freed to their delights, delved into the thickness of the hair at the nape of his neck, blond, silvered, and rakishly wavy.

It was everything Anne had subconsciously waited for and wanted. His kiss set her afire, his embrace fed the flame. The heat had aggregated in rosy clusters on her cheeks and lips by the time he finally set her back from him.

"That was quite some hello," she gasped, in truth bereft at his retreat, "but it wasn't quite proper. . . ."

The smoldering light in his eyes seared through her body, settling in her core, knotting in frustration. Proper or not, she wanted him to continue with this heady seduction of which he was a master. Chewing on her lower lip lest she blurt out her love, her eyes spoke in their own persuasive way, begging him for something more, something deeper.

As he silently fought the divine allure of the woman before him, experienced yet innocently vulnerable, his own need overwhelmed him. When he reached down to renew his embrace, she sighed aloud at the instant relief brought by his touch. Her soft lips sought his, satisfied to be crushed by them with a strength that excited her even more.

Her hands crept around his waist, slender fingers finding the ribbing of his sweater, then slipping beneath to lovingly caress the length of manly flesh. Through her delight she was barely aware of his own fingers on her shoulders, pushing off the slim straps of her nightgown, until he drew back to release her arms completely, letting the fine, silken fabric fall to drape softly about her waist.

His gaze caressed the ivory glow of her up-tilted breasts, their rosy tips swelling before his eyes. "How lovely you are, Annie," he rasped hoarsely.

"You've seen me before . . ." Her whisper trailed off self-consciously.

His eyes, deep green with passion, sought hers. "Yes, when you were sick with a fever, the chills, and a hacking cough. The beauty was there, but I hardly had time to admire it. Now I have that time. You are a magnificent woman, Annie! I'll tell you that over and over again, every time I hold you, every time I make love to you. . . ."

Her insides quivered at his very words. The hand which cupped her breasts heightened that sensation, the thumb and forefinger teasing her nipple until she grabbed at his shoulders for support. "Mitch," she cried aloud, "how can you be so cruel?"

She felt his grin against her ear, where his lips had been nibbling contentedly. "You bring out the worst in me, my lady," he declared huskily, even as his hands continued their agonizingly sweet play without a fault.

The flames within Anne burned higher and hotter, threatening to reduce her to a fragmented mass of embers. Sensing her spiraling need and driven by his own, he eased her down gently onto the bed as his fingers were replaced by his mouth, which enveloped the auburn aureole of her breast in its mind-shattering entirety. Unconsciously she arched her back to offer herself more completely, her fingers clutching at the knit of his sweater helplessly.

When she thought she could bear no more, he released his hold of her breast with a hoarse moan, his tongue flicking over its bud with shocking lightness before he straightened and whipped his sweater over his head to reveal the expanse of his sinewed chest to Anne's love-dazed eyes. He struggled to steady his breathing as her palms explored him, thrilling in the textured roughness of the tawny tufts of hair.

The strength of the attraction brought her to a seated position, from where her lips could explore his muscled breadth, her tongue sampling the tang of his skin with heady satisfaction. His manly scent drove her to distraction, complemented by the sensual move of his large fingers over her naked back. A shudder of ecstasy ran along her spine as he traversed it, again and again, the thrust of desire shooting through her and settling, at length, in her loins.

"Oh, Annie," he groaned, crushing her against him to stop her own form of torture. She gasped at the sensation of his chest against her own, the rapid thunder of his heartbeat echoing hers.

"I need you, Mitch," she whispered, when breath returned for an instant. Pulling her head back, she searched past his chiseled chin and straight nose to his eyes, which flamed back at her brilliantly. "Please . . . ?" At that moment she craved his total possession more than she'd ever craved any man's touch. The need was to be his, and his alone, to give him everything her body could offer. He had succeeded in alighting her every sensitivity. Now only a complete and utter union would satisfy her.

"Do you know what you're doing?" he asked huskily, then sucked in his breath when her hand fell to the snap of his jeans, fingertips slipping inside to grasp the waistband and settle against the flatness of his abdomen. "My God, Annie . . ." For long moments of indecision he stared down at her, reading in her eyes that which her tongue could not seem to say.

"Mitch, I—I—I—" The depth of her love, her longing, brought tears to her eyes, adding a fluidity to their sparkle that told the story even more potently.

But as she held his gaze, oblivious to the emotion spelled out in her own, she saw a sudden and unfathomable hardening. "Damn it!" he swore, as he thrust her away abruptly, standing and pacing to the window, where he stood for a moment, hands on hips, legs wide apart, head hung low, shoulders heaving under labored breaths. Then, muttering the oath once more, he stalked past her and left the room.

CHAPTER SEVEN

Anne sat in stunned silence for what seemed an eternity, unable to move, to think, to feel. It was only the chill in the air, compounded by that from within, that stirred her finally to huddle down beneath the quilt once more, pulling it to her chin. Even then the trembling hit her in recurring aftershocks from his abrupt departure.

Grasping in vain for a foothold to reality, she fell short, time and again, unable to comprehend what had driven him to reject her. It made no sense. Wasn't it more often the man who drove on, the woman who demurred at the last moment? What had happened here?

Anne had blatantly offered herself to Mitch, the man she loved. He had as blatantly refused her offer with a show, no less, of anger. Did he resent her? Did he dislike her? Without doubt he found her physically attractive. His own part in their lovemaking attested to that fact, as well as the physical arousal of which Anne, well-attuned to it, had been certain. Yet he had cast her away! *Why? Why? Why?*

As she lay curled into a tight ball of misery, but one answer came to her. There had to be someone else, the "obligation" to which he had referred once. It had to be his feelings for that other woman that prevented him from taking advantage of her own willing offering. For that she had to give him begrudging respect, yet it didn't help to ease her own problem in the least.

Once again she faced the dilemma of whether to leave immediately or stay the week. Once again she came to the same conclusion. Self-destructive as it might prove to be, she had to stay, to be near Mitch, though she knew the game of self-delusion would be a short-lived one.

With hollow satisfaction at having faced the problem and come up with a decision, she climbed slowly out from beneath the quilt, let her nightgown slide over her thighs and calves to the floor as she stood, then walked to the dresser to get clean clothes. As she pulled on a pair of corduroys and a turtleneck sweater, she made one vow to herself, the only condition under which she could allow herself to remain for the rest of the week under the same roof as Mitch. Never again would she do what she had done earlier that morning. Never again would she humiliate herself as she had done then. Never again would she offer her body as proof of her love, until the day she knew that it would be received in that very same spirit.

With this resolve she descended the stairs with her head held high. But her show of confidence was wasted; Mitch was nowhere about. He had had something to eat; the dishes in the sink graphically illustrated that fact. And the blue Honda was parked outside, as it had been left when he had arrived last night. But there was neither hide nor hair of the man himself. The elements, gloomy and damp as they had been the day before, were far from conducive to hiking. Yet, by a process of elimination, it appeared that he was out in the woods somewhere.

Resigned to spending the afternoon alone, Anne built a roaring fire, then plunked herself before it. With her was a short essay to be translated—in actuality, the last of the little work she had brought—and a new novel, of the best-seller type, to be read. Once more she felt transported back in time to that September visit. But oh, so very much had changed since then.

Late afternoon blended into early evening without a sign of Mitch. More restless than bored, more concerned than angry, Anne wandered into the kitchen. Where was he? The temptation to go ahead and prepare dinner was squelched quickly by her total absence of hunger and the knowledge that Mitch could be all hours in returning. Rather than add a ruined meal to the growing list of disturbances, she returned to the fireplace.

Not long after, the back door groaned open, then slammed shut, and heavy-booted feet traversed the floor to bring the slicker-clad figure within Anne's range of vision. Her eyes riveted to the doorway, held in uncertainty by the shadowed eyes that speared her.

Without a word he crossed the space between them, shucking the slicker along the way and draping it over the back of the straight wood chair at the desk. Then he moved to where she sat, hunkering down to add another log to the fire. Only when it had begun to sizzle and smoke did he swivel on his haunches to face her.

"Angry?" The fire behind him threw a maddeningly angelic halo around the silver shock of his hair, leaving his face and its expression as maddeningly in shadow. Unable to tell whether he empathized or taunted, she could base her response only on her own emotions.

"No. What right have I to be angry?"

"Well, I did disappear on you for the day."

"Wasn't it awfully wet out?" It seemed far safer to make small talk than to analyze motives.

"You might say." The smile on his face was audible in his tone, relaxing her immediately. "But the walk was good. I needed the time to think."

Her own smile teased him gently. "You sound as though you have the weight of the world on your shoulders."

"It sometimes seems that way." His voice was softer, more rueful. "It's been a bad week."

"Work?" she asked timidly.

He shook his head. "No. Fortunately all is well on that score. I have a good second-echelon team; they keep things running, even when I fade out. . . ." His low voice followed his words, tinged as they were with self-directed impatience.

Anne sat still, waiting for him to offer more. If it wasn't business, this problem of his, it had to be personal, as she'd originally suspected. Suddenly, and in a complete turnaround, she didn't want to know.

Clearing her throat awkwardly, she stood with a start. "I'll—ah—I'll go get some dinner on to cook."

"No." He caught at her wrist, halting her escape, his eyes studying her downcast ones intently. Would he tell her everything now? Would she find out where his own heart lay? Would her humiliation be complete? But he had something else in mind. "It's my turn. You did it last night. This time I'm making dinner for us."

The abrupt swell of gentleness in his tone threw her, as did his gaze, which implored her, silently, to let him have his way. Knees weak, she sank back into her chair, rescuing her wrist from his searing touch as she did so. Her whispered grant was barely audible, her hands held up in a sign of concession. "Be my guest."

"That's a funny twist." He chuckled in a suddenly lighter mood. One agile movement brought him to his feet, another, unanticipated on her part, brought him to her, and a firm kiss was planted on her cheek before she had time to pull away.

"What was *that* for?" she asked, for not the first time.

His grin shot back at her from the kitchen doorway. "That's for being such an understanding hostess!"

Astonished all the more, she could only sit and stare at the spot, long after he had disappeared from it. When the sounds of activity filtered in to her—the opening and shutting of the refrigerator door, the clatter of pots and pans, the running of the water from the faucet—she guessed that he must have come to some tentative conclusion during his afternoon of soul-searching.

In her wildest dreams she imagined that his feelings for her might be as strong as those she felt for him. In her more realistic reining-in, however, she understood that he must merely have reached a compromise in his mind, whereby he would make this time they had together simply as pleasant for both of them as was possible, given the placement of his heart elsewhere.

It was in this spirit that dinner passed in comfortable conversation, reverting in essence to those earlier, more heart-free times they'd spent together. And when Tuesday morning brought with it a bright and warming taste of the sun, she was not at all surprised by his early arising to join her for breakfast.

"It's a perfect morning to set in the spouts," he began, when the dishes were cleared and he wiped to her washing.

"Spouts?"

"Sure! With the cold nights and warmer days we've had, the sap will be flowing like water!"

Anne laughed aloud. "Maple-sugaring? You mean we can do it ourselves? I'd fully intended on visiting a local farm to watch one day this week!"

His grin was a well-satisfied one. "Why go elsewhere when we have everything we need right here?"

She could not have agreed with him more. "Do you know what to do?"

His voice was low and chiding. "Do I know what to do?" Strong hands took her shoulders, turning her to face him. The wicked gleam in his eye mocked her. "Since when have you had cause to question my expertise . . . on anything?"

Dazzled by his warmth, she could only muster a feeble retort. "Hmmmm, modesty seems to have escaped you entirely."

"Well," he clipped, with a short laugh and a quick release of her shoulders, "no one is perfect."

In Anne's biased judgment Mitch was as close to it as anyone could be for that day and the ones that followed. Though there was time to hike, to read, to rest, the bulk of their joint attention focused on the maple-sugaring, about which he did indeed know almost everything.

"The best trees have to be big, forty years old or more," he explained, when they left the house, laden with the tools that he had mysteriously produced from a back shed. Anne watched, fascinated, as he drilled small holes in the trunks of each of the huge maples, then plugged each hole with a small metal spout that extended several inches beyond the bark.

"We're using metal spouts. This is really an old-fashioned method of tapping the trees, but it works well for me."

"You've done it before?"

He answered as he worked. "Uh-huh. Whenever I'm up here during this period. The sap flows, generally, during the weeks from mid-March to mid-April, with some variability by the year." With a shove, another spout was in place and he moved on to insert one into a hole on the back side of the same tree.

"I thought you could only have one spout per tree," she halted him.

"With a tree this size, there will be enough sap for two. Here, you slide this one in, while I get more buckets."

By the time he returned she had successfully completed the chore assigned her. The finishing touch was added by his knowing hand as it adjusted the bucket securely onto the spout. "I've never seen sliding lids like these before," she commented, closely examining the seemingly unnecessary top piece.

His eyes glittered humorously, his smile touching the corners of his lips with manly arrest. "Then you've never seen a stray horse or a field mouse devour the sap as it accumulates."

She laughed. "No, I haven't. Then this lid is very clever."

"It doesn't always keep them out. A persistent animal—of any sort"—his eyebrow lifted with devilish flair—"can get what he wants. But"—he returned to the more pertinent discussion—"it does help."

"How much sap will we get?" Together they picked up their equipment and moved on to the next tree.

For the moment that he stood, debating where to drill, Anne could not help but admire the majestic image he conveyed. Bundled warmly in a high-collared sheepskin jacket, he was every bit as bold and commanding as the towering Douglas fir high up on the farther hillside.

Kneeling before the tree and applying the drill at last, he answered her. "Oh, on a good day the bucket could fill and overflow. On a poor day we could get just a few inches. If we were to continue"—he grunted, pushing the bit forward into the tree—"for the entire length of the sapping season, we might get ten or twenty gallons from each tree."

Her dark eyes widened in surprise. "That's phenomenal! But what would we ever do with all that sap?"

The hole drilled, he straightened and motioned with his finger for her to insert the spout, which she deftly did this time around with the aid of a hammer. " 'All that sap' boils down to very little!" Her furrowed brow brought out a spontaneous laugh. "To get *one* gallon of maple syrup," he went on patiently, "you have to boil down anywhere from thirty-five to fifty gallons of sap!"

She groaned aloud. "Now I can understand why genuine Vermont maple syrup is as expensive as it is."

Mitch's lesson resumed as he continued his work. "New York and Vermont produce the most syrup in this country, though the province of Quebec yields more than the two states combined. Today, most of the commonly used syrups are actually a combination of maple syrup, cane sugar syrup, and corn syrup. It's the straight stuff, though, the real thing, that beats all, in my opinion!"

Unable to disagree, Anne just nodded, succumbing to the feeling of contentment that had settled over her. For a while they proceeded in silence, a friendly silence, an intimate silence. She noted that, as always, he favored his right arm, cranking the hand drill around with it, while the other held the shaft in position. When she offered to take a turn, he indulged her, enjoying her fated struggle with a smug smile. When she turned the chore back to him finally with a sheepish glance of apology, he comforted her. "That's all right, Annie. I could never have cleaned the house the way you did before I got up here."

"You noticed!" Quickly tempering her eager question into a more droll statement, she savored the fact that her efforts had not been in vain, though how much, at the time, had been motivated by boredom, she didn't know.

"How could I help but notice," he accused her with a grin. "I was nearly blinded by the sparkle." Anne knew the feeling, nearly blinded, as she now felt from the sparkle in the eyes that held hers so magnetically. When he thrust two more spouts into her hand, she was disoriented temporarily, so carried away had she momentarily become. "In the tree?" he prodded, with a knowing grin, leaving her to recover her steady keel as he turned for a bucket.

That first day, the largest of the maples in the near vicinity of the house were drilled, spouts inserted, and buckets attached. On succeeding days the chore consisted of collecting the sap that had flowed. It was no mean feat, carting heavy buckets from tree to house and back.

"Now, if we had all of the most modern equipment," he had informed her mischievously, as she massaged the nagging muscles of her shoulders at the end of one such toting stint, "we would have used plastic spouts, attached to plastic tubing, which would take the stuff directly from tree to sugarhouse. It's much more efficient in terms of time and labor."

"That's all right." She stated the obvious. "Since we haven't got a sugarhouse. Besides, I'm gaining weight. The exercise will do me good."

He arched an eyebrow in challenge of her self-evaluation. "I must admit that you're no longer scrawny, but . . . in danger of being overweight? Not a chance!"

Anne shook her head in half jest. "I don't know. It seems that you've done most of the work this week." Luxuriant lashes blunted the directness of her upward gaze. When an arm settled across her shoulders, she let herself be drawn to his side.

"You deserve it, having put up with me the way you did when I first arrived. Most women would have packed up and left."

She smiled. "The thought did cross my mind. . . ."

"Well, I'm glad you stayed." It was a warm moment, preserved in Anne's memory along with the silver gleam in hazel eyes, the gentle fingers curved to the contour of her shoulder, and the velvet edge of the croon that, in itself, was ample reward for her having stayed.

By Friday morning, the last full day of Anne's stay, since Mitch had convinced her successfully to give deference to their project and wait until Saturday to leave, there was sufficient sap gathered in the large vat to begin the boiling process.

"They usually do this in long, shallow pans called evaporators. The one we're using is a little deeper than we need, but it will have to do. When all the water has evaporated, we will have ourselves some pure maple syrup." He may have gone through the whole process before, yet his enthusiasm and genuine enjoyment of it now was in no way watered down. If anything, Anne's excitement was contagious.

"How can we get maple sugar?" she asked, enchanted as the colorless and watery liquid bubbled into a gradually thickening golden brown color.

"If we had the time and patience to keep it boiling past the syrup stage, we would eventually get maple sugar."

On impulse, Anne slid an arm around Mitch's waist, happier in this moment, as they stood watching the sap boil, than she could remember ever being. Even if they parted tomorrow, never to meet again, she would have this moment always in memory to cherish.

Mitch read her thoughts. "You look very pleased about something," he challenged softly.

Feigning nonchalance, she shrugged. "It's been a fun week. This"—she pointed to the huge pot—"is a great finish to it." As the implication of her words sank in a sadness crept into her love-gentled features. Again Mitch was in step with her.

"I'd rather a more . . . personal finish. Better still, I'd rather no finish at all."

The dark eyes that gazed up at him drank in the tenderness of his expression, so much like her own, if only for that short time. She loved him so; how she ached to tell him. But, for the moment, it was not to be. Just when she thought he would kiss her, the solution before them gurgled furiously in fateful diversion from their sensual interchange.

"It shouldn't be long now," Mitch commented, lifting a large wooden spoon to stir the solution and test for its thickness. "Should we have pancakes or French toast for dinner?"

"For dinner?"

"Sure! I don't know about your willpower, but I have no intention of waiting around until breakfast to sample this."

Anne drew a slender finger across the back of the cooling wooden spoon, then licked the sweet syrup from its tip. "Mmmmmm. You may be right." She paused, sending an unconsciously coy smile his way. "How about French toast?"

"Great!" Following her example, he tasted the syrup himself, then repeated the procedure, offering his thick-coated finger to her tongue's pleasure. The syrup was as rich and sweet as the moment itself. Anne thought she could go no higher.

Suddenly, before her intent gaze, a faraway gleam entered his eyes. His voice was filled with gentleness. "Rachel enjoyed this taste-testing stage the most last year, too."

Stunned, Anne froze. *Rachel?* His "obligation"? The other woman in his life? As the tension drew taut her every muscle she backed away from the arm that had encircled her shoulders. *Rachel?* In utter disbelief that he would have made such a blunder to speak crassly of his truer love at a moment of such seeming intimacy, she could merely stare in horror at him.

For a moment Mitch was unaware of his slip, initially puzzled by her abrupt withdrawal and even more sudden emotional recoil. "What is it?"

"How could you?" she seethed, distraught.

"How could I what?" His show of innocence riled her all the more.

"How could you do that to me, Mitch?" she cried. "How could you mention *her* name at a time like this?" Tears had begun to gather at her lids, but she was helpless to halt their flow, much less to worry about it. Her mind was too boggled with other thoughts.

Mitch looked down, his brow furrowed. "Her name?" Then, in the instant, he realized what he had done, and the furrows yielded to a sad cast. "I spoke of Rachel, didn't I?"

The softness in his voice at the mention of her name ravaged her anew. "How could you?" she repeated, tears streaming freely now over her ashen cheeks.

His hand reached out to touch her, but she flinched, moving further from him. "Annie, listen—"

"No! I've heard enough! I don't want to hear about your love life . . . about *Rachel*!" She spat out the name, as though she and that female were archenemies.

"You're wrong—" He tried again, only to be interrupted likewise.

"Yes, I have been wrong," she screamed in desolation. "I have been wrong to want to stay up here with you, when I should be back in New York, trying to build some kind of practical life. I have been wrong to think that you really wanted *me* here, when in one careless moment you can conjure up another woman, like that." She snapped her fingers in a raging blend of sadness and bitterness. His face was no longer distinct, but rather a blurred mask before her. "How could you *do* this to me? Can't you see that I love you—"

Instantly the horror was self-directed as Anne realized what she'd confessed. Whirling around, she ran blindly from the kitchen, taking the steps with reckless speed, stopping only when the door to her bedroom was slammed and flush against her back. The pain within was excruciating. Her trembling hands covered her eyes, quickly growing wet, as was her entire face, with tears. The thunderous pounding of her heart drowned out the sound of footsteps on the stairs.

"Anne, open up." His soft rap echoed against her back.

"No!" she cried in a pitiful pitch of mortification and despair, one that reflected the agony that had overtaken her.

"There are things I have to tell you, Anne. Open the door."

Weeping, she shook her head, hardly aware of the fact that he could not see her silent refusal. "Anne . . ."

"Go away!" she pleaded unsteadily, desirous only of privacy to gather together what shreds of pride might remain to be packed and labeled for the final trip back to New York. Did it really matter what Mitch had to say?

"I love you, Annie." His voice filtered soft and sensuous through the ancient wood of the door, and suddenly it did matter, very much. If this was a cruel hoax, she would never be able to forgive him.

Turning to face the door, she laid her wet cheek against its smooth veneer. Afraid to listen, afraid not to, she waited, mutely, for some indication that she had not willed the words through her own heart's desire.

"Did you hear me, Annie?" Again the velvet sound, too dear to be dismissed, too real to be denied. "I love you."

The pulse that had faltered moments before, now raced forward, driven by hope and fueled by her own undying love. There was that one critical question still to be answered.

A weak hand found the knob, slowly turned it, and drew open the door. Fearfully, lest the newfound shreds of hope be scattered by a sudden or unwise move, she raised her eyes to Mitch's. Therein lay part of her answer, for the light of love, unmistakable at last, burned from their hazel centers, irradiating a warmth that chipped away at her lingering resistance. The moment had come.

"Do you love Rachel, too?" she asked in a faltering whisper.

When he reached to grasp her arms, she did not resist. Neither did she melt toward him, as every other instinct demanded. Rather she held her line, waiting, waiting for the answer she needed.

A smile, sad but tender, curved his lips. Even as his eyes spoke of his love for her, his tongue confirmed that for another. "Yes, I do love Rachel." Expecting her reaction, his hands tightened on her arms, thwarting her attempted retreat. Calmly he continued, his gaze binding hers. "But I love Rachel in a very different way than I love you, Annie. You see"—he sighed, his voice lowering to a near whisper—"Rachel is my daughter."

Shocked into wordlessness, Anne could only stare as she struggled to integrate this new and heartrending information. Was this what her jealousy had been of—his daughter? Had his daughter been at the core of Anne's inane outbreak downstairs? If only she had known.

"Why didn't you tell me, Mitch?" Her words were buried against his neck as she threw herself into his arms, received as joyfully as she might have ever dreamed.

His breath fanned her hair, his arms threatened to cut off all air to her lungs. "I've wanted to, Annie, so many times.

But it never seemed appropriate. I think that at the beginning some part of me wanted to—God forgive me—forget her existence while I was up here. Fatherhood has its merits, but it has been my greatest challenge since Bev's death."

She felt his pain and wanted only to ease it. "Perhaps I could have helped."

"No, no, Annie," he crooned supportively, "you have had enough to face without having to cope with a child."

"How old is she?"

"She turned six last week. And she came down with the chicken pox the day after her birthday. It is the first time she has been sick—really sick—since her mother died."

Finally Anne understood. "That's why you were late arriving last weekend?"

"Yes," he nodded against her silken head. "My parents have been wonderful, taking her for weeks at a stretch. They can often manage to be more cheerful than I can." At the note of self-disgust he paused, moving his head back to look down at her. "But I couldn't leave them with a sick child who only wanted her mother to hold her—" His voice broke as did Anne's heart for the little girl—and her father.

"Why didn't you bring her up here with you?" she asked softly.

His gaze studied her closely. "I wasn't sure how you felt about children. Again that discussion seemed inappropriate. I know that you have none of your own. Was it fair of me to ask you to care for a child, a sick one at that? How could I foist that responsibility on you?"

Anne's reaction was vehement and from the heart. "Mitch, how can you even think that? It wasn't through choice that I have no children. I would have loved to have met your daughter, to have helped you care for her. She's your daughter. And I love you."

His "Oh, Annie" was muffled against her lips the instant before he returned her vow, kissing her in open declaration of the love that welled within and between them. His arms crushed her, molding her femininity to his masculinity as though to reiterate the uniqueness of the love they shared.

Smothered by happiness, she gasped when he released her lips to press her head against his chest, her ear against his heart, which beat as passionately as hers. "I love you . . . I love you . . . I love you," she chanted, the song a whisper of beauty to them both—for Anne the freedom of saying it, for Mitch the reward of hearing it.

When his hands moved down to frame her face and turn her eyes to his, she complied gladly, savoring the devotion that bathed her in untold ecstasy. His eyes asked a question; hers answered. In the instant she was in his arms, being carried back down the narrow staircase to the room with the large bed, his bed. But this time, when he lowered her onto her back and reached for the edge of her sweater, she held his hands.

In answer to the look of hesitancy that crossed his features, she put a finger to his lips to still his question before it could emerge to challenge her motive. "Let me, Mitch. I need to . . . to know you."

He searched her pleading eyes for a moment, then understood. Silently acquiescent, he sat back on the bed and followed her every movement as she timidly, knowingly undressed him. When finally his body lay in all its masculine magnificence before her, she could only marvel at its beauty, at the beauty of the love she felt for him. Slowly her hands explored his every sinew, running with innocent wonder from his shoulders to his thighs, skimming lean planes, tracing manly swells, delighting in the height of the arousal to which she could bring him.

A hoarse groan signaled the end of his endurance. "That's it, honey. I can't take it anymore," he growled as, with bullet speed, he flipped over her, disrobing her with a sensual mastery that she had sampled before, though never in the guise of love.

When they lay, at long last, on the cool sheets, their bodies naked and facing one another, their breathing heavy with need, want, and love, he held her off for those last few infinitely trying moments. The glitter of silver in hazel scaled the peaks and valleys of her body once more before it searched her soul through her own dark orbs.

"Are you sure, honey?" he asked softly.

"I love you" was her only response.

"But it's different for a woman, isn't it?"

"Not when she is in love."

"Then you will be mine?"

A sly grin lit her features. "If you keep me waiting one minute longer, I may attack you. . . ."

He kept her waiting not one minute longer. The early-evening glow of pale purple light swathed them in its soft blanket as he possessed her, fully and emphatically. In that first instant of total union she was blessed with a sense of fulfillment surpassed only by the heavenly flight on which he took her, leading her to peak after peak of explosive ecstasy, then trembling back to earth with her, finally, and in utter exhaustion.

Arms and legs entwined, they slept, the deep and satisfied sleep of two who were content, together at last. Long forgotten was the maple syrup on the stove, cooling to a thick amber perfection. Long forgotten was the French toast that was to have provided the syrup's showcase. Long forgotten was the light of dusk, which faded to a dark and moonlit night as they rested.

The only thing of importance to Anne, when she awoke some time later, was the warm chest that pillowed her head, the lean hip beneath her outstretched palm, the well-muscled leg wrapped around her shapely one. Her first movement brought a tightening of the arm across her back, pressing and caressing with reverence. Smiling, she kissed the fine-matted hair on his chest, then tilted her head back to study his features, one by one, in loving progression. The chin was strong yet relaxed, the angled jaw likewise. Tension was nowhere to be found in the faint lines fanning from the corners of his eyes, but rather they held a depth of maturity and understanding. His hair fell in waves across his forehead, countering that very maturity with a certain boyish charm. But his eyes—his eyes held hers, narrow-slitted as they gazed down lazily at her, speaking of his pleasure.

"How are you, honey?" he asked gently.

A slender finger lifted to trace the line of his jaw. "I've never been better."

"I love you. You know that now, don't you?"

She nodded, fully convinced of his love. For only the presence of love could have engendered the tender passion that he had shown when he'd finally made her his own. "And I love you, too." Her whisper was unnecessary. She too had demonstrated vividly the depth of her love in the abandonment of all inhibition in her eagerness to please him.

As the night passed they would repeat the words, thrilling to prove them to each other and to themselves, again and again, in carefree rapture. For Anne there had never been such a night. She would collapse, breathless, weary of limb and shuddering in the aftermath of passion, only to discover, before long, that Mitch had a new element of his love to show her, rekindling a flame that seemed destined to burn forever.

The sun was high in the late-morning sky when they finally awoke, Mitch first, to adore her every feature, rich and relaxed, flushed with satisfaction, then Anne, to kiss her love good morning. It was a first love after other first loves, made new and fuller by the very past that had brought them together.

"How am I ever going to drive back to New York today?" she asked impishly, doubting seriously that her bones could be propelled to move anywhere, let alone her heart.

The voice against her forehead was an arrogant drawl. "You're not. When I go to make *my* phone call later today, I'll make any you need to make. I'm sure the O'Gradys won't mind."

"The O'Gradys?"

"Our neighbors, about two miles to the east. I came upon them by accident once, but they're quite used to me now. I always call Rachel from there."

Anne's mind returned with wonder to last night's discovery, one of the many. "I'm glad you do keep in touch with her while you're away."

"Whenever possible."

She rubbed her chin against his textured chest. "I really feel guilty that you left her at all to meet me here, especially when she was sick."

"Fortunately she was better by the time I left. But that's nothing for you to worry about," he chided softly, his eyes melting her with appreciation for her concern. Then his voice lowered to a more seductive drawl. "What you *really* have cause to worry about is whether or not I'll let you out of this bed before Monday—"

"Mitch . . . you wouldn't," she protested, feigning shock.

A tawny eyebrow arched to underscore his determination. "Oh, yes, I would."

"You couldn't—" She took another tack, one that proved to be an even more divine error.

"No?" he teased, sliding his vibrant body over hers in proof of his claim. All further protest was lost in the recesses of his mouth, as his lips renewed the ardor of the night's passion, once again proclaiming his love.

Saturday night they had cause to celebrate, toasting each other by first and last names, declaring their love once more. In the end they both returned to New York on Sunday afternoon, Mitch to attend a Monday morning board meeting, Anne to deliver a completed piece of work to the university at that time also.

The moment of parting was a bittersweet one, accompanied by a deep and mutual sense of depression as each faced the rigors of the next few weeks alone. Mitch, in particular, seemed tense, once again preoccupied.

"The next few weeks are going to be impossible for me, Annie," he began, carefully choosing his words. "There are several critical . . . business matters to which I have to attend. And"—he paused, sighing—"I'll want to spend a little extra time with Rachel. Let me call you as soon as things clear up somewhat. Does that sound all right?" Considering their intimacy and the repeated exchanges of vows of love over the past two days, his unsureness would have certainly disturbed Anne, had she not been bothered, herself, by the prospect of the immediate future. The court hearing on the matter of her law suit was a mere week and a half off.

"That's fine, Mitch." She struggled to make her smile express the gaiety she was far from feeling. "I'll be waiting."

CHAPTER EIGHT

Wait she did. Day after day, night after night, she waited. The knowledge that Mitch was suffering through a very busy period was little solace to her aching heart. Only the belief that he loved her carried her through to that evening, ironically, the night before her court appearance, when the phone rang finally.

"How are you, Annie?" His tone was deep and sincere in its concern, though the fine thread of guardedness was impossible to ignore.

"Fine, Mitch. I miss you," she heard herself blurt out, blushing at her impulsiveness, though meaning every word.

"Same here, honey. Are you all set . . . for tomorrow?"

The mere fact that he had remembered the date she'd been dreading for so long—and had called to give her last-minute encouragement—pleased her. "No. I don't think I could ever be ready for that," she answered honestly. "But my family—and Jeff's—will be here first thing in the morning to escort me. I think they're not sure that I'll show."

"They'll all be there?" Her touch of humor had gone unnoticed.

"Most of them. I'll have plenty of emotional support, I suppose."

"I'm glad."

A heavy silence weighted the phone in her hand. Driven by the need to escape whatever was its cause, she perked up. "How's Rachel?"

The deep voice, itself, perked. "She's fine. A few scabs still left, but she's back at school." Again a pause hung soberly between them. "Anne?"

"Yes?"

"I love you . . . very much." There was a melancholy lilt to his words that Anne attributed to their separation. Her answering whisper reflected the same.

"I love you, too." She hesitated but a moment before rushing on. "When will I see you?"

"Soon, honey, soon. I'll talk with you again soon. Just remember . . . that I love you."

Tears filled her eyes at the sense of forboding that shook her suddenly. "I will, Mitch. Good-bye." With a shudder she replaced the receiver in its cradle, shivering with a chill that belied the warmth of the April night. The following day was even warmer, yet the chill persisted. It wasn't until midmorning that she discovered its ultimate cause.

The day was to be filled with surprises, beginning with the ringing of her doorbell at nine o'clock. It was her father-in-law.

"Come on in, Dad," she said, then kissed him as was their usual greeting. She and Theodore Boulton had always gotten along famously; she had no more trouble thinking of him as a father, even after Jeff's death, than he had in relating to her as his daughter.

"Are the others waiting downstairs?" she asked, reaching for her coat and grabbing her purse. The sooner this ordeal was over, the better off she'd be. As it was, she had been unable to touch any breakfast, and her stomach continued to knot.

His words startled her. "Actually, no. There's been a slight change."

"What sort of . . . change?" Dark eyes opened wide in trepidation. The day was going to be trying enough as it was, without new complications thrown in unexpectedly.

Mr. Boulton sensed immediately her tense state. "Don't worry, dear, it's all for the best. Our lawyer has been working diligently on the case. It seems there's to be a slight alteration, however. He just got the call this morning."

"Al-alteration?"

A paternal hand took her arm. "Come. Sit down for a moment and I'll explain." Calmly he led her to the sofa, sitting down beside her. "The hearing has been called off."

"What?" After waiting and dreading this day for so long, the last thing Anne wanted was to have to go through the agony of anticipation all over again. "Why?"

"It's good news, really. There will probably be an out-of-court settlement."

A wave of relief swept her, drawing a cautious smile to her lips. "You mean, there won't be a hearing *at all*?"

He shook his head. "I doubt it."

"Then today? . . ." The hope arose that she would be able to change out of her staid navy suit and into more comfortable jeans, putting the whole matter behind her finally. Unfortunately that hope was premature.

"Today we go to the lawyer's office. The lawyer representing the airline, that is. It seems that SouthEast American Air has counter-filed a suit, one against the manufacturer of the airplane itself." He paused to make sure she followed, then, reading such in her eyes, he continued. The gentleness of his tone reflected his own awareness that Anne had not been enthusiastic about pursuing the case of late, and that it had been he who had urged her on, more so than the others. Now, seeing her obviously nervous state, and remembering how much better she had been over the past few months, he felt no small amount of guilt. Still, she did deserve some compensation for her loss.

"An investigation has shown that it was a weakness in the

design of the craft that caused the accident. There was no pilot error, as we had originally suspected, nor any substandard maintenance procedure that could have caused the accident. SouthEast American Air has a fine reputation, on those scores."

Anne lowered her eyes to the thick carpeting. "Then what is the need for me to do anything at all?" If the source of the problem has been discovered and the guilty party identified, was there any need for her own involvement in what had to be a very painful process?

Understanding her distaste, Theodore Boulton took her cold hand in his. "They need a deposition from you, a statement of what you have suffered and will continue to suffer in the future as a result of the accident. The lawyer will simply ask questions of you, and you will answer, under oath, as explicitly as you can. You see"—he went step by step, so as to make it all much more clear to her—"in order to arrange a settlement, there has to be some assessment of damages, of losses. Not only will our lawyer, the airline's lawyer, and its president be there, but there will be similar representation by the airplane manufacturer."

"I see." She sighed. It did sound much more simple than a larger, more impersonal—and infinitely more threatening—court hearing, though the prospect of this question-and-answer session was less than pleasant. "The deposition," she began uncertainly. "What will I be asked?"

"Oh"—he shrugged with purposeful nonchalance—"they will want to know simple things about you . . . and Jeff. They will want to know how old you were when you met him, how long you were married, where he worked, how much money he earned—technical things like that."

"But . . . aren't those all things that are matters of record, which our lawyer has anyway?" To go over and over the same information, all of which would bring back memories, seemed a waste of time.

"He does, dear." He nodded. "But a deposition is a sworn

statement on these matters. It is recognized as legal and binding. It is just a formality, but one that is important."

Anne rested against the back of the sofa. "I see," she repeated once more, when there seemed to be no other comment to make. Then one came to her. "My parents—they were going to meet us at the courthouse," she began in alarm.

"It's all right, dear." He patted her arm. "My wife will have called them by now. There's really no need for them to be with us, since it will be a very small gathering."

Wordlessly, she nodded, then searched the room with her eyes for all the memories of Jeff that were now warm and gentle, a treasured part of her, memories that had finally found their proper perspectives. When her eyes had completed the circle, they fell once more on the attentive ones of her father-in-law.

"Shouldn't we be going?"

A quick glance at his watch brought a frown to his features. "We don't really have to be there until eleven. Was there something else you wanted to do first?"

"No." She laughed sadly. "I had pretty much chalked off this whole day, not to mention the next few."

"Do you have much work to do?" As in all other things, Theodore Boulton had been supportive of Anne's interest in both interpreting and translating.

As though on signal, she relaxed more deeply into the sofa. "Since I was expecting the worst from this hearing, I gave myself a vacation from work this week."

"And you had a good rest the week before last, in Vermont, I understand." He raised both eyebrows in speculation, an endearing gesture that Anne had first seen in his son.

"*You've* been talking to my mother," she accused lightly, astonished at how the mere mention of her private haven could cheer her.

"We *all* worry about you, dear. But you've been looking wonderful lately. Something must be agreeing with you."

The perfect opening was before her, yet Anne could not get

herself to confess to this warm and understanding gentleman the true nature of that "something." It still seemed so soon, and, in light of the day's anticipated happenings, very inappropriate.

Fortunately Mr. Boulton had no way of knowing the cause of her blush, but appreciated it merely as proof of his words. When she spoke, there was an enthusiasm in her tone that he also enjoyed, though it, too, was only partly understood.

"Things have been much better for me. I do think that I've finally accepted Jeff's death, which is why this whole legal business is so difficult for me. The time I've spent in Vermont has helped."

The genuine concern and happiness in her father-in-law's expression was gratifying to her. "I would suspect, from that sudden sparkle in your eye, that you'd like to be there right now!"

"Hmmmm, I wouldn't mind it a bit—no offense to present company intended, of course," she exclaimed with a smug grin, as the rose blush deepened on her cheeks. In the next instant, however, she wondered whether her father-in-law was more perceptive than she'd given him credit for.

"Have you started to date yet, Anne?"

The uncanny accuracy of his question wiped the grin from her lips. "N-no. Not really," she hedged uncomfortably. What she'd said had been a stretching of the truth, she knew.

At her recoil Theodore Boulton sobered also. "Please, dear, I didn't mean to upset you. But, well, we've been very close and . . . I just wanted you to know something. You *should* date, Anne. You're young and beautiful. And I know how much you and Jeff loved each other. But he is gone. Dot and I have accepted that just as you must. It's been well over a year now, and you still have a full life ahead of you. You're only twenty-eight. You should be enjoying yourself and your friends, finding someone else to love, having babies. You know"—his complexion became suddenly more ruddy—

"come the day you do have a baby, I will think of it as my own grandchild."

Tears welled in Anne's eyes at the gist of what he had told her. Arms outstretched, she reached to embrace him, hugging him soundly as she whispered a soft "Thank you" in his ear. For, in essence, he had lifted a burden of guilt from her shoulders. Come the day that she and Mitch revealed their relationship, there would be solace in knowing that Jeff's family would support her. And that day, she hoped upon hope, would be soon in coming. Particularly once this day was over, her path for love and happiness would be cleared. As Mr. Boulton helped her on with her coat Anne had no way of knowing how wrong she was.

The midmorning traffic was heavy as the car wove in and out. Anne looked about, determined to divert her mind for as long as possible from the upcoming interview. Her eyes fell on the first of the flowers that had sprung up in clusters in the occasional high rise window box or street corner whiskey barrel. The trees that stretched for air and sun along the crowded avenues paled in comparison to the memory of those she had left behind in Vermont.

Though further north, and therefore inevitably later in their blossoming, the trees in Vermont were apt to be swelling with buds now, the barest beginnings of a spring that promised to be rich and fruitful. How wonderful it had been talking with Mitch last night, despite the sadness of not being with him. Soon, he had said. Soon they would talk again; soon they would see each other, and the waiting would be over.

"Are you all right, Anne?" Her father-in-law's voice broke through her reverie. "You have such a wistful look on your face." He glanced at her as they waited for the traffic light to change.

"I'm fine," she assured him hurriedly, recalling in the instant Mitch's comment about her transparency. "I'll be glad when this is over, that's all."

"Don't worry, dear." He gave her hand a confident squeeze. "Everything will be just fine."

Within moments the car pulled off the street into a parking lot, and Anne was escorted into the posh skyscraper that housed the offices of the attorney for SouthEast American Air. The elevator ride to the sixty-eighth floor seemed endless, bringing her closer and closer to a confrontation she wished only to be over. Her palms were moist, her stomach jumpy, by the time they finally passed through the portals of the law firm. In its outer waiting room they were met by Terrence Carpenter, the Boulton family's attorney, who spent several quiet moments with them, preparing Anne, much as her father-in-law had done, for the types of questions she would be asked. Then, with a gentle hand at her elbow, Theodore Boulton escorted her, following the lawyer past the receptionist, through long corridors of bent-headed secretaries, past open doors of office after office, to one at the very end of the hall.

It proved, upon immediate entrance, to be a conference room, dominated by a long, rectangular table of a rich wood hue, which was bounded by leather chairs at its sides and ends. On the wall opposite Anne's eye stretched a glass-enclosed panorama of the city she called home, its throngs of people but a memory from this height, which obliterated all detail below. The walls to her left bore the legacy of past partners of the firm, their antiquated visages preserved in oil for posterity. The walls to her right offered wood-framed blackboards and panels that concealed such pleasures as a television set and a bar.

As her father-in-law drew her further into the room, Anne's eyes fell on the other people there—a woman and several men, engaged in a conversation that broke up at their approach. The group turned, all eyes resting on Anne.

"Coffee, Mrs. Boulton?" her attorney asked, drawing her own attention to the percolator at the side of the room.

"Yes—ah—no," she whispered. The caffeine was the last

thing her jangling nerves would need, she knew. Yet her mouth was suddenly dry, her tongue a thick wad within. "If I could have some water, that would be fine."

Within moments a glass of water was before her, and she was seated on one side of the long table. One of the men separated from the other group and approached her.

"We'll be ready to begin in just a moment, Mrs. Boulton. My client should be here any minute."

Terrence Carpenter, who had taken the seat on her left, leaned toward her as the man returned to the far side of the room to speak quietly with the woman. "That was Peter Simmons, counsel for SEAA. He will be deposing you, since it was at his request that we are here. He will introduce you to the others, but I believe that the tall dark fellow is the attorney for Jet-Star Aircraft, the manufacturer, and the man with him must be its president."

Anne nodded, then took a sip of water, wondering all the while how she would ever manage to make it through this ordeal. It had been bad enough in that instant when they had all turned to stare at her; she had felt like the guilty party then, rather than the one who had been wronged.

At that moment a pleasant-looking woman appeared from the hall, signaling for Peter Simmons, then whispering something to him when he met her at the door. Turning, she closed the door, sealing the group within.

The man named Simmons cleared his throat, then spoke. "Ladies and gentlemen, why don't we begin. My client has been delayed and will join us shortly."

At his suggestion and in keeping with the gesturing of his hand, the others took their seats. As Anne's own attorney had promised, formal introductions were made, ending with the woman, the stenographer, who would be making the transcripts of the meeting, and who, under Mr. Simmons's instruction, proceeded to put Anne under oath.

The next ten or fifteen minutes passed harmlessly enough. Mr. Simmons posed questions; Anne answered them. Again it was much as both her attorney and her father-in-law, who sat on her right, had led her to expect. The questions were straightforward—her name, place of residence, age, relationship to the deceased. For a short while Anne made the mistake of believing that things might not be as painful as she had anticipated. That was before the arrival of Peter Simmons's client.

The quiet sound of the door opening brought all heads toward it. "Ah, my client. Ladies and gentlemen, for the record, this is the President of SouthEast American Air, hereafter referred to as SEAA, Mitchell D. Anderson, Jr."

The only thing that Anne could even begin to appreciate was that for the moment, at least, the eyes in the room were diverted from her face. For it drained of what meager color it had held, turning absolutely ashen. Her dark eyes rounded in shock, her teeth sank into the softness of her lip. Her lap held her clenched fists. Every nerve end in her shaking body grew numb.

Mitch. *It was Mitch.* Dressed in an immaculately tailored blue suit. Groomed impeccably. Tall, well-built, and handsome. It was Mitch. Silver waves brushed to obedience. Graphic jaw firmed with confidence. Hazel eyes aimed everywhere but at her.

It was Mitch. Head of the airline that she was in the process of suing. What was it he had said? He had "other interests" than simply real estate. When she had prodded, he had refused to elaborate. Yet she recalled the fierceness in his eye at the time; now she understood its cause. He must have planned the whole thing; how naïve she had been!

Horror surging through her, she had to fight a rising nausea when he crossed the room to take a seat beside his lawyer, who then interrupted the proceedings to introduce to him the others. When her name was given, in turn, he nodded politely, for all indications a total stranger meeting her for the first time, rather than the man who had professed his love and taken hers less than two weeks before.

It was, perhaps, the unreality of the situation that gave Anne a semblance of inner composure to continue. Her voice was more unsteady than it had been, and she did not even dare to take a drink of water for fear that her trembling would cause her to spill it. If either her lawyer or her father-in-law, who certainly knew her better than any of the others in the room—save one—noted her burgeoning state of distress, they attributed it to the stress of the situation in general, rather than to one specific aspect of it.

And so the questioning went on. When did she meet Jeff? How long had she known him before their marriage? How long had they been married all told? Where did his family live? Where did her family live? Of how many members did each consist? Steadfastly Anne willed her eyes to hold those of Peter Simmons, despite the ungodly urge to study the man to his right.

Then the questions took a more personal turn toward finances. What had Jeff done for a living? How long had he done it? What had his annual income been? Had it been rising or holding steady? What had the financial situation been when they had first married? Had their parents helped them? Did they travel? How often? Had they always lived where she was now? How much rent did she pay each month?

On and on, in endless progression, they continued. Had Anne been her normal self, she would have quickly demanded to know the purpose of this line of inquiry. As it was, during a short break after an hour of nonstop questioning, her own attorney volunteered this information.

"He has to establish a life-style, Anne. He wants to determine the way you live, if a proper estimate of damages is to be made." Anne listened to his explanation carefully, hearing very little. Her mind was a muddled mass of latent grief.

When the deposition continued, the questions grew even more difficult. Had she loved her husband? Had they been faithful to one another? What had she done during the times when he was away on business? Did she have friends? Male friends? Anne responded in a soft voice, willing its steadiness, oblivious to the visible shake of the hand she raised to blot the corner of a moist eye. At that point Mitch whispered something to his lawyer, who gave an almost imperceptible shake as he whispered a response.

Then it resumed with a vengeance. Had Jeff been generous with her? Did he buy her gifts? When he traveled, did he call her? Often? Did he ever invite her along on business trips? By now Anne had broken out into a cold sweat.

"Mrs. Boulton, you were married for seven years. Did you have any children?"

"No . . ." Her whisper floated through the room, echoing in its finality. But this line of questioning was just at its start.

"Why not?"

"We just—didn't have any."

"Did you want a child?"

"Yes." Tears brimmed on her lids.

"Did your husband want a child?"

"Yes." Tears began to trickle slowly down her cheeks.

"Then why—"

"That's enough, Peter." It was Mitch, ironically, halting the proceedings with gruff command. "Mrs. Boulton is upset. Is this necessary?" All eyes turned to him.

Peter Simmons stood. "If you will all excuse us for a moment, I'd like to discuss something with my client. Let's take a short recess here."

As the tension in the room slowly eased, Anne bowed her head and put a hand to her forehead. Inhaling deeply, she tried to steady herself. In her periphery, Mitch's dominating form moved to the far side of the room.

"Are you all right, dear?" It was her father-in-law, his head close to hers.

Her plea was a barely audible whisper. "I have to get out of here. How much longer can this go on?" She reached blindly into her purse for a tissue to wipe her eyes.

"Not much longer. Try to hold up, Anne. Once this is over, you'll never have to face it again."

In her heart Anne knew that the agony was just beginning. But she was given no time to dwell on it, as the side discussion ended and Mitch and his lawyer resumed their seats.

It was Peter Simmons who spoke. "My client feels strongly that we have all the information we need. I therefore have no further questions—"

"Excuse me," broke in the man who had been introduced as Bradbury Parks, counsel for the manufacturing company. "If you have nothing more to ask, I do." Something in his tone, a pregnant rise, was ominous. His client was to be found at fault; he would certainly not go out without a fight.

Peter Simmons exchanged a significant glance with Mitch before he faced Mr. Parks. "Certainly, Mr. Parks. But try to be brief. Mrs. Boulton appears to be under a strain." Then he turned to Anne. "Do you feel up to a few more questions?"

Only at that moment did Anne muster the courage to look at Mitch directly. But his expression was masked. Silently she turned back to the lawyer and nodded. Mr. Parks picked right up where the questioning had ended.

"Now, then, Mrs. Boulton. On the matter of children, we would like to ascertain why, after so many years, and with your expressed desire to have a child, you never did."

Numbly Anne stared at the man. She had never dreamed she would be questioned with such persistence on a matter as personal as this. Anticipating her reaction, Terrence Carpenter leaned sideways to explain.

"They just want to know the extent of your loss in terms of future parenthood. If you and Jeff badly wanted a child and he is no longer here to sire it, the loss is that much greater. Do you understand?"

She nodded, then took a deep breath before answering the original question of the other lawyer. "We wanted to have a child, but we were just never . . . that lucky."

"You mean, you never conceived?" he prodded boldly.

"I did conceive. Twice. I . . . miscarried both times." In the brief silence that followed, the comforting hand of her father-in-law took hers beneath the table.

"I'm sorry," the lawyer continued with shallow regret. "Did you see doctors?"

"Of course!" Her voice had risen in pitch now. As if the memories were not painful enough, the humiliation of airing them before this hostile group was traumatic. "They could find no tangible cause. They insisted that, another time, the baby would be fine."

"And did you keep trying?" he asked callously.

"How could I, Mr. Parks? My husband died." Again her words brought a silence to the room. Had Anne dared to look at Mitch, she would have seen the torment in his eyes. But her own were too fogged to see much of anything.

Abruptly the lawyer redirected the discussion. Anne's relief was short-lived. "Do you date, Mrs. Boulton?" When her brow knit in bewilderment at the sudden turn, he rephrased the question. "Have you begun to date again, since your husband's death?"

The hammering in her chest threatened to rob her of all breath. While her mind flew to the silver-haired man on the opposite side of the table, she lowered her eyes lest they follow that line. "No," she whispered.

"I'm sorry, I couldn't hear that, Mrs. Boulton."

She raised her head, pain gripping her features. "No." It was a mere technicality, she knew, that enabled her to make the claim in good faith; what she and Mitch had was not, in the traditional sense, a dating relationship.

"That's hard to believe, if you'll excuse me for saying so. You're an attractive woman and still very young." Hadn't her father-in-law said the same earlier that morning? Why had it been complimentary on his lips, whereas now it was an indictment? Her periphery took in, once more, Mitch's movement to whisper to his own lawyer. Bradbury Parks went on, undaunted. "Have you no intention of dating?"

"Not now." It was the truth. After what had happened and was continuing to happen, she felt like a frozen wasteland inside.

"Wouldn't you like to marry again?"

"Now? No." How could she, when the man she loved had taken himself out of her reach?

Disappointed at not having ferreted out the information that would have helped his client, the persistent Parks made a final stab, disbelief lending a sinister edge to his words. "You mean, there have been *no men* in your life—"

"I think that the woman answered you once, Mr. Parks," Peter Simmons broke in forcefully. "Now, unless you have any more questions—on a different tack—I suggest we let Mrs. Boulton go. There are still other depositions to be taken, from my client *and* yours."

Reluctantly the other lawyer agreed. "Very well, Mr. Simmons. Thank you, Mrs. Boulton. I have no further questions."

Anne heard nothing of the remaining exchange of civilities. Her being was too distraught to take in anything, save the knees that began to buckle when she stood. A firm arm settled across her shoulders, supporting her graciously as they left. For an instant, in her state of inner upheaval, she imagined it was Mitch. But the height and weight of this champion were all wrong, the touch of the hand on her arm likewise. The voice was wrong. The scent was wrong. It was Theodore Boulton, her father-in-law, who assisted her from the room and promptly took her home.

"There, that wasn't so bad." He feigned cheerfulness as he deposited Anne on the sofa and headed for the liquor cabinet, returning moments later with a glass of straight amber liquid in his hand. "Drink this, dear. It will help to relax you."

With the fabled obedience of a child, she downed the liquid quickly, sputtering in reaction to the fiery flame that seared her throat lingeringly. Unable to think, much less utter a word, she merely let her head fall back against the sofa, and closed her eyes against the world.

Mr. Boulton stood and stared down at the peaked face for long moments. Had he imagined the toll this legal process would take on her, he would have found some other way. She had been so much better; now she was as distraught as she had been following the accident.

"Let me call your mother, Anne. I'm sure she'll want to be with you."

Weary eyes opened to look up at him. "N-no. I'll be fine. I'm just tired."

"Are you sure? Would you like me to stay awhile?"

She forced a smile onto pale lips. "Thank you for offering, but, no. I think I would like to be alone for a bit."

Bending, he kissed her head, a sad smile on his face. "Just remember, dear. It's over now." With a reassuring pat to her shoulder, he let himself out.

Over. That, it certainly was. But Anne and her father-in-law were thinking of different things totally. Her heart grieved for what had been lost on this day of rude awakening, yet her mind clung to its numbed state, refusing to face exactly that which she had discovered. Exhausted, or perhaps more as an escape, she dozed off right where she was on the sofa, having not moved an inch since she had collapsed there. It was the harsh ring of the telephone that brought her back to awareness with a jolt.

"Hello?" she offered her feeble inquiry.

"Anne!" It was her mother's voice, filled with concern. "Ted just called and explained what happened. Are you all right?"

"Yes, Mother. I'm fine."

"You don't sound it."

"I was just . . . resting. The whole thing has worn me out."

"Would you like me to run over and take you out . . . for an early dinner, perhaps?"

Startled, Anne eyed her watch. It was nearly three thirty.

Lunch had somehow fallen by the wayside, along with the bulk of her appetite. Even now the thought of food aggravated the knot in her stomach.

"Anne? . . . Are you there?"

"Yes, Mother. Ah, no, thanks anyway, but I really don't feel like anything to eat."

"Was it that bad . . . the deposition?"

It couldn't possibly have been worse, she rued silently. "Oh, it was a little heavy at times," she lied, the understatement of the year.

"Are you sure there's nothing I can do?" Her mother tried a final time.

"I'm sure." Her soft voice held the forced smile she had managed for the sake of her mother. It vanished the instant the words were out, when it was no longer needed.

The older woman's sigh was clearly audible. "All right, then. I'll call you later. Get some rest, dear!"

"I will. And . . . thanks for calling, Mom."

"You're welcome, darling. Bye-bye."

How much more patient her mother was now, she marveled, as she hung up the phone. Evidently the past year of Anne's self-imposed independence had gotten through finally. Now she wondered if it was what she really wanted, what she really needed. It occurred to her that, more than anything, she needed a shoulder to cry on. But then the tears refused to come, even as she could feel them bottled deep within her.

Wandering aimlessly about her apartment, she found herself in her bedroom, changing into an old pair of faded jeans and an oversized shirt. Barefoot, she padded back to the living room, feeling every bit the hollow shell she must have looked. The view from the window held nothing for her. Nor did a cursory examination of the day's mail. Unable to draw herself from her lethargy, she sank back onto the sofa, lying back on its fluffy throw pillows, resting her legs out upon its length.

Gradually, as minutes passed into an hour, then more, the shock of the day's happenings began to hit her. For starters, the questions she had been subjected to had been bad enough. Yes, she understood their general purpose. But those more personal ones . . . and their implications . . . what had been the need for those? In hindsight, as she avoided deliberately the crux of her depression, she reflected on them.

What that lawyer—*his* lawyer—had begun to imply, and the other lawyer had proceeded to imply, was that her marriage had been far from ideal. It simply wasn't true! There had never been infidelity, nor the slightest thought of it, yet those men had suggested it, subtly, but nonetheless so. And the question of having a child—as though there had been dissension between her and Jeff on the matter! He had wanted a child as badly as she had, though he had refused to pressure her on her failure to carry to term. But that was all in the past. Had it not been for one particular factor, she could have held her head high, secure in her conviction of all these things. Now everything in her existence revolved around that one particular factor—Mitch's presence in that odious conference room.

In that one riveting moment, when she had, along with the others, turned toward the door of that conference room and seen Mitch standing there, her entire world had fallen through. Mitchell D. Anderson, Jr., President of SouthEast American Air! After all these months, after all they'd shared, he had deceived her. Oh, perhaps it had started out quite innocently that first time in September when a legitimate slipup on the part of the rental agent had thrown them together. But, at some point, when he had discovered her identity, he had put the pieces together. Hadn't she had that nightmare? Hadn't she spoken of the crash in which Jeff had died, its approximate date, the fact of the court trial upcoming? Why hadn't he spoken up then? Why had he done this to her? Last night—my God—he had called last night—without a word. Why? *Why?*

Groaning aloud, she clutched her stomach, when, in fact, it was her mind through which the pain seared. Oh, how dearly she loved him; to find that he had knowingly and continually deceived her was more than she could bear! If only she could cry. If only she could scream. Instead she felt drained, heartbroken, half whole.

When the telephone rang again, she sighed. Even two layers of pillows did not succeed in stifling the persistent peal when she refused to answer it. But if, as she was sure, it was her mother again, the woman would be on the doorstep within the hour if Anne did not answer the call.

Listlessly she dragged herself off the sofa to the wall phone just inside the kitchen. "Hello?"

"Anne?" The deeply familiar voice filtered electrically over the wire and through the network of her veins, jolting her with its current and sending a shock wave shuddering through her. It was all she could do to still her trembling hand enough to hang up the receiver.

Wobbly legs took her in a stagger to the sofa, where she fell into a crouch, knees bent and hugged to her chest as she awaited the return call she knew he would make. Mitch was persistent; she knew him well. Sure enough, within a minute, the sound of the ring drilled into her, piercing her with its shrill note, stabbing her, again and again, with the knowledge of who it was at the other end of the line.

Arms encircling her legs with painful intensity, she rocked back and forth, suffering each ring with renewed agony. In an impetuous move she covered her ears with her hands, grinding her forehead against her knees as though an outer torture could alleviate the inner one. But the latter continued, as did the excruciating clang of the telephone, seeming louder and louder, more and more harsh, crueler and crueler, until, at last, it ceased. Only then did she break down and weep.

CHAPTER NINE

The days that ensued were pure hell for Anne. When the crying abated, the self-recrimination began. She had been naïve, she had been irresponsible, she had been wanton. She should never have returned to the cabin, to be alone with that man, after the initial week. For that matter she should have turned around and left that second day, when he had insisted in remaining, himself. It was due punishment, this torment that seemed her life sentence. But had she been wrong to love? Was it ever wrong to love? All she had done and felt had been in good faith. How could she be faulted for that? How could she be faulted for reaching out for happiness?

Self-recrimination gradually yielded to an indictment aimed directly at the one who had, it seemed, led her down the primrose path. How could Mitch have treated her so badly? How could she have misjudged him so? What kind of person could take such blatant advantage of another who had helplessly come to need him?

It was, indeed, an ironic and merciful twist of fate that, in light of the anticipated court hearing, she had accepted no work for the week. For she was no more able to face anything requiring concentration than she was able to face the human race itself.

Each time the phone rang she recoiled, answering, out of necessity, only to ward off the personal visits of her family. On those occasions when the caller was that deep-voiced and commanding one, she hung up steadfastly, refusing to hear one further word from his traitorous lips.

If anything, her seclusion was more total than it had been after Jeff's death. Only Mitch knew of the source of her grief, and it was doubtful that, given his previous disregard for her feelings, he was even aware of the trauma he'd thrust upon her. Her parents sensed that her reaction to the deposition was more extreme than it should have been, but they attributed it to an accumulation of all she'd been through since losing Jeff. It served her purpose to let them go on believing that, rather than to have to confess the extent of her own folly.

During those first days following her fateful discovery Anne could not begin to think of the future. It was once more a void, ominous and terrifying. Each day was enough of a challenge to suffer through. As her thinking did solidify, finally, her only hope was that she could wipe the memory of Mitch from her mind. It was easier, here in New York, with the only times shared having been in Vermont. Never would she return there. Never would she see the lilacs bloom, nor smell their fragrant bouquet. Strangely it was this thought that added to her sense of loss—and the knowledge that never, never would she be able to forget Mitch totally.

Unfortunately, though his calls to her ceased beyond the first few days when she had persistently hung up on him, her hopes of wiping him from mind did grow ludicrous. It was her father, during a spontaneous visit on his way through the city one afternoon, who unknowingly brought home this point.

"I received a call from Mr. Anderson the other night." He raised the matter casually, as a simple point of interest, after other pertinent conversation had been dispensed with. "You know, the head of SEAA?"

Do I ever! "Uh-huh." She choked on her nonchalance, hit anew by a churning in her stomach.

"Seems like a very nice fellow. He wanted to make sure that you were all right, since you seemed to be feeling poorly at the time of the deposition."

"Wasn't that considerate of him," she snipped bitterly. *Guilt feelings. Good. Let him suffer.* "But how did he know to call you? He only knows me by my married name." Her lips clamped shut, her heart pounding in her throat. Had she betrayed herself by her own words? But, no, she had been introduced to him at the hearing, using only her married name. And it had been a Boulton, to boot, beside her.

Her father was undaunted. "He explained that he called Ted first, and that he hesitated to call you directly, for fear of upsetting you more."

"Wise man." Sarcasm drew her lips thin. *Clever scoundrel,* she mused angrily. *Upsetting me more. Huh!* He was still merely at his game.

Anthony Faulke eyed her with gentle reproach at her barely disguised disdain. "It was considerate, dear. After all, his airline has been found innocent in the matter. It's really no concern of his any longer."

That fact served up more pain than solace. In Anne's mind Mitch was still a deceiver. Yet, as many times as she reminded herself of his betrayal, she could not help but recall the image of the man she had thought she'd known in Vermont. It wasn't fair—this life of hers!

Moping about for the better part of each day, the nights were no better. It was a living nightmare that obsessed her, both waking and sleeping. When would it ever end? When, by the middle of the second week, she realized that she was living her grief as she had done, so long ago, it seemed, after Jeff's death, she knew that something had to be done. In that first instance the answer had lain in getting herself busy, in stepping beyond her apartment, little by little. Perhaps that was what was needed now. In a moment of defiance she vowed that she would not let him crush her, that the bullies of the world—like Mitch—should not be given that satisfaction. Dutifully she arranged to resume her work, lining up several jobs quickly, some involving the interpreting that would, of necessity, get her out into the mainstream once more.

The solution, however, was not to be simple. For, just when she had hoped to have a handle on her emotions, she was thrown a devastating setback. It occurred one evening, when the doorbell drew her reluctantly from her blue reverie. Chain latch in place, she opened the door the several inches allowed, peering out to find none other than Mitch, standing on her doormat. Instantly she reclosed the door with a resounding slam. As she had expected, the bell rang again . . . and again. Her legs, which carried her to the most remote corner of the apartment, were jellylike in their weakness. *Let him ring,* she vowed, clenching her fists against the rising anger at his persistence.

What she hadn't been prepared for was the loud pounding on the door that followed. Each blow reverberated through her, as though it were her own soul, rather than the thick metal door, which was being attacked. The bell-ringing was a private matter that could, with some manner of patience, be ignored; not so this earth-shaking racket. Within a few minutes he would have her neighbors with him in the hall, out of curiosity, if nothing else.

With faltering steps she crept back to the door. "Go away!" she yelled, hoping that her voice would carry through his loud ruckus. It did.

The intonation that returned to her was muffled, though its anger was impossible to miss. "Not until I've spoken with you, Anne."

She repeated her cry. "Go away. I don't want to talk."

"You'll have to."

Inwardly she fumed. What did he mean—she'd *have* to? What power did he think he held over her? What right did he have to harass her in her own home? Suddenly furious, she reopened the door those few allotted inches. "I don't *have* to do anything. Now, please leave, or I'll call the police." It took every ounce of restraint for her to remain calm when she would have liked nothing more than to run him through with her carving knife.

She had no way of knowing that he was under as great a restraint. "Anne, I'm trying to be patient. You have refused to talk with me on the telephone repeatedly. Now we must talk. There are certain things I have to explain."

Jaw clenched, Anne seethed. "You had your chance to explain, but you passed it up, didn't you? You had all those days and nights to tell me who you were and exactly what your business was, but you didn't. You were very cagey—I'll see you *soon, Annie, soon.*" She contorted her voice in mocking imitation. "But you didn't bother to tell me *when.* Well, Mitch, I don't want to talk *now.*" Her diatribe finished, she gasped for breath as though having been through a strenuous physical workout. Gathering her strength, she leaned against the door to shut it, only to discover, to her dismay, that a firmly planted foot stood in her way. "Move, Mitch!" she ordered hoarsely. His presence was beginning to wear on her in more ways than one, and with devastating impact.

A gruff oath muttered under his breath filtered through the narrow opening. "Hell, Anne, but you can be a stubborn woman. If we were back in Vermont, I'd know just how to handle you—"

"But we're not in Vermont!" she screamed, uncaring that others might hear, mindful only of the hurt that his words caused. "And I, for one, will never be there again. Now, leave!" Every muscle in her body quivered beneath her bridled rage.

As though sensing her state of near-hysteria, he sighed. "All right, Anne. I will leave . . . for now. But I will be back. If not here, I'll catch you elsewhere. On the street, in a restaurant, even at your parents' house, if need be. I can be very devious. You can't stay holed up in this place forever. And I won't give up!"

Slowly his foot slid back into the hallway, whereupon Anne slammed the door shut, then turned and ran, trembling, toward the bedroom, where she huddled against the headboard of the bed like a hunted animal. *He could be very devious;* that was putting it mildly! It was well past an hour before she mustered the courage to emerge from hiding, knowing that Mitch would have left. Deep within, she knew she *would* see him again, and the thought filled her with boundless dread.

Determined to make good her vow of returning to work, Anne did begin to venture out. But if she had expected relief in this diversion, she found none. For she was ever on guard against running into Mitch. Against her will, she found herself looking over her shoulder wherever she went, half expecting to find the compelling figure ready to pounce on her. It was nerve-racking, to say the least. After more than a week of scurrying from place to place, always with the same haunted look in her dark eyes, she began to fear that she had been defeated. For the pain persisted. And, no matter how wrongly Mitch had treated her, she did love him. Still. Forever. It was an awesome burden she was fated to carry with her. She could not escape it as she had his physical presence, for it hounded her relentlessly at every turn.

Then inspiration came . . . with the help of her parents . . . in the form of an invitation to spend a week or two with them at the shore. Whereas once she had shunned their company as overprotective, now it was the very quality she sought. *Someone* had to protect her from Mitch, and she seemed emotionally unable to do so herself. The change of scenery was what she needed; she was determined to make the most of it.

The first of May found her dressed in a bright yellow sundress, her bags piled by the entrance to the apartment building. Her parents were to be along at one; it was now one fifteen. Nervously she glanced at her watch. Had something happened? With a brief word to the doorman, she returned to her apartment, dialing her parents' home phone, waiting as ring after unanswered ring suggested they were en route, then retracing her steps to the street. What she found stopped her dead in her tracks.

No longer were her bags where she'd left them. Rather, with the doorman's ready assistance, they were being loaded into the trunk of a shiny brown Audi she didn't recognize. She did, however, recognize the man who stepped from its opposite side.

He had, it seemed, carried out his threat, this most devious of devious men, for there he stood, sun-bronzed, in a pullover and white ducks, looking as handsome and menacingly masculine as could be . . . and very, very smug. Before she could rescue her tongue from the hold of astonishment, he turned his back, opened the rear door of the car, bent down, then straightened, turning back to her, carrying the most beautiful child Anne had ever seen. Her breath faltered. How cruel he was to do *this* to her!

"Mitch . . ." she whispered in poignant plea, unable to command herself to say anything further.

His grin was as mischievous as she had remembered it. "Hi, Annie!" he greeted her spiritedly, as though nothing had ever happened. "I hope we didn't keep you waiting too long! The traffic was heavier than we expected." Without hesitancy, he went right on. "I think we've got all your bags. Was there anything you forgot?"

Anne may have been thick in the past; now she saw too many things awfully clearly. He had known she would be waiting. He had known just what time. He would never have taken a chance bringing this little girl with him . . . had he not had that certain confidence. Her parents . . . *my God* . . . they had betrayed her too! They had collaborated with the enemy!

For an instant Anne stood frozen. Then, slowly, frantic

shreds of reality gave her movement. Had it been Mitch, alone, she would have turned and run. But her eye trained on the child, and she knew she was lost. The six-year-old wore pink bib-topped shorts and a white jersey, with a pair of clean white sneakers on her feet, leaving expanses of freshly tanned arms and legs, long but delicate, to dangle by Mitch's thighs. Golden cascades of curly hair fell halfway down her back, held off from her face by gaily painted barrettes high above either ear, leaving short wisps of curls to escape in tendrils here and there around her face. The face, itself, was something to marvel at, slim and rosy cheeked, with a swarm of bright freckles over the bridge of the button nose. But it was her eyes that captured Anne with their soulful depths.

"Ah, I've almost forgotten the introductions in my rush to get going." Mitch covered for Anne's speechless state. "Anne"—he looked playfully at her—"this is my daughter, Rachel Anderson. Rachel, this is Anne Boulton."

With a poise well beyond her years, the blond-haired child extended a small hand toward Anne, who instinctively reached out to hold it. "How do you do, Anne. I'm so pleased to meet you. Daddy has told me all about you."

A dark eyebrow arched into Anne's forehead. "Oh, he has, has he? I hope he's only told you the good things."

The child's brown eyes rounded quickly. "Oh, my daddy would *never* say anything bad about *you.* He—"

"That's quite enough, pumpkin," Mitch broke in, a deliberate smile playing on his lips. "You can't give away all our secrets, now, can you?"

The child burst into a wide grin, displaying a mouthful of small white teeth with a very visible gap smack in the middle of the top row. Against her very will, Anne was enchanted.

"Say, that's quite some hole you've got there," she teased. "Did the good fairy bring you something nice for those teeth?"

Again the grin; the child was delightful! "Oh, yes. I got a

whole dollar for each of them." She emphasized her prize with owl eyes. "Daddy says he only got a quarter, when he was a little boy, but that the good fairy was afraid I might swallow a coin, so she gave me paper. I'm really glad," she bubbled on, then lowered her voice in mock confidence, "'cause you can't really buy much for a quarter!"

With total spontaneity Anne burst into a laugh. "You're a very perceptive little girl, Rachel!" Having forgotten all about Mitch in the perfectly charming interchange with the child, now Anne stiffened when she suddenly looked over at the pride on his face. He did have a right to be proud of this youngster, though he should be absolutely ashamed of using her as a shield against Anne's anger.

Having caught the harsh edge to Anne's gaze, Mitch cleared his throat. "Ah, perhaps you ladies are ready to go. The sooner we leave the city, the sooner we'll reach the cabin."

The cabin? My God, he really intends to carry it all the way! She couldn't go! She absolutely couldn't! Yet Rachel's eyes were glued to hers and Mitch's bore clear warning. "Rachel," she began softly, glancing back over her shoulder for a moment, "do you think you might wait here while your father helps me out with one last thing upstairs? Maurice, the doorman, will keep you company."

The child looked to her father for permission. He kissed her, then set her back in the car. "We'll be down in a jiffy." He spoke gently, repeating the same for the doorman. Then, taking Anne's elbow firmly, he escorted her back inside. There was no need to go upstairs; as soon as they rounded a corner and were out of the child's sight, Anne turned on him in loud-whispered vengeance.

"I'm not going, Mitch. You arranged this with my parents, didn't you?"

A leisurely grin played at his lips. "They are wonderful people. When I explained the situation in full, they were more than glad to help out. Very accommodating!"

"I'm not going!" She repeated her vow more loudly. "For all your smugness and the crafty little wheels in your head that set this whole farce into motion, *I'm not going!*"

His gaze narrowed. "I told Rachel that you'd be spending the week with us—"

"You had no right to do that!"

"But it's done. And she is counting on your being there. Would you disappoint her?"

Exasperation sent sparks of pain through Anne. "How can you use her like this? You know I couldn't do anything to hurt her—"

"I was counting on that."

At least, on that score, he was honest. "Well, *you're* going to make sure I don't. Now, *you* go out there"—a shaky finger motioned toward the street—"and tell her that I can't go."

"But you can." His confidence was a thing to marvel at. "Your bags are packed and loaded. All of your work has been cleared for the next two weeks. There's nothing left to hold you here."

Even Anne's determination was no match for his resolve. With a sigh of fatigue she slumped back against the wall.

"Why don't you just leave me alone? Can't you see that I don't want to see you?"

For the first time since his arrival Mitch grew entirely serious, even grim. "I can see that very clearly, Anne. And I can see that you are too stubborn to listen to reason. I tried, more than once. You wouldn't answer my calls or let me in when I banged on your door. You wouldn't give me the simple courtesy of hearing me out. Now," he went on, anger bridled into a taut smoothness, "I'm asking you, for Rachel's sake, if nothing more, to come with us. Just this once. At the end of the week, if you still feel this way, I *will* leave you alone." His eyes bore into her relentlessly.

Hearing his words and knowing of her own emotional exhaustion, Anne wondered if it was the only way out. After all, the child *would* be with them . . . as a chaperon of sorts.

"Is that a promise?" she asked, her voice mirroring the hardness of his gaze.

"Yes."

There was no point belaboring the matter. With a defeated lag to her step she moved away from the wall and allowed Mitch to escort her back to the car.

Given the lightning turnaround of her plans for the week, Anne could not quite assimilate it all. Instinctively, however, she knew that for those days she had so reluctantly agreed to spend with Mitch now, her greatest enemy would be herself. Even knowing how badly Mitch had hurt her, she couldn't stop loving him. His appearance this morning, affecting her beyond words, was proof of that. Whether she would be able to maintain a distance from him for the length of the week, she didn't know. Therein lay her most awesome challenge.

CHAPTER TEN

Within the hour they had left the traffic of the city behind to speed northward. "When did you get the new car?" Anne asked, groping for conversation with Mitch as Rachel knelt on the backseat, studying the receding skyline.

"About a week ago. This is her maiden voyage. The Honda was a bit small for three." The tawny eyebrow that arched her way was subtle, yet Anne could not help but wonder at the need for a new car for one simple trip. The Audi was luxurious, to say the least.

Demonstrating her hearing of every last bit of their conversation, Rachel poked her golden head between the bucket seats, rubbing her cheek kittenlike against the soft velour crush. "I like this one. Daddy says the color matches my eyes."

"It does, at that." Anne smiled warmly. It was impossible to be any other way with this child, she mused sadly. If only there were pouts, crankiness, and temper tantrums, it might be easier to face saying good-bye to her at the end of the week.

As though to compound this one particular issue, during those first few days at the cabin, Anne found herself growing more and more attached to the little girl. Even her belief that Mitch contrived it did not detract from the pleasure that

Anne received in simple custodial things, such as bathing her, combing her long blond curls into a semblance of order, helping her tie the shoelaces that managed to constantly escape the loose bows that Rachel, herself, labored over. Then there were the more substantive things to cherish—the cookie-baking project, the hikes in the woods, the story-reading before the fire at night. It was a luxury for Anne, this affection that Rachel had so freely developed for her.

The only drawback to the perfection of the moment was the constant struggle she had to maintain an indifference toward Mitch. He never pushed. Anne slept upstairs, he slept down. Rachel was camped, mercifully, in a sleeping bag—treat of all treats for her—on a throw rug on the floor in his room. Never once did she complain about the hardness of her mattress; rather, she delighted in her little bed in the corner. And to share a room with her daddy—that was the best part of all!

By Wednesday morning Anne felt herself walking a tight-rope, torn between love and disdain, trust and paranoia, hope and fear. There seemed to be no clear solution, particularly with Mitch's watchful eye on her from morning to night. For what he searched, she did not know. Nor could she begin to analyze his behavior, so wrapped up was she in her own torrent of memories.

What nagged mercilessly at her was the image of beauty and joy that she had found here once, the love and fulfillment that had been hers during those days of innocence. All that had been tainted by one eye-opening morning in a large conference room, her own Armageddon. Now she grieved for all that she thought she had had, all that she might have had, all she had lost. In the final analysis Mitch's words of love had been meaningless. If his opinion of her was low enough for him to have deceived her as he had, there was no possible way he could have ever truly loved her.

"I'm going for a walk," she burst out after a postbreakfast fit of brooding.

"I was just going to suggest that very thing," Mitch intoned quietly, his gentleness but another example of the week's torture. "Why don't you make it a long one. I think I can manage Rachel for a few hours." The mockery she expected was absent, replaced by a doe-skin softness of expression.

Despite the little girl's high-pitched protest, Anne left. It was, in actuality, the first time she had been truly alone—save those lonely night hours—since they had arrived. And she needed it badly. With her composure becoming more and more precarious, she had to find some way of surviving the next two days, until she was once more back in New York and free to lick her wounds in private.

Spring was everywhere about as she walked. What had been damp and gray a month before was now a fresh and vibrant green. The scent was of rebirth, spreading upward from the lush carpet of new grass and through the lime-hued leaves that gaily clothed the long tree branches. The sounds of spring were enchanted ones, the chirping of birds from nest to nest, the rustle of newly emergent ferns beneath the light step of resurgent animal life. Waters bounded downward over rocks and silt, running freely, at last, roaring with the force of the snows, now melting, still further up the mountain. The sight was of a glowing pasture of yellow dandelions and a pink-crowned crab apple tree. It was the countryside at its gayest and most promising.

Not so Anne's heart. It bore a cloak of sadness made all the more poignant by contrast with the bounty surrounding her. Pebbles scattered haphazardly before her shuffling feet; more than one solid boulder felt the anger of her rubber-edged heel as she sat on its makeshift stool. When finally she buried her head on her arms, the tears flowed fast and free, much as the water of the brook beside her. But whereas the brook's course was one of liberation, Anne's was the opposite. She loved Mitch and would love him always. In that intangible prison lay her anguish.

The frigid water against her hot eyes refreshed her, as she knelt on the stones and splashed her face, gasping at its coldness, savoring its odd pain and accompanying invigoration. Sufficiently revived from her tearful bout, she headed slowly back toward the cabin, winding in and out among the forest paths, feeling herself physically relieved from the outpouring, though no closer toward a solution to her predicament.

Under the warmth of the high noon sun, she arrived at the house to be greeted by an unexpected refrain of silence. Immediately assuming that father and daughter were out in the woods themselves, she passed through the kitchen to the living room, only to stop short in her tracks at the sight of Mitch, tall and lean, standing before the front window. His hands casually filled the side pockets of his jeans in a pose more idle than she would have expected, given the tireless presence of a vivacious six-year-old.

"Where's Rachel?" she demanded, when a fast scan of the room produced no hint of the child.

With infinite slowness he turned around to face her. "She's left."

"What are you talking about—'she's left'?" The source of Anne's concern was twofold. Rachel was both a treasured being and a precious buffer.

Hazel eyes searched her face coolly, chilling her much as the brook water had done, though without the same invigoration. "My parents stopped by to pick her up. Thcy are continuing up to Montreal for a few days, before returning to the city."

"W-what? You mean, she's *gone*?" . . . Safe with her grandparents, leaving Anne in peril.

"Yes." His gaze held hers firmly, a slight frown therein. "You've been crying?"

Her lie was immediate. "No." Rachel was no longer here; what was *she* still doing here, then?

"Your eyes are red," he challenged softly. Mercifully he made no move to approach her.

"I have hay fever," she snapped testily, because with the awareness that she was on her own, came a growing fury. "You planned this, didn't you? You had it all prearranged with your parents. You orchestrated this whole thing, using Rachel to get me up here, then managing conveniently to have her vanish." Every muscle in her body had tensed. Instinctively she lifted a hand to slide beneath the heavy curtain of her dark hair and massage the sudden ache in her neck.

"Yes." He offered no excuse, simply admitted his guilt to her charges.

Anne's eyes blazed darkly now. "And you really think that I'm going to stay, now that she's left? Hell, *she* was the only reason I agreed to come up here in the first place!"

With pantherlike grace he began to move toward her. "Was it, Anne? Was it really? Be honest with yourself."

Nerves jumping higher as the distance between them decreased, she was suddenly afraid. "I am! That *was* why I came up here." An unsteady hand warded him off as she took a step backward. "Don't come any closer, Mitch. Don't you dare touch me—"

"Or what? Haven't we been through this before? We're right back at the beginning, Annie. Face it. No child. No deposition-taking. No other pretense. Just you and me."

"It's not that simple!" she cried, swallowing convulsively, as she took another step back. He was far too tall, far too attractive, far too near. "I can't forget all those things. They're all here, even if you try to deny them. And nothing can change the fact that I didn't want to see you, that I *don't* want to see you or have anything to do with you!"

Even as she spoke, the traitorous yearnings of her body contradicted her, the trembling that began at her core, moving upward and out. Finely attuned to her conflict, Mitch continued his advance until she was backed against a wall with him no more than an arm's length from her.

"I don't believe you, Anne," he informed her smoothly. "I think it's just the opposite that you want." His bold form towered inches from her. Determined to withstand the awesome draw, she kept her head down, shaking it gently in denial.

"Don't, Mitch. Get away from me." Her warning was a faltering whisper. Flattened against the wall, it was as unyielding behind her as the muscular wall before her. Glancing to the side, she contemplated lateral escape, only to have that plan thwarted by the long arms that came up to rest against the wall by either shoulder, caging her effectively.

Determination verged on anger in his words. "Like hell I will. This has gone on long enough. I'm going to talk now, and you are going to listen, if you know what's good for you. My patience is wearing very thin."

In a final burst of frantic argument Anne ignored his warning. "*Your* patience?" she screamed, raising her eyes the distance to his. "What about mine? And what about my feelings, for that matter? But then you never were all that concerned about what would happen to me after you'd taken everything *you* wanted! You are the most selfish, arrogant, ruthless—"

The list of scathing expletives would have gone on forever, had it not been for the mouth that halted them. With every bit of strength she could summon Anne fought the onslaught of his lips, wrenching her head from side to side in attempted escape, using her hands to try futilely to push him away. But her meager might was no fair contender against his superior strength.

With the force of the latter he pulled her from the wall, circling her back with the steel band of his arms, crushing her own hands flat between his chest and hers. Her lips were plundered brutally, her breath cut off until darkness swarmed before her lids. At the instant she would have collapsed, he eased his grip, gasping raggedly for a moment against her whimpered protest, then capturing her lips again.

But this was different. Having broken the backbone of her fight with the cruelty of his lips, they now commenced a more persuasive form of dominance, moving with sensual sureness over her ravaged mouth.

Had the harshness continued, Anne might have been able to resist the headiness of him. But this firm seduction was another matter. Her limbs were weakened, her consciousness muddled. From the maelstrom emerged the electrical charge that had always sparked her before, and was no different now. While her arms continued to apply a token pressure against the wall of his chest, her lips betrayed her. Gradually they softened, then opened, then helplessly drank in his kiss with a thirst that was faint, at first, but grew greater with each instant of mindless caress. By the time he drew his head back her fingers clutched at the fabric of his shirt for support. But his arms were there, holding her up until her knees held their own weight at last.

As the realization of her surrender hit her Anne bowed her head to let its black-sheened top rest against him. Uncaring, she dissolved into quiet tears, the irregular rise and fall of her shoulders punctuating her distress.

"Don't cry, Annie. Please." His voice was infinitely more gentle than it had been earlier, as though his own anger had been spent in the embrace, but it only added to the torment that welled uncontrollably within Anne. The torrent had begun; she could not stop it. Realizing this, he merely held her, tightly and protectively, until she gradually quieted. "I won't hurt you. Please believe me, honey. I've never meant to hurt you," he crooned softly. "I just want you to listen to what I have to say."

A hushed whisper, tinged with bitterness, broke the ensuing silence. "Do I have a choice?"

Manly lips twisted up against her hair, appreciative of even that last bit of spunk. "No."

She remained docile as he led her to the chair before the cold hearth. Its wings, which once had served as blinders to blot out the darkness, now acted to blot out all but Mitch, the very source of her darkness, as he stood straight and uncharacteristically rigid before her.

A lean hand raked through the thatch of silvered waves in subtle indication of his own distressed state before he began. "I know what you must be thinking about me. But you are wrong. It is totally unfair of you to blame *me* for what happened to Jeff." Anne had never blamed him for the crash, yet her frown of puzzlement went unnoticed. She could only stare through the residue of tears as he unburdened himself.

"It wasn't until February, when you were so sick and had that nightmare about the plane crash—when you mentioned the upcoming court hearing—that I began to suspect that Jeff had died in my craft. Contrary to your apparent assumption, I did *not* run right back to New York to check it out." A surge of anger whipped through him, turning him from her to approach the hearth. One arm on its mantel, one foot on the charred and ash-strewn grate, he stared at nothingness in silence for several moments. "I guess I didn't want to know. My guilt feelings about that accident were bad enough, without having to bear your scorn, as unjustified as it might have been."

Anne's dark brows drew together; he seemed to have totally missed the crux of that very scorn. But she was given no chance to enlighten him, as he spoke again. Even amid her own rising anger she could see that his was self-directed.

"You have no idea of my torture when I first arrived back up here in March. I knew I had to be with you, yet I was acutely aware that you might hate me even more afterward." He sighed in resignation. "You were bound to learn the truth sooner or later. Although I wanted to tell you myself, I just . . . couldn't . . ."

Slowly he turned to face her, his eyes bearing a pain she couldn't comprehend. "When we made love, Anne, it was magnificent. As much as we always fight, when we came together that day, it was heaven. It was a spontaneous expression of something so very deep. Afterward I hoped that if you knew how much I loved you, you would forgive me. If I could have ever prevented that accident . . ." As his voice trailed off, his body sagged in defeat.

He was far off, in another time, but Anne was too choked by her own emotion to notice. "I never blamed *you* for that crash, Mitch! That's not the point—"

He went on, as though he hadn't heard a word she'd said. His voice was low and sorrowful as he spoke his thoughts aloud. "The guilt has been unbearable. It's irrational and unjustifiable . . . but it's very, very real. You have no idea. Between the plane and the car . . ." He shook his head in pained remembrance.

Anne stiffened, feeling lost, missing a vital link to the puzzle. "Mitch . . ." She spoke quietly. "What are you saying? What car?" Without realizing it she stood up to face him, her legs strengthened by an intuitive need to probe the psyche of this man she loved. "What car?" she repeated softly.

To her astonishment it was Mitch who turned away in agony, his head bent, his voice a steady moan. "My wife was killed in an automobile accident three weeks before that plane crash. It was very late at night. The roads were icy. Our car was hit head on by a man who had had too much to drink." He looked back over his shoulder, keenly awaiting her reaction. "I was at the wheel."

Too stunned to move, Anne could only stare dumbly at him. Her own guilt was overwhelming; amid her self-pity, it had not occurred to her that Mitch had such similar cause for grief. "But . . . it wasn't . . . your fault. . . ." she reasoned.

His eyes flashed an explosion of self-anger. "*I was driving!* If only I'd driven a bit slower . . . or faster . . . or taken a different route. . . ." He looked down, then sighed deeply, his anger spent as quickly as it had burst forth. "I'm sure that with both accidents occurring so close together, my feelings about each had to be affected. Do you remember your nightmare, Anne?" At her nod he continued. "Well, mine was no dream. I was able to pull Bev out of the car, only to watch her die in my arms. There was nothing I could do. A battered arm was the least of my punishment. The plane crash seemed an extension of it. Then"—he looked up—"I found you."

Anne swallowed hard, unable to interrupt him. Her eyes followed his lean frame as it crossed the room; he seemed to roam aimlessly, as though it no longer mattered. His voice came from a distant and strangely crestfallen stranger.

"I had fallen in love with you long before I made the connection between Jeff's death and my airline. In an odd way I felt you were my only chance at happiness, at building a new life. And you seemed to need me as badly as I needed you." Before Anne could voice her agreement, he had gone on. "I was frightened . . . frightened to death of losing you. I didn't know what would happen when—if—I told you everything. I thought I could count on you to understand . . . but the stakes were so high. I never lied to you about the crash, Anne. I simply didn't offer you the full truth. And it's tormented me for months. But"—he pivoted toward her with an intensity that rattled her—"the longer the deception went on, the harder it was to face risking your love. I feared that once you knew, you might despise me." For long and heart-rending moments he stared at her. Then he cursed quietly. "Ach, what's the use. It's happened . . . and I deserve it. I was too blinded by *my* need for you to see that you *needed* to know the truth." The deep breath he took was ragged. "I just wonder when the punishment will end." Turning on his heels, he stalked through the kitchen and out of the house, leaving Anne alone and in shock.

It was the slam of the back door that jolted her out of her paralysis. She had to explain; she had to tell him. If *he* thought *her* a passport to his happiness, the reverse was no less true. What kind of a person was she to have distrusted him so? Why ever had she assumed the worst without giving him a chance to explain?

It was all very clear, at last, and every second counted. So much had already been wasted. And life was too dear, too precious, too short to waste. At a run, she followed him, leaving the house, stumbling on the back porch steps, the hammering of her heart making breathing difficult.

His tall form was in the distance and fast disappearing down a verdant path. Frantically she followed, calling his name aloud, managing to produce nothing more than a desperate plea. Mindless of the low growth that scratched at her legs and arms, she pursued him, stopping only at the opening to the clearing in which he sat, back to her, a darkly brooding figure among the golden dandelions. The sun glanced off his hair in sparkles, though his hunched form was ominous. Love gave her the courage to push on.

"Mitch? . . ." When he made no response, she chanced to creep nearer. "Mitch . . . I'm sorry, so sorry." A tentative hand reached out to touch him, then pulled back with lightning reflex when he flinched. Somehow she had to make him understand. "I've been so wrong. Please forgive me. It was cruel of me to hold everything against you the way I did. After what we'd shared, to know that there was this awful thing we hadn't. . . . Even worse, I was wrong to refuse to listen to you. *Because* of what we had shared, I should have given you that chance. But . . . I loved you so much. And I was so hurt to discover who you were . . . like *that.* You have to try to understand." This time when she touched his shoulder, he did not resist. She took a breath to steady herself. "I've always been naïve. Life was so easy and happy. I must have felt myself immune to tragedy. I'd never known any. Until the crash. I just couldn't believe that Jeff was gone. It simply couldn't happen to me. Then . . . I found you." Her hand tightened its grip on the sinewed swell of his shoulder as she moved closer and knelt down beside him to gaze at eyes that stared straight ahead. "I love you so much, Mitch.

I fought it for a long time, afraid to open myself to the kind of pain I had suffered, loving Jeff, then losing him. When I saw you in that lawyer's office, the two worlds came together. It had been hard enough to believe that I'd found you; I was sure that I was meant to lose you. I didn't think I could bear it. Call it self-pity or whatever else you choose—I don't think I'll ever forgive myself for it. I should have trusted you. I should have known that there was an explanation. So help me, I was afraid to listen. Perhaps I was punishing myself, exorcising my own guilt at having found happiness with you—" Her voice choked into an emotional silence.

In one heart-stopping moment his eyes captured hers. The feeling in them, the same vulnerability she felt, gave her the last bit of strength to finish. "My God, Mitch, haven't we *both* suffered enough? Isn't it time to end the punishment? I love you. I always will."

Her face was mere inches from his as he studied her. "Do you, Anne?" he asked softly, unsurely, huskily, hopefully. "Do you love me enough to want to wake up in my arms for every day of the rest of our lives? I can't have it any other way."

The exquisite spark of joy that exploded within her brought tears to her eyes. "I love you" was her only verbal response to his proposal. But more was needed. Timidly she edged forward until her lips touched his, shyly at first, awaiting his confirmation of her acceptance. When it came, her heart spiraled madly.

"I love you, Annie," he murmured against her lips, then held her—crushed her against him—for an eternity of rediscovery and healing, long moments in silent vow of trust. "Don't ever, *ever* turn away from me, Anne. I may make mistakes here and there, but I can't live without you. Don't shut me out again; I don't think I can survive it." With a gruffness born of adoration, he reached out to twist her down onto his lap, where he promptly renewed the embrace, deepening it this time with the fullness of love. It was only the taste of salt on their lips that drew him back. "Tears?"

Her smile was brilliant in spite of them. "Happiness. You'll just have to bear with me."

A large finger traced her jaw, then brushed the tears from her cheeks with infinite gentleness. "I think I can manage that. I do love you."

That certain gleam entered Anne's eyes first, then its suggestiveness spread to her soft whisper. "Show me."

He did. With utter adoration he undressed her, meeting each newfound expanse of creamy soft flesh with the warmth of lips pliant to her curves. His lean fingers splayed across her body, seeking her nakedness, probing it, reveling in it. Her breasts swelled to him, her thighs quivered. The tenderness of his touch drove her to distraction.

His was a gift of pleasure to Anne's love-drenched gaze when he stood back to remove his own clothes. She drank in the sight of his body—his broad and muscled chest, his long legs, his narrow hips. He was a man, bold and proud, a man to fill her for eternity. When he lowered himself to her, she trembled in urgent desire.

As he loved her, he worshiped her, touching every inch of her body in wonder, setting her every cell afire with that wandering touch. She cried to him of her own love, ever building, ever deepening. And there, on the soft, fresh carpet of grass and dandelion puffs, he made love to her, convincing her forever of the force of his love. Their bodies merged, then soared, reaching explosive heights in instant satisfaction. When much later they lay still, the sun stroking their naked bodies, she nuzzled his neck with a purr of contentment. "Mmmmmm, this *is* heaven."

Playfully he patted her bare bottom. "Let's hope there is no poison ivy around here."

He burst into a loud guffaw when Anne bolted upright. "Is there?"

"Relax, my beauty, and come back here, where you belong," he teased, pulling her head once more onto his finely matted chest. "No poison ivy. Only me."

"Will *you* give me a rash?" She joined the game merrily.

The glitter of silver in his eye came through in his laugh as his hand slid over the soft and silken length of her body. "Hopefully one very special itch every now and then; never a rash."

"Oh, Mitch." She sighed, stretching happily against his warm and manly shape, her hands drifting over him recklessly. "You have no idea how I love you."

His challenge was as pleased. "Not as much as I love you, Annie."

"Wanna make a bet?" Her dark head cocked pertly.

"You're on, woman," he growled, rolling over onto her to settle the matter.

To their mutual delight it was far from settled by the next morning. Awakening with the sun in her glow of happiness, Anne crept from his bed, stealthily, so as not to disturb his slumber, pulled on his large shirt, discarded carelessly in the heat of passion the night before, and walked to the front door. As it opened the sweet scent of the lilacs met her winging senses. In the week's tumult she had not noticed them before. Now she cooed in delight at the shapely pinkish-purple clusters and the fragrance that spoke to her of the richness of life.

Snapping off a small cluster, she returned to bed, shedding the shirt as she slipped back quietly beneath the sheets to lie on her stomach and watch Mitch. As magnificent asleep as awake, his features showed that he was at peace, at last, as was she.

Touched by no more than her visual adoration, one sleepy hazel eye opened to smile at her lazily. "The lilacs," she whispered, laying the lavender flower on the pillow. "They're in bloom. Spring is truly here." As her lover's hand wound through the dark silk of her hair to draw her lips to his, she knew that, indeed, it was.

LOOK FOR NEXT MONTH'S
CANDLELIGHT ECSTASY ROMANCES™

90 BREATHLESS SURRENDER, *Kay Hooper*
91 SPELLBOUND, *Jayne Castle*
92 CRIMSON MORNING, *Jackie Black*
93 A STRANGE ELATION, *Prudence Martin*
94 A WAITING GAME, *Diana Blayne*
95 JINX LADY, *Hayton Monteith*
96 FORBIDDEN FIRES, *Nell Kincaid*
97 DANCE THE SKIES, *Jo Calloway*